A STORE

Joanna Toye joined the production team of *The Archers* after reading English at Cambridge University, and was a scriptwriter for the programme for over twenty years. She has also written a number of spin-off books about the long-running radio drama. On television she has written for *Crossroads*, *Family Affairs*, *Doctors* and *EastEnders*. *A Store at War* is her first novel.

Find out more about Joanna on Facebook.com/joannatoyewriter/

A Store at War

JOANNA TOYE

HarperCollins*Publishers*

HarperCollins*Publishers* Ltd
1 London Bridge Street,
London SE1 9GF

www.harpercollins.co.uk

First published in Great Britain by HarperCollins*Publishers* 2018

3

A catalogue record for this book is available from the British Library

ISBN: 978-0-00-829823-4

Typeset in Sabon by Palimpsest Book Production Ltd, Falkirk, Stirlingshire

Printed and bound by CPI Group (UK) Ltd, Croydon CR0 4YY

MIX
Paper from
responsible sources
FSC™ C007454

This book is produced from independently certified FSC™ paper
to ensure responsible forest management.

For more information visit: www.harpercollins.co.uk/green

For my grandmothers –
and all the women of their generation.

Chapter 1

June, 1941

'Well? Will I do?'

Lily Collins hovered in the doorway of the small back parlour. Her brother Sid, shirt sleeves, flannels, wavy blond hair, broad shoulders – Sid was the looker of the family, and no mistake – his injured foot propped up on a stool, glanced up from his *Picturegoer* magazine.

'Come in, then, Sis, give us a closer look!'

Coming in was just what she didn't want to do. What she wanted, no, needed, to do was to get Sid's swift approval, then shoot out of the house faster than a firecracker before her mum could see that Lily

1

had dabbed on a bit of her powder and even (before quickly blotting most of it off) a smudge of precious lipstick. She'd only dared sneak down to seek Sid's approval because she'd seen from upstairs that her mum was out in the back garden, sitting on a canvas stool in the sun, shelling peas.

'Come on!' urged Sid. 'Let the dog see the rabbit!'

Lily edged forward. She was horribly aware of how young she still looked in her faded print frock and – horror of horrors – ankle socks.

Sid scrutinised her, his head on one side.

'Um . . . your hair. What exactly were you aiming for?'

'A mind of its own' was the kindest description of Lily's own fair hair. It made life interesting, she supposed, because she never knew when she woke up which way her strong-minded curls would have decided to arrange themselves overnight. She imagined them in the small hours, debating long and hard.

'I'll flop over her right eye if you stick out at an angle at the top.'

'No, hang on, I stuck out at the top yesterday! Why don't I do the flopping? And for a change, you can spring off her ear?'

It hadn't used to matter that much. At school she'd had to force her hair back any old how with grips and a hairband, but for a job interview, and with hairgrips just one of the things that had started to disappear now the war was in its second year . . .

The best she'd been able to do was a complex arrangement with as many grips as she could muster and a couple of combs – also her mum's. The effect she'd been aiming for, since Sid was asking, was side-parted and crimped at the side – Bette Davis in *Dark Victory*, basically – but her brother's face told her the effect was more like something from *The Wizard of Oz*. And not Judy Garland, either.

'Sorry, Lil, I'm not sure . . .'

'It hasn't worked, has it?'

'You're ahead of your time, that's all. Give it six months, a hairdo that looks like you've stuck your finger in the socket's bound to take off.'

'Sid! They're never going to give me the job!'

'No. They won't. Not unless you get a shake on, have you seen the time?'

In her anguish, Lily hadn't seen or heard her mother come in.

'Now sit yourself down and let's sort that hair out.'

Dora Collins crossed the room. Lily was her youngest child but neither being the baby of the family, nor, after two boys, being a girl – at last! – meant that she was in any way indulged. If their father had been around, it might have been different – a lot of things would have been different – but he'd died of a heart attack the year Lily was born and Dora had been left a widow with three children under five.

Lily's stomach took a plunge.

'Here we go,' she thought. 'She'll see the make-up. I've had it.'

But if she noticed – and she would have done, Dora missed nothing – her mother said nothing. Instead she sat Lily down at the table, snapped her fingers for Sid's comb, and began with practised eye and hand to tame her daughter's hair. Miraculously she managed it with half the amount of hairgrips Lily had used.

'Now you're presentable,' she said with brisk satisfaction. 'If Marlow's don't take you on, well, it's their loss.'

Marlow's. Simply hearing the word set Lily's stomach somersaulting again.

It had first come up at the end of the Easter term when her headmistress had called the girls in Lily's year in one by one for the customary interview. She'd been sorry, she said, to hear that Lily wouldn't be staying on to take her school certificate.

'I'm sorry too, miss,' said Lily with real regret. 'But Mum can't afford for me not to be working.'

Miss Norris sighed. As a bright girl unable to make the most of her chances because of her family situation, Lily wasn't alone. It had been the case through all Miss Norris's teaching career – all the previous decade and the one before – despite the Great War, despite the vote, despite the new opportunities that had supposedly opened up for women. And now another war, which had brought with it more opportunities – of a sort.

Miss Norris sighed again. It had come so close. In 1939 there'd been debate about raising the school leaving age to fifteen, but the outbreak of war had put paid to that, for the time being at least. And now that unmarried younger women had to register for war work – it'd be married women next, including those with children – there was even talk of women being conscripted before the end of the year – it also meant that girls like Lily were in demand for the jobs they'd left behind. Shops, cafés, laundries, pubs, hotels . . . there were plenty of jobs for fourteen-year-olds. In fact the country was relying on them to 'do their bit' as well.

'What do you think you might do?' Miss Norris enquired.

'They're looking for someone at the Fox and Goose – general assistant, they call it,' Lily replied. 'Or Mum's got a friend that works at a laundry . . .'

Miss Norris looked pained.

'Lily. You're better than that,' she protested. 'You don't want to go skivvying!'

'Well . . .'

'And I won't let you. Let me make some enquiries.'

And so Miss Norris had made her enquiries, and within a few days told Lily of the opening at Marlow's – the biggest department store in town. It was only a junior's job – skivvying too, in its way, Miss Norris had explained apologetically – but it would at least have prospects – promotion, if she worked hard. And from the very start it would be better paid and what Miss Norris called a 'better working environment' than either of Lily's other possibilities.

Lily had tried to look grateful – and she was. It was really kind of Miss Norris to have taken the trouble; she didn't have to. But Marlow's! Their motto was 'Nothing but the best'. They might as well have added 'for the best' because who could afford to shop there? Not the likes of Lily's family, for sure: she'd never been further than the black-and-white mosaic tiles in their doorway, and that was only because she'd sheltered there from the rain once, when she'd been in town buying a present – a scarf ring – for her mum's birthday. Which she'd bought from the haberdasher's in the market, of course.

And now Miss Norris expected her to work there? Marlow's, with the drift of scented air which had escaped when the commissionaire had opened the door; Marlow's with its oak-and-glass counters, polished parquet floor and dove-grey carpeted staircase – Lily had made sure to take a good look inside. Marlow's . . . only the poshest shop in town. And Lily just a girl from a back street.

And now here she was, at two o'clock on a Monday in June, ready for her interview. Or was she?

Her mother jerked her thumb over her shoulder, jolting Lily back to reality.

'Scullery, and double quick,' she said. 'Wash all that off your face. Wasting my powder like that! The nerve!'

Sid shot her a look that mixed sympathy with 'might have known' as Lily went to do as she was told. This never happened to Bette Davis, she thought wistfully, drying her face on the rough roller towel. Even at my age.

'She doesn't mean it, you know, our mum,' said Sid consolingly as he walked, or more accurately, limped, alongside Lily into town.

Their older brother, Reg, had been eighteen the month war was declared, and had signed up straight away – Sid, too, enlisting for the Navy the minute he was old enough in April. Reg was doing well – going to be made up to lance corporal soon, he'd hinted – but poor Sid hadn't got much further than training camp. He'd managed to crack a bone in his foot landing badly from the vaulting horse and, to his frustration, was now stuck at home till it mended. Not the sort of thing, he'd remarked ruefully, that you ever saw happening to James Cagney in the films – unless it led to him meeting a pretty nurse. Which in Sid's case, it hadn't, only an unsympathetic naval doctor with bad breath, apparently.

'Thing is, she's had to be mum and dad to us, hasn't she?' Sid continued now. 'That's why she lays it on a bit strong sometimes.'

'I know,' said Lily.

She knew her mum wasn't really that cross, because after checking that Lily's face was scrubbed as clean as the day she was born, she'd lent Lily her white fancy-knit cardigan, with her lucky horseshoe brooch pinned to it, and given her a hug and a kiss before she left.

'So have you got all your answers ready?' smiled Sid.

'I don't know what they're going to ask!'

'They probably only want to see that you haven't got two heads. Let's face it, they're not exactly spoilt for choice at the moment, are they?'

'Thanks very much!' retorted Lily. 'If you weren't already on crutches I'd put you on them!'

But she knew he was only joking. Sid was four years older than Lily, but since they were children they'd always enjoyed teasing each other. Reg, Sid's elder by eighteen months, was the quiet one, good with his hands, good at mending things. He'd spent the war so far being sent here and there for unspecified 'training' – Reg was very discreet – but after all that had ended up back at the searchlight battery in Nottingham where he'd started. This was a mixed blessing in the Collins household: it wasn't what Reg had joined up for; on the other hand, Dora's worries could be contained. Then, at last, his technical skills were appreciated – he'd been an apprentice mechanic when war broke out – so after more training, which this time he was happy to tell them about, he was going to be transferred to REME – the Royal Electrical and Mechanical Engineers – to his great satisfaction, but their mum's growing anxiety. Reg would be twenty in September, which meant he'd be considered for overseas service. The Mediterranean? The Middle East? The Western Desert? It was all much too worrying to think about.

'Here we are, anyway.'

They stopped before the sandbagged façade of Marlow's, its corner site bridging the town's two main shopping streets. Even the Splinternet tape stuck criss cross against the huge plate-glass windows – four down one street, four down the other, and two graceful curving panes each side of the entrance – couldn't mask the elegance of the approach. Anyway, Lily thought, it gave the place a sort of charm, like the latticed windows of a cottage, albeit a cottage more the size of a mansion. The store's name stood out above the entrance in stylish black on gold and was picked out again in gold on the mosaic tiles of the entrance. The huge clock which overhung the doorway showed five to three.

'Right then. "The time has come, the Walrus said . . ."' Sid squeezed her arm.

Lily gulped.

'Don't leave me, Sid.'

'Of course I'm not going to leave you. I'm going to look at the ties,' said Sid airily.

Lily's eyes widened. At Marlow's prices?

'You're never going to buy one here! Anyway, you've got a dozen ties already!'

'Looking's free, isn't it? And they can't stop me.'

The uniformed commissionaire gave them a hard look as he held the door open, but Sid's salute and rueful glance at his foot brought a twitch of recognition from an old serviceman to a younger one and he swept them through with a gracious wave of his arm.

Once inside, Lily froze again. Now she was inside, properly inside, she could appreciate Marlow's true magic. She'd never seen anything like it – or imagined such a place could exist in Hinton, their workaday Midlands town.

'War? What war?' she felt like saying, because there didn't seem to be any shortages here. Overpowering scents wafted towards her from the cosmetics and perfume counters in front of her. To her right, scarves and gloves were fanned out in a rainbow of summer colours – palest pink through mauve to cornflower blue, and white through cream to lemon. Beyond were umbrellas both furled and twirled, handbags and shoes. Behind them, notices pointed to menswear, footwear, stationery, and gifts.

'Come on, Sis, you don't want to be late. Who is it you're to ask for?'

The name was imprinted on Lily's mind.

'Miss Garner, staff office.'

Sid motioned her towards the enquiry desk.

'Now you really are on your own.' He squeezed her arm again. 'You'll be fine, kid. Just be yourself.'

With that he was gone, swinging himself athletically on his crutches, and attracting as he passed, Lily noticed, interested looks from Elizabeth Arden and Max Factor – or at least their immaculately-presented salesgirls.

The enquiry desk was on her immediate right. Behind it was a woman in her fifties who regarded Lily over spectacles whose design made them look as if they wanted to take flight.

'My name's Lily – Lily Collins. I have an appointment. With Miss Garner. Three o'clock,' she said – or squeaked. Her voice seemed to have been replaced by Minnie Mouse's.

'Let's see. . .'

The woman ruffled a couple of sheets on a clipboard and placed a satisfied tick against a typewritten line. She replaced the clipboard in a wooden slot to her right.

'They didn't tell you, then?' she enquired.

'Tell me what?'

The woman raised her eyebrows higher than her aerobatic glasses, but her smile was kind.

'This'll be the last time you use the customer entrance. The staff entrance is in Brewer Street, at the back. That's if you get the job.'

If I don't get the job, thought Lily, it'll be the last

time anyway. I'm hardly likely to set foot in here again!

On the third floor, Miss Garner, the staff supervisor, was holding forth on her favourite subject – the difficulty of getting what she called 'the right type of girl'.

'I never thought I'd see the day' – she indicated Lily's letter of application, written not so much with the help of as by Miss Norris – 'when Marlow's had to take girls from anywhere but the grammar school!'

Cedric Marlow shrugged. He was sixty-three, the son of the founder of the original Marlow's ('Capes, mantles and bonnets – all the latest designs from Paris!') and had been in the business since he was twenty. He'd seen plenty of commercial ups and downs, plenty of staff come and go, and more to the point had seen one war that was supposed to end all wars be followed by this one. If he'd learnt nothing else – and he'd learnt a lot – it was that a business had to adapt to survive and accepting reality and adjusting requirements to suit what was available was the only sensible strategy.

'We don't have a great deal of choice, do we?' he said mildly. 'And I can't see things improving when—'

'When they bring in conscription for women. I know.'

Miss Garner looked briefly at the floor. She didn't ever mention it, but she'd done her bit. She'd served in the First Aid Nursing Yeomanry in the First War. She'd met her first love, too, when she'd nursed him back to health after the second battle of Ypres. Before he left for the front again, he'd asked her to marry him, and had become her fiancé, then her missing-in-action fiancé, then her missing-presumed-dead fiancé. His body, the body she'd bathed and tended back to health once already, was never found.

Miss Garner was too old now for nursing, or any interesting war work, and too useful anyway, doing what she did at Marlow's, keeping the home fires burning, or rather somehow finding the staff to sell the coal scuttles and hearth rugs that flanked the home fires – while hearth rugs and coal scuttles were still available. Making do and mending, cutting her cloth . . . seeing the young, then middle-aged, staff leaving and replacing them with the halt, the lame, the very old – and the very young. Fourteen-year-olds, in fact.

A shaky tap on the door told them that the girl they were expecting had arrived.

'Enter!' called Cedric Marlow.

Lily's interview was about to begin.

Chapter 2

'So when do you start?'

'Next week. Monday.'

'That's brilliant, Sis! Well done!'

Sid folded Lily in a huge hug and she relaxed for the first time that day. He was in the garden now, in an old collarless shirt and some ancient trousers, once their dad's – nothing was ever thrown away in the Collins household. They were too big for him round the waist, so he'd found a huge leather belt which pulled them in tight and his braces were hanging down. Somehow, using the handle as a support, and putting as little weight on his bad foot as possible, he'd been hoeing between the lettuces, which were dangerously close to bolting, their mum said.

Now things were getting scarcer in the shops, Dora had taken 'Dig for Victory' to heart. She'd never done more than nurture the odd Christmas cactus or aspidistra for the front room, but now they grew what they could in a couple of small raised beds at the back of their terraced house. It had been nothing but a yard, but Lily and Sid had carted the soil in barrows half a mile from a bigger, boarded-up house with a garden. Every little bit they grew helped cheer up a diet that was becoming more and more repetitive and meagre.

Bacon, butter, sugar . . . they'd been rationed since almost the beginning of the war; even margarine had been rationed for almost a year now. Meat, tea, jam . . . sweets, of course . . . last month cheese and this month, eggs. One egg each a week!

Still, if it helped the war effort . . .

'Where's Mum?' asked Lily. 'I wanted to tell her straight away!'

'Ah. She's out,' said Sid mysteriously.

'She never goes *just* out.' Lily looked puzzled.

'She won't be long,' soothed Sid. 'Anyway, you can tell me. Who was there? What did they ask you?'

'Ohhhh,' said Lily, covering her face. 'It was dreadful. It wasn't just Miss Garner, it was Mr Marlow himself! I mean, he seemed very nice, but . . . he asked what I'd liked at school and I said "all of it" and how I'd have liked to stay on, and then I thought that was the wrong answer 'cos he'd think

15

I didn't want the job . . . and then I blabbered on about how I liked meeting people, and talking to them, and about how I really really wanted to work there . . .'

'Well, you do, don't you? Better than that steamy laundry any day of the week. Or the Fox and Goose, with old Pearson trying to put his hand up your skirt.'

'Sid!'

Sid grinned. 'It's true. There'll be none of that at Marlow's. Everyone there's ever so well brung up, ain't they?' He lapsed deliberately into the strong local accent.

'I suppose so,' mused Lily.

'Well, don't sound so sorry about it! So no mental arithmetic or spelling? You were dreading that.'

'Nothing like that,' said Lily. 'It's only a junior's job – in the Children's department. I don't suppose they'll let me near a customer. And anyway I don't know if I can take it. I haven't got the right clothes!'

'What, no uniform?'

'They've scrapped it 'cos of the war. A dress in a plain dark colour, they said, or dark skirt and white blouse. And plain black shoes.'

'Well, you've got those.' Sid nodded at Lily's best Sunday shoes.

'They'll never last the winter!' cried Lily. She steadied herself against Sid's shoulder and balanced stork-like to show him the soles, which were already worn. 'As for a dress—'

'Mum'll come up with something. Or we'll ask around. You know how it works in our street.'

Lily knew all too well. Hand-me-downs, making do. That was one thing the war hadn't changed.

Sid went back to his hoeing.

'Surely though, you'll get some kind of discount? Buy some decent stuff?'

'What, like a tie for you? On their prices, 90 per cent off wouldn't be enough!'

'They had some smashers,' said Sid wistfully. 'Silk. Still . . . one day, maybe . . .'

'One day,' sighed Lily. 'When the war's over . . .'

'Dear me. A nice enough girl, but no polish.'

Miss Garner was assembling Lily's staff manual, letter of engagement and terms and conditions of employment. Cedric Marlow was standing at the window of his office, looking down into the well at the back of the shop. A grimy pigeon was fluffing out its feathers in the sun and he was ashamed to realise that all he could think about was how good it would taste casseroled with bacon, mushrooms and shallots. His household could afford to buy its way out of the worst of rationing, and he could always eat out, but there was less and less variety on the menu.

'I think she'll suit very well,' he said mildly.

'She'll need a few rough edges knocked off her.' Miss Garner tapped the pages straight and pinioned them with a precious paper clip. They'd be the next

17

thing to disappear. She'd make sure the girl gave it back once she'd signed her contract.

'I daresay. But we've had worse.'

'I'll say.'

Her thoughts swung immediately to Beryl Salter on Toys. A year at Marlow's had knocked off her rough edges, it was true, but at the expense of the girl giving herself a most uncalled-for air of superiority and what she obviously thought was a 'refined' accent.

Shaking her head, Miss Garner returned to the latest candidate.

'Miss Collins is a little too keen to pipe up, I thought. "Likes talking to people" – she'd better not try that with the customers! She'll have to learn to speak when she's spoken to. But Eileen Frobisher will keep her in line.'

Miss Frobisher was one of Miss Garner's protégées, having soared rapidly through the complex sales hierarchy to the dizzy heights of buyer on Childrenswear. They'd been so lucky to get her back. She wasn't really a 'Miss' of course, else she'd have been in a munitions factory or the services by now, but Marlow's convention was that all saleswomen were addressed as 'Miss' whether they were married or not. And Eileen was, with a husband serving overseas and a little boy of four, which excused her from war work. An elderly neighbour looked after him during store hours.

Cedric Marlow let the net drop back as the pigeon fluttered off.

'How's that new young man on Furniture and Household getting on by the way? James Something-or-other.'

'Oh! You mean Jim. Jim Goodridge,' confirmed Miss Garner. 'From what I can gather from Mr Hooper,' she named the Furniture buyer, 'he's made quite a good impression. He's rather quiet, not the most pushy, but as third sales he doesn't have to be. There's plenty of time for him to learn. And with experienced salesmen like Maurice Bishop to learn from . . . Why do you ask?'

'Oh . . . he simply popped into my head for some reason,' Cedric Marlow replied. Then: 'Did you notice that poor kid's shoes? Literally down-at-heel.'

'I'll make sure her presentation on the sales floor is up to scratch, Mr Marlow, don't you worry.'

'That's not what I meant.' He turned away from the window. 'The Queen may feel she's able to look the East End in the eye, but sometimes . . . I wonder. I mean, I don't suppose Lily Collins' family were exactly flush before the war, her mother being a widow, but so many like them are suffering more than ever now. As is anyone who can't buy their way out of it. And here we are, selling only the best . . . '

Miss Garner cleared her throat. Mr Marlow wasn't usually given to sudden enquiries about random members of staff, nor to such outpourings – and certainly not this kind of sentiment. It had been a long day, clearly.

'It's got very warm in here,' she said. 'Might I suggest you open the window? And I'll ask the restaurant to send you in a tray of tea.'

'Lay the table will you, love?'

Her mother's voice carried over the clattering coming from the scullery.

Lily went to the sideboard for the knives with the yellowed bone handles and the tarnished forks and started doling them out on the cloth.

After the elation of getting the job, it had all been a bit of a comedown. Her mum had been pleased, of course, and Lily could see the relief on her face. But on hearing of the uniform requirements, she'd jumped up, gone upstairs and come back down with a hideous dress in navy gabardine.

'Cousin Ida's,' she announced. 'I knew it'd come in useful!'

Cousin Ida. Her mother's cousin – a shrivelled spinster who worked as an assistant in a chemist's so old-fashioned they practically had leeches in jars. Hardly a fashion plate at the best of times, this particular dress was at least ten years out of date, Lily could tell from its straight up-and-down shape. It was already seated in the behind and sagging at the hem, but Dora Collins loved nothing like a challenge. Lily had had to stand while her mother forced

20

her to put it on – smelling of camphor and itchy in the afternoon heat – and primped about with a pincushion, tucking and pinching, prodding and poking, telling Lily to stand up straight, before proclaiming that with a few darts, a nice Peter Pan collar, and cuffs if they could run to them, it would do fine. A Peter Pan collar! Cuffs! As if they'd make it look any better!

Out came the cruet, the mismatched plates . . . What was the point, thought Lily, of getting a decent job if she was going to look such a frump? She might as well have been stuck slaving over a mangle at the laundry.

Sid came downstairs, spruced up after his stint in the garden. Dora had fretted that he'd overdone it, standing all that time on his injured foot, but she and Lily knew sitting about wasn't his style – he wanted to be up and doing. He'd got to report to the local medical officer weekly, but the doctor had advised against going back to training too early. 'You'll only set yourself back' had been his advice, so it looked as though they'd have him around for a while yet. Lily was glad. She loved her mum dearly, but Dora had always been so occupied with making ends meet and keeping them fed, clothed and shod – even more so nowadays – that there wasn't much time or maybe energy left over for the smiles and cuddles which Lily had craved since she was a little girl. That was another reason she was happy to have

Sid around. He was always ready with a joke and a hug.

On trailing feet Lily carried through the breadboard and breadknife with the inevitable loaf – they seemed to live on it – the pot of dripping, the dish shaped like a lettuce leaf with, yes, lettuce on it. A few tomatoes, a dish of radishes, half a pot of green tomato chutney. Was that it? Hardly a celebration tea. She'd hoped her mum might have conjured something tasty from some- where – potted meat? Pilchards? Or at least fried up a few potatoes – Sid had dug some up, she'd seen – but it looked as though this was going to be their lot.

Sid carried the tea things through one at a time – he used a stick inside the house – and dispensed pot, milk jug and cups and saucers. Maybe that was the celebration, no milk bottle on the table. Lily thought he was limping more than he had been at the start of the afternoon and gestured to him to sit down, bringing him the rush-topped stool.

'I could get used to this!' he smiled as she stuck a cushion under his foot.

'Well, don't!' she retorted. 'Who's going to look after you in the Navy? One of the Wrens? You hope!'

Sid winked.

'Wouldn't say no.'

Lily was pouring tea when her mother finally appeared, so she didn't notice the serving dish till it went down in front of her. She lowered the pot in wonderment.

'Oh, Mum!'

There, in all their jelly goodness, were three fat slices of pink, speckled brawn. Lily bent and sniffed the plate. It smelt heavenly.

'Meat? On a Monday tea? Where did it – how did you . . . ?'

Her mother sat down in her place with that little 'Oof' which she so often gave these days when taking the weight off her feet.

'Never you mind,' she said. 'I wanted us to have something special. To celebrate.'

'But – how could you be sure I'd get the job?'

Lily sat down too, almost in slow motion, still transfixed by the sight and smells in front of her. Sid was watching it all with amusement. Dora served a slice of brawn on to each of their plates.

'I never had a minute's doubt! I knew you'd impress them. If you ask me, they're lucky to have you!'

Lily bit her lip. It was one of the nicest things her mother had ever said.

Her mother put her hand over hers.

'You've done very well, love – and thank you.'

'You're thanking me? Why?'

'Oh, Lily,' said Dora. 'You know and I know you should have stayed on at school. And you know as well as I do that you could have gone to the grammar school back along if things had been different.'

Lily knew. But she hadn't even taken the exam,

because she also knew her mother could never have afforded the uniform.

'You've had to give up so many opportunities already,' Dora went on. 'I hope this job'll be the start of something good for you. And it could be, you know, if you work hard.'

'I know, Mum. And I will. I'll do my very best to make them like me and keep me on.'

'Course they will,' Sid assured them. 'Give her a few years, she'll be running the place, won't you, chick?'

Her mother squeezed Lily's hand and they both had to squeeze back tears.

'Oh, blimey,' said Sid, offering his handkerchief to each in turn. 'Women! Give over, will you? There's a slice of brawn with my name on it in front of me! Can we get stuck in?'

Chapter 3

'Are you coming, going, or going to stand there all day thinking about it?'

Lily's feet had brought her as far the staff entrance of Marlow's, but they were showing a complete inability to take her any further.

'Oh, never mind!'

A sharp-shouldered blonde pushed past her in a swirl of cheap perfume and peroxide and disappeared through the door.

'Take no notice,' said a voice at Lily's side. 'She's like that with everyone.'

Lily smiled gratefully. The girl was shorter than Lily, and plumper, with straight brown hair in a pudding-basin shape. Under a too-small jacket, she was wearing a plain black dress. With her intimate knowledge of second-hand, Lily could tell from its greenish tinge that, like her own, the dress had had at least one previous owner. The girl's white lacy collar, too, had suffered many launderings – but never mind her clothes. Best of all, from Lily's point of view, she was wearing a smile.

'You wouldn't happen to be the new junior on Children's?'

Lily nodded.

'I was the same on my first day – stomach feels like it's in a lift!'

Lily nodded again. Her head would fall off at this rate.

'Don't be. It does get better. I'm Gladys, by the way. I'm a junior on Children's too. Well, I suppose I'm the senior junior now! We'll be working together!'

'Lily.'

'Pleased to meet you.'

They shook hands awkwardly.

'Come on, I'll show you what's what.'

Gladys pushed open the door and Lily entered another world.

If what she'd seen of Marlow's on the day of her interview was like something from a fairy tale, this was more like the reality Lily knew. There was nothing fairy tale here. The corridor walls were scuffed where pull-along wagons delivering goods had bumped against them, the lino was worn, and the stairs which led to the basement staff cloakrooms were stone, dipped from years of footfall and as far away from the soft-carpeted dove-grey staircase inside the store as it was possible to get.

All around them staff moved purposefully this way and that. Men in brown coats rattled past with sack trucks or shoved metal cages full of boxes into a creaking goods lift. Shop-floor staff, some in outer coats going in their direction, others without their coats and ready for the day ahead going in the other, pulsed and flowed in a human tide. Lily dodged as best she could until Gladys pushed through a swing door into a long, low room alive with noise and movement. Wooden benches with pegs above ran down the centre and the walls were lined with pitted metal lockers.

'My locker's along here,' explained Gladys, leading the way. 'Let's see if we can find you one close by.'

'Oh, look, it's Slow and her new friend Slower.'

The girl who'd accosted Lily outside was patting her hair in a cracked mirror fixed to the wall before retying the bow at the neck of her blouse.

'Don't ever go to the zoo, you two, will you? You might get dizzy watching the tortoises whizz round!'

She smiled to herself at her witticism and turned away.

'Who is she?' whispered Lily. 'Or who does she think she is?'

'Beryl Salter,' muttered Gladys. 'Junior on Toys –

well, fourth sales she calls it, though there's no such thing. And Toys is right next to our department, unfortunately.'

'There's always one, my mum says.'

Gladys said nothing more, so Lily bundled her gas mask, bag and cardigan into the locker Gladys indicated and checked that the clean handkerchief her mother had insisted on was still tucked up her sleeve.

'But we don't have to take it, you know.'

Gladys shook her head. 'You don't answer Beryl back.'

Lily had already noticed that, in front of Beryl, Gladys looked like a rabbit being hypnotised by a snake.

'You may not,' she responded. 'But I'm here now.'

'Well, Lily, you join us on something of an unusual day.'

Lily was hardly listening to a word Miss Frobisher, the Childrenswear buyer, was saying, so dazzled was she by her appearance. Though Lily was no judge of age – anyone over twenty-five was simply 'old' – Eileen Frobisher was probably not much over thirty. Tall and imposing, she had a proper figure (hour-glass, Lily would tell Sid later) outlined in a fitted grey pinstriped costume. Her enviably smooth toffee-blonde hair was swept round her head into an elegant French pleat in which not one single hairpin showed. How did she do it?

'For reasons that . . . well, reasons you don't need to know, Furniture and Household are having to move down from the second floor to join us here on the first. So we shall have to condense our stock. The good news for you, Lily, is that you'll get to know everything we sell straight away. The bad news for the two of you' – she included Gladys – 'is that we'll be losing a display counter, drawers and several racks. So in future you girls'll be running back and forth to the stockroom a lot more.'

Lily and Gladys nodded dutifully. The department's two saleswomen – or salesgirls, as Lily learnt they were called – Miss Thomas and Miss Temple – were already going through the racks, removing the covers that protected the stock from dust and dirt overnight. As the morning ticked away, along with Miss Frobisher, they pondered party dresses and picked out little summer coats. Beautifully smocked romper suits, tiny embroidered blouses, fluffy pram covers and soft leather bootees piled up on the counters as they made their decisions over what should stay and what should go.

As she smoothed and folded, Lily marvelled at the detail, the workmanship in every garment – all in miniature – and tried not gasp when she saw the contrastingly enormous prices. Not that she had much time to gasp. Her job, with Gladys, was to carry armfuls of tiny clothes and boxes of accessories to the stockroom and stow them away under the supervision of Miss Thomas, who was now stationed up there. Occasionally, to rest their legs, they folded fresh tissue and cut holes for the hangers to protect the clothes from the stockroom's much dustier atmosphere.

But their main task, as it turned out, was trying to avoid Beryl, whose own department was also being reduced in size. Despite her self-styled senior status, Beryl had been set the same job, carrying boxes of Meccano, train sets and soft plush toys off the sales floor and up three flights of unforgiving stone stairs to the fourth-floor stockrooms – with accompanying moans.

'I wouldn't mind,' she complained as they toiled up the stairs for the umpteenth time. 'But Toys have already moved once to make space for the Red Cross and St John Ambulance stalls. Now I've got to lug this stuff about again! Where are the porters?'

'Helping bring the furniture down, I suppose,' panted Lily as she plodded on up.

'Children's has moved too,' pointed out Gladys mildly. 'From ground to first. That was soon after I came,' she explained to Lily. 'To make way for the Permits Office and the interpreter's desk. For French and Belgian refugees,' she added, when Lily looked blank.

Lily couldn't help but be impressed. It seemed there was nothing Marlow's wouldn't do to attract custom. Mr Marlow must have a very shrewd brain.

'And now it's the Air Ministry!' snorted Beryl, grabbing at a velveteen monkey as it tried to make a break from the armful she was carrying.

'What?'

'Oh, hasn't Frosty Frobisher taken you into her confidence? I wonder why?'

'I don't think she's frosty.' Lily was defensive. 'She seems very nice.'

'Thinks a lot of herself, if you ask me.'

'She's not the only one,' muttered Lily to Gladys, thinking that Miss Frobisher had a lot more right to than Beryl, about whom you could say the same.

'I suppose she knows you two dumbclucks'll do as you're told without asking questions. I asked Mr Marlow.'

Gladys's eyes widened.

'Robert Marlow. Floor supervisor,' she mouthed to Lily. 'Mr Marlow's son.'

'The management have known about it for weeks but the communiqué' – Beryl rolled the word around triumphantly like a diver surfacing with a rare pearl – 'only came through on Friday. They've requisitioned half the second floor for aircraft parts.'

'Come along, come along!'

Miss Thomas was waiting for them at the double doors to the stockroom.

'Come along, girls! The war'll be over before we get our stock moved at this rate!'

But she gave them a smile and when dinnertime

finally came – Lily's stomach had been growling for over an hour – Miss Frobisher let them both go off together as it was Lily's first day – as long as they only took forty minutes instead of the usual hour.

At last, in the basement canteen, where Marlow's provided a daily hot meal for all their employees, Lily got a chance to take stock instead of moving it.

As they chewed their rissoles – not as good as her mum's, but they were grateful for anything; you had to be these days – Lily learnt that Gladys was six months older than she was and had started at Marlow's just before Christmas. As soon as she heard where she'd been born – Coventry – Lily had a horrible feeling she knew what Gladys was going to say – and she was right. Worried for their only child's safety, her parents had sent her to stay with her gran in Hinton soon after Dunkirk – and they'd also been right in their thinking. When Coventry had taken its pounding from German bombers the previous November, the cubbyhole under the stairs where Gladys's parents had been sheltering was no protection against a petty burglar armed with a paper knife, let alone the Luftwaffe. The house had been completely obliterated and Gladys's mum and dad with it. With no home or other family to go back to, Gladys had had no option but to stay on with her gran – and since she'd never enrolled in school in Hinton in the first place, she thought she might as well find herself a job. She thanked her lucky stars every day, she said, that she'd been taken on at Marlow's – her chances boosted by the fact that her parents had run a small corner shop and she'd always helped out there.

'What happens if there's an air raid here?' asked Lily. 'I mean, there must be over a hundred staff, more maybe, and with customers too . . .'

'I'll show you when we've finished.' Gladys forked up a final shred of cabbage and a chunk of watery potato. 'There's an air-raid shelter down here, big enough for all the staff and as many customers as Mr Marlow thinks could be in the store at any one time.'

Lily couldn't help but be impressed again by Cedric Marlow's foresight.

'And he's had a door cut through that leads into Burrell's basement too.'

'Burrell's! But that's way down Market Street!'

Burrell's was another big store and, Lily would have assumed, a rival.

'Their basement and ours meet in the middle. Weird, isn't it? So if there was a raid and we got hit, we could get out through their shop, and the other way round.'

'What are you two gassing about now?'

Beryl plonked her tray down on the table and plumped down beside them – naturally assuming there'd be no objection. Lily noted that, however much she appeared to despise them, she didn't seem to have anyone else to sit with.

'Air-raid precautions.' Lily sipped her water.

'Hah! I suppose Little Miss Muffet's been telling you how they say it's all about "protection not profit". Has she told you how long we have to wait till we can go down the shelter?'

Lily shook her head. Beryl sprinkled salt and pepper vigorously over her rissole and pushed her cabbage disgustedly to one side.

'It used to be that we all went down the minute we heard the siren. But now they've got plane spotters on the roof – with flags.'

'So have Burrell's. And Marks and Spencer. And Boots. And—' added Gladys.

'Yes, thank you, we don't need the entire Trade Directory.' Beryl didn't appreciate being interrupted. 'White for the alert, shop to shop, then red once they actually see a plane,' she continued matter-of-factly. 'Then it's all bells and whistles on the sales floor and everyone scuttling down as fast as they can. Well, you have to make way for customers, of course.'

She didn't sound too impressed with that, either.

'But sometimes the air-raid warnings can last all night,' objected Lily. 'What then?'

'You're stuck, ducky.'

'It's never actually happened,' said Gladys consolingly. 'And we've never actually been seriously bombed, have we, in Hinton. There's only a couple of factories, and nothing big like Birmingham or West Bromwich or . . .'

She obviously couldn't bring herself to say 'Coventry'.

'No, but . . . well, they can always get things wrong,' said Lily. 'Burrell's got hit last winter.'

'That,' said Beryl dismissively. 'A couple of incendiaries the Jerries couldn't be bothered to lug back with them.'

'I suppose.'

Lily was glad she'd be able to tell her mum about the precautions at Marlow's. She knew it had been bothering her. Dora would be relieved Lily had had a hot lunch too. It wasn't just Lily's wage which was going to be a help to their household budget.

'Why does Beryl have to be so snide all the time?' she asked Gladys as they made their way back to the sales floor. 'I notice she still had to sit with us. Obviously nobody likes her. And fancy asking the boss's son what was going on!'

'I know,' Gladys sounded resigned. 'But that's Beryl. She seems to get away with it. "If you don't ask, you don't get" is what she says.'

'Yes,' replied Lily. 'And one day you might get more than you're asking for, like the sack!'

Gladys shook her head.

'Not Beryl. Mr Bunting, the buyer on Toys, you've seen him—'

Lily had. Short, plump, with a frill of white hair round a bald crown, he looked like the old toymaker in the fairy story. It had come as no surprise to Lily to learn that he doubled as Santa at the staff Christmas party.

'He's been here years. He's a soft touch – that's what I heard Miss Frobisher call him.' Gladys hesitated. 'Beryl calls him something quite different, of course.'

Beryl would, thought Lily.

Lily was on her hands and knees, trying to brush up the nap of the carpet where a set of glass-fronted drawers had stood, when she was aware of a little cough behind her.

'Excuse me . . .' It was the first time a male voice had spoken to her since she'd stepped through the staff entrance and the first time that day that anyone who might be senior had given her, however nicely phrased, anything but an order or an instruction.

Without looking round – surely it wasn't Mr Marlow Junior, the floor supervisor? What had she done? What hadn't she done? – Lily scrambled to her feet. Her hair, tamed by her mum that morning, had gone its own way with the effort of her scrubbing, and she pushed it out of her eyes with the back of her hand. With the other she smoothed down the skirt of her dress, horribly aware of the dust and fluff it had attracted. And she'd been congratulating herself on being put on a carpeted department instead of having to stand on a hard parquet floor all day!

'Will you be much longer? Only I rather fancy the dining set that we've got on promotion in that little area. Sideboard in carved oak, Tudor – well, Tudor style – to the right, draw-leaf table central, a couple of chairs . . . Think I'll have room?'

'Erm, probably, as long as you're not planning on Henry VIII sitting there with a goblet and throwing a chicken bone over his shoulder as well,' offered Lily.

'Hah! Hadn't thought of that!' said the young man. 'But now you mention it . . .'

'I was only joking!' said Lily quickly.

'I realise that. But I could set the table to make it look more tempting. Sorry, I should introduce myself. James Goodridge. Jim. Third sales, Furniture and Household.'

'Lily. Lily Collins.'

Lily found herself looking up into deep-brown eyes behind wire-framed glasses. And looking a long way up. Sid was tall, but this lad – Jim – must be well over six foot, and skinny with it – a right bean-pole, her mum would have said.

'I'm sorry if I'm holding you up. It's my first day,' she added.

'I thought I hadn't seen you before. Well, seems we're going to be neighbours.'

'Looks like it.'

She couldn't place his accent. Not Midlands, definitely, but not posh, like old Mr Marlow, and not put on, either, like she could tell Beryl was trying to do. It was sort of natural, gentle, like the hills on the calendar her mum kept in the kitchen, the one that had come as a pull-out with *Woman's Weekly* at the turn of the year. And then she heard herself saying – a bit forward, perhaps, but he seemed so normal and friendly . . .

'Perhaps once you've set the table I can come for tea.'

'You're on! So what do we need? I'll half-inch some stuff from Small Household – tray, tray cloth, crockery, teapot . . .'

'Cake stand,' suggested Lily. 'No cake, we'll have to pretend that . . .'

'Cake stand! Of course! You're going to be good at this sales lark, Lily.'

'Well . . .' Lily was pleased with the compliment, but cautious. 'I've got to be good at being a junior first.'

'It's not so bad. You can soon work up.'

'I hope so.'

Then, in case anyone was looking, she added quickly:

'I'd better get on. Or you'll never get your stuff moved in time for breakfast, let alone tea! You should probably check with Miss Frobisher, but she told me and Gladys she wanted our old sales space clear for you by three o'clock.'

'Perfect. See you later!'

Lily watched him go, skirting a display of soft toys in his dark suit, watched him stop by Miss Frobisher, checking with her as she'd suggested, presumably, and then bound back up the stairs. He was all angles, tall and gawky, nothing like as smooth as the other salesmen she'd observed, with his wrists poking out from his shirt cuffs, his thatch of dark hair, and his glasses ever so slightly askew.

He seemed awfully nice, though. Friendly. And he'd spoken to her like a human being although he was a salesman proper, and she was a very junior junior.

She might be bounded on one side by bitchy Beryl in Toys, but with Household and Furniture on the other, Gladys an ally on her own department, and Miss Frobisher to learn from, Lily, as she went back to her brushing, felt very fortunate indeed.

Then it happened. The air-raid sirens began their wailing in the street outside. Above her head a bell shrilled, across the floor a whistle sounded, then another, sharper, longer . . . There was a flurry of alarm, then the buyers took charge, shepherding customers towards the stairs, prising people who were insistent on completing their purchases away from counters, making sure they had their own belongings and, crucially, their gas masks, with them. Lily looked round, not sure what to do, but Gladys was at her side.

'Wait till Miss Frobisher tells us we can go. Or gives us a customer to take down.'

'A customer?' Lily looked horrified.

'Don't worry, it's never happened yet,' Gladys assured her.

Luckily, because of the disruption of the move, there weren't many customers on the first floor and within seconds Miss Frobisher beckoned them over and told them to take the back stairs as quickly as they could. Lily had hoped to get away from the ear-splitting bell but another was clanging on the stairs, which with the ringing of feet on stone and the carrying of voices up and down the stairwell – some anxious, some bored, some annoyed – was even worse. And then, worse still, there was Beryl.

'All we need!' she cried. 'Me and Les are going to the pictures tonight! Well, supposed to be!'

She glared at Lily.

'I hope you're not going to be bad luck!'

Chapter 4

Lily's first impression of the shelter was its size. It seemed to stretch for miles – well, it must do, if it connected in a sort of dog-leg with Burrell's basement way down the street. She'd seen newsreels at the pictures, of course, of big air-raid shelters in London and people sleeping in the Underground's own tunnels. She'd watched grimly as they tucked small children up with their teddy bears, tried to read in the gloom, or knit, or play cards to pass the time, and not to flinch too much in front of the camera when the air juddered with explosions on the streets above. The sirens went often enough in Hinton, because of planes flying over and back to other, bigger towns, but Lily had never had to spend a raid in a public shelter. She didn't count the one at school, because you knew everyone; you were among friends, and the teachers were in charge, and however frightened you might have been you had to put on a brave face for the younger kids and try and keep them amused – or at least not let them get upset. And if the warning went when she was at home, their next-door neighbours had an Anderson shelter in the back garden, and she and her mum had always taken refuge there.

It had been a right performance getting it installed, Lily remembered. Their neighbours' backyard had been concreted over, so Sid and Reg, before Reg had joined up, had helped break up the concrete with pickaxes and dig the deep hole to fit the shelter in. Lily had helped pile all the soil from the hole back on top of the shelter, and the biggest slabs of concrete and some fresh cement had been put back to make a sloping roof. Lily had wondered why – was it to make it look nicer? But Mr Crosbie, their neighbour, had laughed in a scornful way and Reg had quietly explained that no one cared about the look of the thing. It was so that any incendiaries would slide off and not burn through.

Lily had hated every moment she'd spent in there. Obviously, there was the being scared, and not just from the moment you heard the whine of the siren. Sometimes, often, she was scared even before. She couldn't say exactly why, but it was as if since the start of the war – from the time she'd realised what it actually meant – she'd been living with her head constantly on one side, her heart beating that little bit faster, her mouth dry yet needing to swallow, her stomach turning over, the blood in her ears constantly pulsing, alert to anything that could be the sound of a plane. As if that wasn't enough, there was the damp earthy smell of the shelter, the raw slats of wood to sit on, the battery-powered lamp which would often give out, the stink of the paraffin heater and worst of all, the bucket in the corner, which they'd all had the embarrassment of having to use. Fear played its part there as well.

Mr Crosbie was a warden at the public shelter two streets away, so if there was a raid he wasn't usually there, just twittery Mrs Crosbie and their son Trevor, who was eight, and had adenoids and sniffed a lot. Lily sometimes wondered, when the war was over and she thought about it all, what she'd remember most. She hoped it wouldn't be smells: the smell of stale breath, and the bucket, and the graveyard smell of the shelter making her feel she was dead already, when being walled up in this tomb was the very thing that was supposed to be keeping her alive.

'Oy! Dopey!' Beryl waved her over. 'There's a space here.'

Somehow, in the crush, Lily had lost sight of Gladys, though she could see her now, lucky thing, sitting with Miss Thomas on one of the benches along the walls. Lily squeezed in beside Beryl who, relieved from her duties on the shop floor, seemed to have decided to use the hours that lay ahead to interrogate Lily. Not about her family, or where she lived, or what she was like as a person, but if she had a boyfriend, what film stars she fancied, and whether she owned a pair of stockings. Needless to say, Lily did not, but Beryl did, of course, and soon, unsatisfied with Lily's disappointing answers, was happy to hold forth about her own likes, dislikes, and achievements. Rather too happy for Lily, especially in a public place, as Beryl divulged details of some of her past boyfriends and advised Lily on suspenders. Though she did learn one useful piece of information: in the fullness of time, and still using precious coupons of course – there was no getting round that – she'd be able to put her name down at the hosiery counter at Marlow's for stockings to wear to work.

'Not the best, of course, not fully fashioned,' explained Beryl. Lily wasn't quite sure what that meant, but she wasn't going to admit it and open herself up to more teasing. Doubtless Sid could fill her in: he'd probably had to buy them for girlfriends. 'But at least then you can stop wearing those stupid ankle socks!'

Having to wear socks to work had been another thing that had depressed Lily about her appearance, but she'd noticed all the other juniors wearing them, Gladys included. Let's face it, grown women were having to wear ankle socks these days, at least for everyday.

Not Beryl, who extended a stockinged leg.

'These are only rayon, I'm working up to nylons,' Beryl went on. 'If I play my cards right with Les . . . who knows . . . ?'

She gave Lily a sidelong, smirking look, including her in the conspiracy. Lily felt instantly sorry for Les, poor mug. He must be the one forking out for stockings already. Lily wondered how he could afford it.

So the time passed, awkwardly for Lily. Beryl prattled on, reading out snippets from the *Reveille* and *Picture Post* magazines that were being passed around. The hands on the clock passed five o'clock, then six . . . The ladies from the canteen came round with meat-paste sandwiches, and you could get a drink of water from a big urn if you wanted. Lily had one, but only took sips – she was sure there'd be a better arrangement than a bucket in the corner, but she was embarrassed to ask, and didn't want to find out. But she had to admit, spending time in the shelter at Marlow's, even with Beryl as company, was preferable to hours with Mrs Crosbie and Trevor. Though she couldn't help thinking about her mum. She hoped she was safe in the Anderson shelter. Dora didn't know yet about the safety precautions Marlow's had taken, though surely she'd assume that a place with its sort of reputation wouldn't take any risks with its staff, let alone customers. Lily had no

way, anyhow, of letting her know she was all right
– in fact that she felt safer here than she'd felt in
any raid so far. At least she could breathe. At least
she could stand upright if she wanted to. And at
least there was light.

Finally, finally, Beryl turned away to torment her
other neighbour, Mr Bunting, her boss. Lily saw him
reluctantly put down his *Just William* book ('Research!'
he'd claimed with a twinkle) to listen to Beryl's
chatter. He really was a softie, bless him.

At last Lily was free to look around. Though there
was no aircraft noise that sounded close by, still less
any bombs, Gladys was sitting stock-still and staring
straight ahead of her. However bad the raids might
be for Lily, she reflected, how much worse for Gladys,
every one a reminder of what her parents had gone
through. Miss Thomas was chatting to Miss Frobisher,
she saw, Miss Frobisher as immaculate as ever, her
skirt and jacket still looking crisp, her stockinged legs
crossed, though in a concession to the situation, she'd
kicked off her shoes. The other Childrenswear sales-
lady, Miss Temple (Lily couldn't imagine ever feeling
familiar enough with them to think of them as 'girls'),
was sitting not far away. She must have come down
with a couple of customers. They had their coats
with them, and handbags; the older woman had a
couple of parcels. They looked like a mother and
daughter, the girl not much older than Lily. They
were holding hands, and tightly, Lily noticed.

She was just thinking about her own mum again, and that at least she had Sid with her, who'd be some comfort, and would talk sense about Lily being bound to be safe, when it happened. It came out of nowhere. One minute there was a hum of chatter from the hundred and fifty-odd people in the room, the next there was the sound of a plane and a terrific tearing, screaming sound, followed by a massive chest-constricting thump. Somehow, deep down as they were, however many floors of concrete and steel of Marlow's were above them, it rocked people back in their seats and almost winded them. The lights suspended from the ceiling shook, flickered and went out, before coming back on again in time for Lily to see the girl opposite – the one who'd been holding her mother's hand – jump up and start screaming.

'Violet!' Her mother tried to pull her down again. 'Violet, it's all right. We're all right! Stop that!'

But Violet couldn't. She stood there, shaking and screaming, screaming and shaking, all eyes on her, her mother trying hopelessly to calm her. Miss Frobisher wriggled her feet back into her shoes and got up to try to help, Miss Thomas following behind. A couple of other salesladies crowded round, offering a handkerchief dipped in water and smelling salts. Soon the girl was surrounded by well-meaning do-gooders, who were doing no good at all. Lily couldn't bear it. Jumping up, she crossed the floor, found a way through the crowd, grabbed the girl's

47

shoulders, and shook her, hard. Violet stopped screaming momentarily, then started again. Without hesitation, Lily raised her hand and slapped her. Violet took a step back, opened her mouth to scream, then raised a hand to her face and sank down into her seat. Her mother put her arms round her and leant her head against hers as the girl started to cry. Then, apart from Violet's sobs, there was a deathly silence broken only by the far-away clanging of fire engines as they rushed to the scene of the blast. Lily slowly raised her head and met Miss Frobisher's eyes. Miss Frobisher shook her head. Lily put her own hands to her face, both of them. What had she done?

'You're all right! Oh, Lily! Thank God!'

Lily's face was pressed to her mother's shoulder, against the old plaid dressing gown with its frayed yellow piping. It smelt of her mum, of lily of the valley talc, of camphor, of home.

It was nearly midnight. The raid, or the danger to Hinton at any rate, had been over by ten, but it had taken Lily over an hour to get home in the blackout, trying and often failing to pick out the now patchy luminous paint on the kerbs. She stumbled a few times, often finding her way more by the glow of lit cigarettes than anything else. There weren't many of those – though enough for her not to feel scared – but at least there were some people about, trapped in town, perhaps, like she had been, by the raid. She was more shaken by what she overheard. The bomb had dropped near Tatchell's, the only decent-sized factory in Hinton, that had made carburettors and speedometers for cars before the war and was now making aircraft parts. But if it had been aimed at Tatchell's, people were wondering, why not a bigger payload? Why only one bomb? Everyone had an opinion or had heard something different. The plane had been winged by an ack-ack gun . . . no, it had been hit in the fuselage and been leaking fuel . . . no, it was the pilot; he'd been wounded, so had hit the button to offload the last of his ordnance and headed for home . . . No one knew for sure and they probably never would, unless the plane had come down somewhere this side of the Channel, so what was the point of guessing, thought Lily. It was a sign of how tired she was that she didn't care. She was usually the first to want to know; to try to make some sense of the nonsense of it all, death dropping from a summer sky on to a blameless row of houses and a pub, apparently . . . a few more lives and families destroyed. Again, rumour had anything between two and twenty dead, plus, people speculated, those dying, injured, trapped, survived . . .

It was all too much for Lily. She'd got home in a daze and was still in a daze when Sid pressed a mug of cocoa into her hand. He was dressed – he'd been out looking for her and couldn't think why he'd missed her on her way home.

Lily looked down through the coiling steam of her cocoa. She felt the warmth of the mug and held on tight. It seemed like the only real thing in the world.

'I came through the park,' she confessed.

'The park! What were you thinking?' cried her mother. 'You don't know who could have been hanging about in there and—'

But at Sid's warning look, Dora held up her hands in submission and turned away.

'You were just trying to get home double quick, weren't you, Lil?'

Sid was trying to help her out and Lily nodded. She couldn't tell them she'd walked home in such a state she hadn't really noticed which way her feet were taking her. She'd been too busy replaying the awful aftermath of what she'd done.

Violet and her mother had been quickly led away to another part of the shelter. In fact, Lily had learnt, there was a sort of dormitory where anyone who wasn't feeling well could go and lie down. There were half a dozen camp beds screened off from the rest of the space by a wooden partition, and the store's nurse had a basic medical kit for use in emergencies. Lily had been led away too, by Miss Frobisher, out on to the stairs.

'I don't quite know what to say.'

Miss Frobisher was lighting a cigarette. Like everything else about her, the whole action was elegant – the cigarette tapped on a green enamelled case and lit with the snap of a matching lighter. She drew a deep breath and the tip of the cigarette glowed in the gloom. She seemed as cool and in command as ever but smoking on the premises by staff, except in the canteen, was strictly forbidden, so Lily could gauge the extent of her boss's agitation.

'I've simply never had to deal with anything like this before.'

'I'm so sorry, Miss Frobisher,' stammered Lily. 'I don't know what came over me.'

Except she did. She knew, because she'd seen one of the teachers do it, when they'd been caught in a raid at school, the very first time the sirens had gone, and Deborah Lowe, with her silly fringe and freckles, had gone glassy-eyed with fear, and started an awful wailing, and one of the teachers had given her a good smart smack which had sorted her out.

'Only . . . no one else seemed to be doing anything much and what they were doing, well, didn't seem to be working. And I do believe that' – Lily was basing this on a newsreel she'd seen – 'if one person gets upset and panics, it . . . well, it can affect other people too.'

'That may well be,' said Miss Frobisher, puffing a ribbon of smoke up the stairs with a toss of her head. 'But it's beside the point. If it had been another staff member, even someone senior to yourself – well, that would have been one thing. Bad enough, but we

could have dealt with it internally. But a customer
. . . !'

Lily hung her head. Was she going to break all
records at Marlow's, and not in the way she'd hoped?
The first person to be sacked before they'd even
completed a full day's work?

'I shall have to take it to Miss Garner. As I said,
it's beyond anything I've ever had to deal with before.'

'I'm really sorry if I did wrong, Miss Frobisher,'
said Lily again.

'And she'll have to take it to Mr Marlow, I should
think. Oh, Lily. And I really thought I could perhaps
make something of you.'

Looking down now into her cocoa, Lily bit her
lip. She'd let everyone down, her mum, Sid, Gladys,
herself. It'd be the laundry or the Fox and Goose
after all. And thinking about the opportunity she'd
lost somehow unfroze everything she'd been keeping
in. Her lip wobbled and tears dripped into her cup.

'She's washed out, Mum, get her to bed,' Sid took
away the mug. 'She'll have to be up again in a few
hours.'

Dora put her arm round her daughter, regretting
her previous outburst. She'd only spoken that way
because of the fear and the worry. Why did anxiety
so often come over as anger?

'I'm sorry, Mum. I'm sorry,' said Lily obscurely,
apologising not for the park, but for something her
mother didn't even know about.

'Don't be silly. I'm sorry for going off like that. It was only because . . . oh, never mind. We're all a bit beyond ourselves, aren't we?'

Lily nodded.

'Bet this feels like the longest day of your life, eh, Sis?'

Sid patted Lily's shoulder and she nearly crumpled. Please don't be nice to me, she thought, forcing her eyes wide to stop the tears, or it'll all come out!

'Tell you what. You can sleep in with me tonight, love,' offered her mum. 'Would you like that?'

Lily nodded dumbly.

'Yes, please,' she whispered.

She didn't imagine she'd sleep much, wherever she was.

Miss Frobisher had told her not to go down to the lockers the next day, but to take the service lift up to the third floor, the floor where Miss Garner – and Mr Marlow – had their offices. The floor where only a week ago, Lily had had her interview, and had left with such high hopes. She wasn't sorry not to have to mix with the others, to see the stares and the nudging. She was sorry not to see Gladys, to say goodbye if nothing else, but never to see Beryl again could only be a blessing.

She had to squash into the lift with a cage of gents' socks and caps steered by a grizzled man with a moustache, presumably on his way up to the stockrooms.

He manoeuvred his load wordlessly aside so Lily could get in with her gas mask and bag, which contained the contract of employment she'd signed only yesterday and hadn't had the chance to drop off at the staff office. Nice waste of paper and ink that had been!

'It's you, in't it?' the man said as they creaked up past the first and second floors. 'The little miss who slapped that other little madam down the shelter last night?'

'Don't, please.'

'No need to apologise, love. There's plenty on the staff who'd love to land one on a few of our customers, and without the excuse of a Jerry over-head! And on a few of the management, come to that! You only did what no one else dared. It raised a smile with some of us, I can tell you.'

'Oh, well, that's all right then!'

'Sorry, chick. I didn't mean . . . you're new, ain't yer?'

'Newer than new. Yesterday was my first day,' Lily confessed.

'Dear oh dear! Start as you mean to go on, eh?'

'I don't think there'll be any going on,' said Lily sadly.

Her new friend shook his head.

'That's a pity. Even more of a pity there's no union here that might fight your corner. We're trying to set one up, but these family firms . . .' He tutted and rolled his eyes. 'You wouldn't be able to join till you was sixteen, of course, but at least a union'd look out for you if you was in trouble.'

'Well, that's good to know. For other people,' said Lily. 'But it won't come in time for me, I'm afraid.'

'In that case you'll have to stick up for yourself, won't you? You don't seem backward in coming forward.'

'Oh, I don't think so,' said Lily sadly as the lift clanked to a halt at her floor. 'That's what got me into trouble in the first place.'

'My forms from yesterday, Miss Garner.'

Lily placed them on the desk.

'I'd already signed them, I'm afraid. I'm sorry about the waste of paper. But I know you wanted the paper clip back especially.'

'I did, Lily. Thank you.'

Miss Garner was still trying to come to terms with all she'd learned about the events of the previous evening from Eileen Frobisher, who'd sought her out to explain the situation. This was, of course, precisely the sort of thing Miss Garner had dreaded with the type of girls she was having to take on. She'd anticipated most things – or thought she had. Slapdash appearance, grubby fingernails, slatternly habits, dropped aitches, mispronunciations . . . chatting amongst themselves or, worse, over-familiarity with the customers . . . that was as far as her imagination had taken her. Assaulting the customers had never occurred to her. But . . .

'The thing is, Lily,' she said, 'I've had a telephone call. From Mr Marlow.'

So he knew as well! Lily's cheeks flamed.

'And he . . .'

Miss Garner removed her treasured paper clip from Lily's forms and stowed it in a little japanned box on her desk.

'He'd had a telephone call from Mrs Tunnicliffe. Violet Tunnicliffe's mother,' she added, inscrutably.

Lily bit her lip. Hard. Was Miss Garner going to deliver the killer blow, or would Lily be passed on to Cedric Marlow? Would he rant and rage? She didn't somehow think that would be his style. More a sort of sad disappointment that she'd turned out so badly. Either way, it'd end with her being shown the door.

But Miss Garner was speaking again.

'It seems that Violet's very highly strung. They've had trouble with her before in air raids. The doctor prescribed a bromide, but they didn't have any with them yesterday.'

'That's awful,' said Lily. 'I'm sorry.'

'Yes, well, it gets some people like that, doesn't it?'

The little japanned box had a picture of a temple or a palace or something on it, brilliant in gold and turquoise. When the sun poked through the taped-over window, it throbbed with colour. Miss Garner saw her looking at it.

'My brother sent it to me. He's out in Syria. Perfect for paper clips.'

'I see,' said Lily automatically, though she couldn't believe they were talking like this, about paper clips of all things.

Please. Get on with it, she thought. Why are you dragging it out?

'The fact is' – Miss Garner couldn't keep the surprise out of her voice – 'Mrs Tunnicliffe's actually rather grateful to you. She can't do anything with Violet when she gets like that. If it had gone on much longer she'd have screamed herself into fits, and it needed someone to bring her to her senses.'

Another 'I see' would have done well here, but Lily was too stunned to speak.

'In fact, Lily, if you really want to know—'

Miss Garner herself sounded amazed as she pulled a piece of scrap paper towards her.

'I wrote this down so that I could relay it correctly. Mrs Tunnicliffe couldn't praise you highly enough. "Quick-thinking" was the phrase she used. And she told Mr Marlow to make sure you were properly thanked.'

'Never!' The word was out before Lily could help herself.

A brief smile touched Miss Garner's lips.

'That's what she said. But—'

She couldn't let this go without delivering something of a lesson.

'You crossed a line, Lily, and I can't recommend you ever do the same in future. Though let's hope the situation won't arise.'

'No, Miss Garner. Of course not. But – have I got this right? Shall I . . . can I . . . can I stay on?'

'Yes. You can consider yourself reprieved.'

Lily looked blank. It wasn't a word she knew.

'It means that it'll go in the incident book, though I'm not quite sure under what heading . . . but when it comes to your staff record – well, it's more likely to be entered as a mark in your favour than against. Anyway, leave that to me. We'll say no more about it. Well, go on!' she chided. 'You'd better get to your department! Or you'll be late!'

'Yes, Miss Garner.' Lily was beaming. 'Of course! And thank you!'

She scuttled down to the basement and stowed her things away. As she straightened her hair in the mirror – no Beryl to hog it today, just a few stragglers, as the ten-minute bell had already gone – she still couldn't stop smiling. She'd somehow got away with it, she'd lived to fight another day. No, bad choice of words – lived to work another day. And at Marlow's, not at the laundry, not at the Fox and Goose!

'Thank you, God,' she breathed, as she walked on to the sales floor. 'Thank you, thank you, thank you.'

Miss Frobisher looked surprisingly unsurprised to see her – Miss Garner must have tipped her off. Miss Thomas raised an eyebrow to Miss Temple but gave Lily a smile. Gladys was open-mouthed, her face a pantomime of astonishment, delight and relief. But best of all was Beryl, whose mouth also fell open – in shock.

'Not so unlucky after all,' she hissed as she passed Lily later that morning. 'How did you do it? Who do you know up on the third floor? Got a mate up there, have you?'

'No,' said Lily.

'Well, you've got away with it this time,' said Beryl nastily. 'But you'd better watch your step.'

'Oh, I will,' Lily assured her. With you and everyone else, she thought, as Beryl turned back to her own department.

She wouldn't be taking any more chances.

Chapter 5

Over the next few weeks, as a thankful Lily settled in, she began to feel more and more at home at Marlow's.

Miss Frobisher was certainly determined to make sure she 'got to know the department'. Day by day she took Lily round the racks and display cabinets, pulling out drawers, showing off leather bootees with embroidered flowers (pink or blue), tiny but fully fashioned socks and miniature vests. In the toddler section for boys there were flannel shirts, elasticated bow ties, velveteen shorts, and child-sized braces. For girls, there were Liberty lawn dresses, corduroy pinafores and Viyella blouses. The party dresses, their protective tissue removed for the day's trading, hung stiffly on their racks, crying out for jelly, ice cream and streamers. Some hope these days, thought Lily – though maybe not for the sort of children whose parents could afford these prices on top of their child's coupons. Miss Frobisher pointed out again where items were missing – the sizes and styles Lily and Gladys had carted up to the stockroom. These were the ones the juniors would be sent to fetch.

Lily's bond with Gladys was strengthening every day and Lily was so relieved that it was Gladys she worked with, not someone like Beryl, who continued to smirk when she saw them leaving the store arm-in-arm, and mockingly called them 'the lovebirds'.

'She's just jealous,' Lily reassured Gladys. 'She doesn't seem to have a single friend of her own on the staff.'

'She's more interested in boyfriends, isn't she?'

They'd both seen Les, who, Lily learned, worked as a driver in Despatch, lounging with a cigarette by the staff entrance as he waited for Beryl to complete her elaborate toilette at the end of the day.

But there was something admiring and envious in Gladys's tone, and Lily knew there was nothing her new friend would have liked more than to have a boyfriend of her own. But if Lily despaired about her looks, at least she had a pert little nose and wide-set blue eyes, unlike Gladys whose hair was poker-straight, whose looks were unremarkable, and who was prone to the odd outbreak of angry spots.

Gladys was almost as potty about the pictures as Sid, though naturally she preferred a 'nice romance' to the action-adventures Sid enjoyed. Her search for a Hinton-based Errol Flynn was hardly likely to be satisfied soon, though, if ever, and not just because of her looks. It was a shame, because Gladys was so kind and generous – such a good person – but the sort of person people took advantage of. As Lily had realised on that very first day, it was a good job Gladys had Lily to be her protector, even if only from the likes of Beryl.

Despite her bravado, Lily was still a bit nervous of Beryl herself. She had such a bold manner with men, and such a sharp tongue. Beryl would smile quite brazenly at Robert Marlow when he toured the first-floor departments, whereas Lily and Gladys tried, as the staff manual urged the juniors, to make themselves helpful but invisible.

Only with Jim did Lily risk a smile and a word on the shop floor. The day after the air raid, he'd arranged his Tudor-style dining set in the corner he'd identified, and set the table with cloth and crockery, but Lily hadn't been invited to tea. He hadn't witnessed the shelter incident but he'd heard about it, of course, because he'd grinned at her and asked where she'd learn to throw such a powerful right hook. Lily had blushed and he realised he'd perhaps gone too far.

'One way to get yourself noticed, I suppose,' he'd commented.

'I shan't be repeating it, don't worry,' was Lily's response.

After work, as they walked to their respective bus stops, Gladys took her to task.

'How do you do it?' she demanded.

'What?'

Lily wasn't aware she'd done anything.

'Talk to people – boys – like that Jim – the way you do.'

The question baffled Lily but it was true, Gladys blushed and stammered if anyone in trousers, staff or customer, young or old, gave her so much as a polite nod of the head and a 'good morning'.

'I suppose,' said Lily thoughtfully, 'it's because I've grown up with them. Boys, I mean – my brothers. I'm used to having them around. I don't think anything of it.'

Gladys sighed enviously. Apart from the father she'd adored, she'd never been exposed to male company the way Lily had.

'Come to tea,' said Lily impulsively. 'One night soon. Then you can meet Sid for yourself. You'll see, it's impossible to be shy with him around!'

Gladys's face lit up.

'Oh, Lily, I'd love that!' she cried. 'Thank you!'

'I'll have to ask my mum,' warned Lily. But she knew Dora wouldn't mind. She was over the moon that Lily had found such a good job. Her wages helped with the housekeeping, and with Sid at home to help with the veg plot, life was easier all round. His foot was healing, but he needed to give it a while before he could fully put his weight on it without doing further damage, the doctor reckoned.

Before Lily knew it, she'd been at Marlow's a month, and Miss Frobisher took her to one side. Her probationary period was up.

'So, how are you liking us?'

'Oh, Miss Frobisher, I love it!' exclaimed Lily. 'I feel so lucky, I really do!'

'Well, that's good to know. You've certainly knuckled down after your rather . . . rocky start.'

Lily knew what she meant and hung her head.

'It's all right, Lily,' said Miss Frobisher kindly. 'I think you'll do very well. I need a bright girl like you. There used to be six staff on this department – myself, three full-time salesgirls and two juniors. Now all my full-timers have gone off to do war work, so there's only you and Gladys, and Miss Thomas and Miss Temple, who retired years ago, really – and Miss Thomas only part-time. You could be serving customers sooner than you think.'

Lily glowed. And gulped.

'Don't worry,' Miss Frobisher smiled. 'Ask the others if you're not sure. Gladys will give you all the help she can, I know, and the salesgirls if they're not busy. But never let a customer see you look confused. Take your troubles away to a colleague. Is that clear?'

Lily nodded.

'I'll try not to let you down, Miss Frobisher,' she assured her. 'I really am grateful for this job. And, well . . .' Her eyes met Miss Frobisher's cool grey ones for a moment. 'A second chance.'

'Then prove it to me,' she replied, but with a smile. 'And you can start by tidying away those vests, please.'

As usual, without even seeming to move her head, she'd noticed that Miss Temple had finished serving a customer and was now escorting her to the lift. Miss Frobisher herself swooped off to attend to a woman dithering by a display of little Argyll pullovers.

'Mrs MacRoric! How good to see you . . . how are your boys?'

Lily moved to the counter and started re-tying the ribbons on the little crossover vests. As she slid them as neatly as she could back into their cellophane packets, her gaze drifted to Household where she could see Jim serving a tall, bulky man with a military moustache. The man was jabbing his finger repeatedly, evidently making a point. And making sure Jim took it . . .

'I said "usual arrangement", didn't I?' he boomed. 'What part of that do you not understand?'

Jim paused in wrapping the purchase, a fancy chrome ashtray on a stand.

'All of it, I'm afraid, sir,' he replied, genuinely puzzled. 'The usual arrangement for a purchase like this nowadays can only be "Cash and Take" or "Account and Take". Is that what you mean? I take it you have an account with us?'

Sir Douglas Brimble looked at him coldly.

'Of course I have an account! Do you think you're being funny, young man?'

'No, Sir Douglas, I wouldn't dream of it.'

'Not your idea of a joke? Nor is it mine. I'm not talking about my account!'

Jim still looked baffled.

'Oh, for heaven's sake, the same arrangement that I have with Mr Bishop. Look, just fetch him, will you?'

Maurice Bishop was Second Sales on the department, a sharp-faced chap in his twenties – an Army reject on account of his supposed asthma.

'I'm sorry, sir, Mr Bishop has taken his annual holiday this week.'

This was not the answer Sir Douglas wanted. Irritably, he leant further over the counter and the jabbing forefinger made contact with Jim's lapel.

'Do you know how much I've spent in this store over the years? This past year, even? It's customers like me who keep places like this going, especially in these straitened times. We pay your wages!'

Jim had certainly seen Sir Douglas in the store, indeed on their department, but he'd always been served by Maurice Bishop until now.

'That may well be, sir, but—'

'Account and Take indeed!'

'Don't you have a car, Sir Douglas? Is that the problem?'

'Of course I have a car! Impertinence!'

Sir Douglas Brimble of Holmwood House, stock-broker, landowner, former councillor, and past Mayor of Hinton, was a man accustomed to getting his own way. Instantly.

'My problem, as you put it, is that my wife dropped me off. I shall walk to the station where I am catching a train to Birmingham for a business lunch. If you think I'm going to lug an ashtray on a stand round with me all day, you've another think coming!'

There was a pause while the bristling moustache bristled.

'Usual arrangement!'

The one thing Lily was still uneasy about was going to dinner alone. For the first few days after the incident in the shelter, she'd had to endure a lot of sidelong looks and questions and it was hard to explain away how she'd managed to be kept on without revealing what Miss Garner had told her. Even a few weeks on, she still felt some of the staff were looking at her, judging her, and, not knowing of Mrs Tunnicliffe's intervention, wondering how she'd managed to hang on to her job. Lily certainly didn't feel she could share the real reason for Violet's hysteria – the secret wasn't hers to tell – on top of which she felt strangely protective towards Violet. In any case, if she wanted further vindication, customer confidentiality, she'd learnt when she finally got to the end of the staff manual, was paramount. At the same time, she knew that her first day's dinner break with Gladys had been an exception: the two juniors couldn't be off the department at the same time. Today, however, as she left the sales floor, by great good fortune Jim caught up with her and they walked down to the canteen together. Lily was still getting used to the menu and brightened when she saw it was Irish stew.

'Don't get excited. Gravy with gristle,' warned Jim, but Lily eyed the ladleful on her plate with relish. There were the usual collapsing potatoes too, and cabbage – again. But there was roly-poly with currants ('If you can find them,' warned Jim) for afters – and Lily intended eating every mouthful. They carried their food to a long table, squeezing with their trays held high past men from the warehouse playing cards for matchsticks.

It was then, as they ate, that Jim related his odd encounter with Sir Douglas.

'But what did he mean?'

'That's what I didn't know. But I wanted to find out. So I had to pretend I did.'

'How?'

'Come on, you go to the pictures, don't you?' grinned Jim. 'You know the bit where our hero has a sudden thought, or realises something, or remembers. They do this knowing sort of look. So I gave him one of those.'

'Knowing?'

Lily stopped with a forkful of stew halfway to her mouth. She'd never heard anyone talk quite like Jim. Not to her, anyway, not even Sid, who had a pretty vivid turn of phrase when he liked, the more so since he'd joined the Navy – and not in a good way, Lily's mum often scolded. Jim's tone was sort of casual, but confidential, and chatty. Now he tutted impatiently.

'Like this!'

He mimed an expression somewhere between surprise and 'Aha!'

Lily nodded uncertainly.

'I don't think Clark Gable's got anything to worry about,' she smiled. 'And then?'

'And then I apologised profusely. Claimed I understood. So Sir Douglas huffed and puffed, said he should think so too. We made out his account as "Account and Take", he signed it, I put the docket in the tube, it came back receipted from the cash office, he crammed his hat on his head, and off he stomped.'

'Leaving you with his ashtray! But if you only pretended to know . . . and he left without it . . . what are you going to do with it?'

'Not going to do, already done,' said Jim triumphantly. 'Are you eating that potato?'

'Yes!' said Lily.

'Just thought I'd ask. You eat a lot, don't you, for a girl.'

'Oh, go on, have it then.' Lily forked the potato on to his plate. 'It's got an eye in it, though. Be careful.'

'Thanks.' Jim attacked it eagerly.

'You eat a lot, for one that's so skinny,' said Lily. 'Doesn't your landlady feed you?'

'Not much,' said Jim ruefully. The potato had already disappeared.

Lily returned to the subject in hand.

'So, the ashtray. What have you done with it?'

'Well,' began Jim, leaning in and dropping his voice, obviously relishing the telling. 'I don't know if you've been told, and maybe it doesn't apply to those tiddly little baby things you sell, but with petrol restricted to essential work only, we can only deliver larger items. Sofas and chairs and tables and beds and wardrobes – if we can get them to sell in the first place – but – well, you get the idea.'

'Definitely not ashtrays on stands.'

'Absolutely not. Anything like that the customer has to take away. Though evidently not in Sir

70

Douglas's case. So here's the good bit. He goes off, I wrap the thing up, address it to him and take it down to Despatch. The office assumed it was an add-on to some bigger item, told me it was Les Bulpitt's round, so I went and found him.'

'Les . . . ?' Lily frowned. 'Beryl – you know, on Toys – she goes out with someone called Les who works in Despatch. Same one?'

'Tall, a bit of a swagger and a lot of Brylcreem?'

'That sounds like him.'

'Interesting . . . Anyway, I offer up the parcel, and say the magic words. "Usual Arrangement for Sir Douglas Brimble." At which Les does a double-take and says, "You're in on it now, are you? I suppose Maurice filled you in . . ."'

'Maurice Bishop? In on what?'

Jim had demolished his pudding (not a bad number of currants, actually) in about four mouthfuls and was now eyeing Lily's. She curled her hand protectively round her bowl. Defeated, he took a sip of water.

'Les was due a break, so I went and stood on the loading bay with him while he had a smoke. Did the "all boys together" act. Pretended Bishop hadn't had the chance to explain it all to me before he left. Asked a few discreet questions. With my coat collar turned up, of course, best gumshoe style,' he added.

Lily never knew when Jim was joking. He was very like Sid in that respect.

'Turns out,' Jim went on, 'Sir Douglas and a select few of his cronies still have everything they buy delivered, large or small. There's a salesman in the know on every department they might use – Wines and Spirits, Tobacco and Cigars, Gents' Outfitting, Household. There's a "consideration", naturally, for any salesman involved for adding the stuff on the van, and any driver involved for adding the delivery on to his round when he's next in the immediate area. In fact, it turns out that's how Maurice Bishop is spending his annual holiday – not in Stoke-on-Trent with his aged mum but in Blackpool, if you please. It obviously all tots up.'

'But that's . . .' Lily hadn't yet memorised every single line of the staff manual but 'Private arrangements with customers are strictly forbidden' was one sentence which she very much remembered reading. 'That's a sacking offence!'

'Worse than that,' said Jim. 'It's illegal. How are they getting their hands on the extra petrol, for a start? Les, Maurice, all the others involved and, worse, Marlow's itself, could be prosecuted – and found guilty!'

'But, Jim,' Lily was aghast, 'if you've given Les the parcel, you're involved now, you're as bad as the others!'

'This is the clever bit,' explained Jim. 'I told him to hang on to it. Told a little white lie – well, a big white whopper. Said Sir Douglas might be adding a couple more small things to his order. Les was fine about it. He wasn't going anywhere near Sir Douglas's today anyhow.'

'Fine,' said Lily. 'But now what are you going to do about it?'

'Good question.'

Jim returned to his pudding bowl and scraped at an all-but-transparent smear of custard.

'You'll have to report it, surely?'

'I will. But . . .'

'But what?'

Jim leaned forward.

'Thing is, I need to find out a bit more. Who knows, exactly who's involved, names, how often it happens, how long it's been going on. That sort of stuff.'

'Can't you ask Les?'

'How can I? It's not as if I know the bloke. And as I'm supposed to be in on it, I can't pretend I've no clue what's going on. I've asked enough already. It's going to look too obvious.'

'You're stuck then.'

'Not entirely.'

A cunning look, much more believable than his 'knowing' one, crossed Jim's face.

'Not if you're right and Les and Beryl are—'

Lily could see where this was heading.

'Hang on!'

'No, listen – it's brilliant. You know Beryl. All you

have to do is get her at tea break, or go for a drink or something after work—'

'A drink?!'

'Only a lemonade!'

'But, Jim, I don't know her! And what I do, I don't much like. And she positively hates me!'

'Don't be ridiculous. How could anyone hate you?' Jim smiled.

And instantly, still shaking her head in disbelief, Lily knew she'd do it. Quite how she was going to win Beryl's confidence – and before Sir Douglas started wondering where his blessed ashtray was and caused a stink – was another matter.

'I'd be so grateful. You see, Beryl, I haven't really got a clue.'

Leaving a baffled Gladys to walk on her own, and gasping that she'd explain everything in time, Lily had managed to catch up with Beryl as they left the store. Now they were standing in the evening sun by the sandbagged Post Office on the High Street.

'I'd be so grateful. Truly I would.'

Beryl took a step back and smiled. Though her smiles always seemed more like a sneer to Lily.

'Well, I'm sorry, but where exactly do you expect me to start? Hair, clothes, shoes, socks – socks! – make-up – or lack of it – I mean, really!'

Lily looked meekly down at the offending shoes and socks. Her appeal had been one she calculated

Beryl would not be able to resist – to offer the hapless Lily advice on clothes and make-up.

'This is what I mean, Beryl. Anything you could do to help – not that I can afford much . . .'

She suddenly realised with alarm that Beryl might actually expect her to buy something to prove her new-found interest. Lily handed most of her wages over to her mum and did so gladly. The first thing she was going to spend her savings on, she'd decided, was a better birthday present for her mum than something from the market. And the second thing would be a tie for Sid. Only then was she planning on spending anything on herself.

'Well, I hardly expect you to start off in Marlow's! But I tell you what . . .'

Lily's ruse had worked. Beryl was clearly flattered to be asked, though it would have killed her to have shown it.

'Woolies'll still be open. We'll go there.'

Five minutes later, as the Woolworth's sales assistants sighed and looked at their watches – they stayed open half an hour later than Marlow's, but it was very nearly closing time – Beryl was demonstrating lipsticks.

'If you're serious, you ought to get in quick,' she advised. ''Cos this is the next thing that's going to disappear. So, I mean with your next wage packet.'

She twirled a lipstick up from its case and displayed it.

'Tangee Uniform lipstick,' she said. 'I wouldn't touch it, but for a baby like you, it's just a hint of colour, see? First step up from Vaseline. Good for starters. But still looks natural.'

Lily nodded, her eyes widening when she saw the price. The whole thing was impossible – but Beryl was so carried away with her own sense of importance and so enjoying imparting information that she didn't notice.

'Yes,' she lamented. 'They say Coty's going over to making foot powder and anti-gas ointment, and the metal in lipstick cases and compacts has all got to go for shells. So much for keeping up morale, eh!'

Lily tried to look as shocked and disgusted as Beryl about it, though privately, and despite her desperation to look older, it seemed to her a much better use of resources. The important thing was that Beryl believed she was genuinely interested in all this and was a willing disciple.

'That was so kind of you, Beryl,' she said as sincerely as she could when they stood outside again. Behind them the staff were covering the counters and bolting the doors. 'Thanks so much for explaining it all. I'd never have known all that any other way.'

Basking in the false flattery, Beryl preened, while Lily waited for a thunderbolt to strike her down.

'So,' she added oh-so-casually. 'Which way do you walk home from here?'

'I'm not going home,' said Beryl. 'I'm meeting Les. By the bandstand.'

'Oh, I can cut through the park!' said Lily, adding boldly, 'Shall we . . . ?'

This was where Beryl would surely say she wasn't being seen with a frump like Lily, and the plan would fall to bits, but to Lily's amazement, Beryl hooked her arm through hers and gave her a grin.

'Come on then, kid. At least there's no swings, so you can't embarrass me by wanting a go.'

Like the park railings, they'd been taken away for armaments last summer.

'It'll be the blooming bandstand next,' mourned Beryl. 'I hate this war, don't you?'

Lily shrugged. 'Yes, of course, but what choice do we have?'

'I'm sick of it, no this, no that, nothing decent to buy that we can afford, rotten food, and not much of it, nothing nice or fun—'

'You have fun with Les, don't you? Going to the pictures and stuff.'

Lily couldn't believe how easy it had been to bring his name into the conversation.

'Oh, Les!'

'What about him?'

'He's all right, I suppose. I mean, he'll do for now. Until someone better comes along.'

'He's got a good job at Marlow's,' started Lily, but Beryl looked at her with narrowed eyes.

'A driver in Despatch? I hope I can do a bit better than that for myself. But at least he knows how to give a girl a good time. We don't sit in the cheap seats at the cinema, I can tell you.'

'The circle? How can he afford that?'

Beryl gave her a sidelong look and another smile-cum-smirk.

'You don't have to stick with what Cedric Marlow pays you. If you know how to play the system.'

Lily did her best to look both curious and impressed.

'Beryl . . . How do you mean?'

They'd reached the park now and her new confidante drew her down on to a bench. In front of them was what before the war had been a flowerbed full of salvias. Now it, and the grass around it, had been ploughed up for allotments.

'All right,' began Beryl. 'I'm going to tell you something. There's a bit of a racket going on with some of the wealthier customers. Those who've been used to snapping their fingers and having everything done for them.'

There was admiration and bitterness in her voice.

'Well, they don't expect the war to change that. So to keep them happy, to keep the wheels turning so to speak, Les and some of the other drivers and sales people make it easier for them. Oil those wheels if you like. So they'll do that bit extra.'

Lily goggled obligingly as if this was the first time she'd heard all this. Beryl looked gratified.

'Les has got to be careful, of course. All his mileage is logged, but if he organises his round carefully, and filches some petrol from the vans whose drivers aren't in on it, or tops up with petrol from . . . well, that he's got hold of . . . he can hide the odd bit of extra distance. With road blocks and the Home Guard doing their stuff, who's to say if he's had to go a bit out of his way?'

'Very clever,' said Lily acidly. Caught up in her story, Beryl didn't notice.

'People might have to wait a day or so to get their things, but they don't mind that. And the other bit extra – the bit of money he gets from doing it – he's taking a risk, after all – well, it all helps, doesn't it?'

'So hang on, you're telling me certain customers can get stuff delivered that they shouldn't?'

'You're quick, aren't you? Of course, management mustn't know. Well, with certain exceptions.'

'Managers are involved?'

'Why not? Everyone's on the make, aren't they, given the chance?'

'I can't believe it!'

Now Lily genuinely was shocked. She could well believe the racket – it only confirmed what Jim had been told. But managers! When they were so trusted and, well, respectable – and earned, surely, a decent salary anyway? That really did amaze her.

'Who?' Lily sat forward. 'Which managers exactly?'

Beryl looked at her, long and hard. Lily could see

the emotions fighting within her: self-importance and the satisfaction of imparting what she knew versus discretion. It wasn't a long struggle. Beryl swooped towards her and whispered in her ear. Lily fell back as if she'd been thumped in the chest.

'No!'

'Oh, yes.'

'Not really?'

'Yes, really! Well, you said you wanted to learn, kid.'

As Lily shook her head, still disbelieving, Beryl sat back herself, pleased with the effect she'd had. She examined her nails and found them pleasing too, even without the crimson nail polish she'd have preferred – forbidden of course for Marlow's staff, who were only allowed clear – not that any was readily available now.

'Well, there's your first lesson,' she pronounced. 'Everything and everyone may not be quite what they seem.'

Chapter 6

'Jim? Jim?'

Jim looked round, startled. Robert Marlow, in his pinstriped suit, with stiff collar and firmly knotted tie, was striding towards him. Jim had snatched off his own tie the minute he'd left the shop, rolled up his sleeves and hooked his jacket over his shoulder. The sinking sun was still warm and after a long day cooped up inside, he was longing to feel the rays on as much of his bare skin as he could.

'What's of such gripping interest?'

Robert had arrived beside him now and Jim caught a waft of cologne. He was surprised and a little perturbed to be accosted like this. He didn't know much about Robert Marlow except that he was, of course, heir to the business – and so to everything that Cedric Marlow had lovingly created Marlow's to be.

Jim and Robert were much the same age, Robert just a few years older, but there, quite apart from status, any likeness stopped, physically and, Jim suspected, on pretty much every other level. Jim was well aware of his physical shortcomings, with his hair which stuck up in a tuft at the back and specs he was always fiddling with, so which were always bent out of shape. His tie was most often adrift, however much he tried to straighten it, the seat of his suit trousers was shiny, and his shoes, though polished, had seen better days. Robert, on the other hand, had the buffed and glossy look of a man who'd known nothing but privilege since birth. He had thick well-cut fair hair, a rosy face that looked as if it had been scrubbed with a Brillo, and his clothes were always immaculate. His hands were pink and clean and his nails clipped. He was, in short, a perfect physical specimen. As for their interests – well, Jim could only guess, but he hazarded that Robert's were cars, cricket, and pretty young women – definitely not the quieter pursuits Jim enjoyed. In the few months Jim had been at the store any conversation with Mr Marlow Junior that wasn't about stock levels, a customer query or a complaint had been confined to pleasantries about the weather. But now a friendly-sounding Robert indicated the lime tree into whose canopy Jim had been peering. Jim explained.

'It's a nest. Blackbird. Listen.'

In the stilled air – so few cars on the road had to bring some advantages – a demanding cheeping could be heard.

'Must be a second brood. Mum and dad are off foraging for food, I suppose.'

Robert's eyebrows telegraphed surprise.

'Birdwatcher, are you? Still, that goes with the territory where you come from, I suppose. The wilds of Worcestershire!'

He grinned as Jim dipped his head.

'There's a bit more wildlife there than in town, yes, but it's amazing what thrives here. Nature's pretty hard to keep down. Which is encouraging, really. When everything else is limited or rationed or being pounded to bits.'

Robert Marlow pulled a face.

'Crikey! This is all getting a bit deep!'

'Sorry. But when you see bombsites – buddleia and loosestrife starting to grow – don't you think that's incredible? That huge mess of rubble and dust but they always find a way into the light.'

'What, there's a message there somewhere?' Robert pulled a face. 'Like I said, all a bit deep. Come on, enough philosophy for one night. I'm taking you for a drink.'

'But—'

'No arguments. We'll find a place with a beer garden. You can commune with nature with a pint in your hand!'

They found a place with not so much a garden as a yard – this was Hinton after all. It did, however, have a free table, a sawn-off, upturned barrel partly in the sun with a couple of rickety chairs round it. It even had beer, which was never a certainty.

'Cheers!'

They knocked glasses and each took a cautious sip. Watery, as they expected, and their expressions showed it. Jim looked guardedly at Robert, who'd insisted on buying the drinks. This was unprecedented, and they both knew it.

'Smoke?'

Robert produced a gold cigarette case engraved with his initials, flicked it open and offered it to Jim.

'I don't, thanks.'

'Of course not. Clean living. Very wise.'

Robert extracted a cigarette, lit it with a lighter which matched the case, took a deep draw on it and sat back.

'You're probably wondering what this is all about. I don't make a habit of waylaying people in the street. Forcing them into public houses. But, well, my father and I have been having a chat. He's given me special responsibility for the junior staff. So when I saw you . . . I thought I might as well start somewhere!'

'And this "responsibility" entails what exactly?'

A group of drinkers nearby erupted in raucous laughter. Robert waited for the hilarity to die down before continuing.

'It's about staff morale, Jim. Now the war's dragging on, and we don't seem to be making much progress . . . shortages starting to bite, not so much stock to sell, customers getting tetchy, the store turned upside down and inside out, and now to cap it all we're a storage depot for the RAF . . . Dad and I want to know how the staff are bearing up. Because as the old man's fond of saying – happy staff make happy customers.'

Jim could not in a million years imagine Cedric Marlow saying anything of the kind. Though he had heard a rumour that Marlow's was changing its advertising agency from a small local firm to a bigger one from Birmingham. Perhaps they'd been coming up with slogans. They were probably the same outfit that had invented 'Doctor Carrot' and 'Potato Pete'.

'So come on, Jim – how are things? Tell me about life behind the scenes. The chat, the gossip. The stockroom and the staff canteen.'

Jim considered. He wasn't sure about this. Wasn't Robert being a bit over-friendly all of a sudden? Was he being pumped for information, or was the interest sincere? But he had to say something, not that he really knew.

'Things are fine – I think. As far as you can tell.

There's a bit of grumbling of course, but that's inevitable, isn't it? Everyone grumbles – about queuing, about the blackout, about rationing . . .'

'But the shop itself? Any specific complaints there? A feeling that one department's being favoured over another? Moans about being cramped for space? Hours of work? Conditions?'

Jim suddenly realised what Robert was getting at. 'You're worried about a strike!'

Strikes had been banned for over a year under Defence Regulations and arbitration was compulsory. But there was a lot of discontent, even in some of the industries most essential for the war effort, like engineering and mining, and the unions were starting to believe that you could strike in wartime and win. There was no union at Marlow's – only bigger stores like the Co-op had one – but Jim felt the day had to come when all workers had some sort of protection from unscrupulous bosses. Not that Marlow's were unscrupulous – they looked after their staff pretty well, considering. Though when, along with the rest of the staff, Jim had heard about Lily and the incident with Violet Tunnicliffe, he'd wondered what would have happened to her if things had turned out differently and she'd faced the sack. Would anyone have spoken up for her? Would he?

Robert raised an eyebrow, waiting for Jim's reply.

'I certainly can't say I've heard or seen anyone that

disgruntled,' Jim said. 'Strike, what about? Why? What for? Have you heard something different?'

Robert took a swig of his drink and pulled a face. Jim couldn't help thinking wine or whisky would probably have been more to his taste, even if the beer had been full-bodied. But Robert had presumably felt obliged to go with this blokeish man-of-the-people act.

'Not within Marlow's, no. But there's trouble brewing at Burrell's. Or could be. Some of the women workers agitating for equal pay, can you believe!'

This was the talk in pubs and homes up and down the country. Privately Jim couldn't see anything wrong with it, provided women were doing the same jobs as men – as many were, now. But he could see the worry for shop and factory owners who employed so many women – their wage bill would rocket.

Judging rightly however that he and Robert might not agree on the subject, Jim bought time by taking a sip of his drink too. Robert had finished his cigarette and ground it out grittily underfoot.

'When I say not within Marlow's,' Robert went on, 'I suppose I mean not yet. But some of the staff we've had to take on lately . . . that new little girl on Childrenswear for instance?'

'Lily?' Jim was incredulous.

'That's the one. You know about that business in the shelter. With the Tunnicliffe daughter.'

'Yes, of course. But . . .'

'She got lucky there,' mused Robert. 'Turns out she did the right thing. But in other circumstances . . . With that sort of attitude, if she turned her mind to workers' rights . . . she could be a proper troublemaker.'

'Lily, a troublemaker!' Jim burst out. 'She wouldn't dare, not now, anyway. I think she feels lucky to have kept her job. I can only say again,' he repeated, 'I've heard nothing about strikes from the people I talk to.'

Jim didn't add that he didn't really talk to many people at all. Lily and Gladys, yes – and they were nice girls but only kids – junior even to him. On his department, apart from the buyer, Mr Hooper, and Mr Seddon, first sales – both retired staff brought back for the duration – and a couple of juniors, there was only Maurice Bishop, who'd seemed jealous of Jim from the start and had never been over-friendly. In the canteen, the nearest Jim had heard to a complaint was the lack of a decent football team to follow or the comments when a promised cottage pie turned out to be thickened Bisto topped with mash.

Robert, however, seemed relieved.

'Well, that's good to know. And look, Jim – I don't want you to think I'm sounding you out as a sort of spy in the camp. I wouldn't ask you to do that. I'm going to be talking to other younger staff members – men and women, all grades, all departments.'

'I didn't think that for a minute,' Jim reassured him, though he had, of course. What he was pondering now was his next move. Since he had Robert's attention, should he or shouldn't he say something about Sir Douglas and the whole delivery business? There might never be another chance.

'You won't only concentrate on the departments the customer sees, will you? I mean, you'll go into Despatch too?'

'All of it! Especially there, actually, as those bods are far more likely to have Labour views!'

'Not necessarily,' ventured Jim. 'I've got the feeling there are some who are more out for themselves than they're collectivists.'

'What are you getting at?'

Robert Marlow may have looked like he was all for show, but there was a shrewd brain in there, Jim was sure. He took a breath, sat forward, and out it came. The full story of Sir Douglas Brimble's chrome ashtray, the nod, the wink, the racket being operated with Despatch and selected sales assistants, the 'consideration' paid to them. Jim didn't mention any names – he didn't want to, not at this stage anyhow, but he told Robert enough to see the other man's handsome face toughen into something much less attractive.

'Let me get this right. You're telling me you know and have proof – well, verbal proof – that some of the staff are taking tips, and some of the drivers are ripping off petrol or getting it on the black market, to make deliveries they shouldn't?'

'That's exactly it,' nodded Jim. 'I don't know how many or how far up the . . . well, the hierarchy, it goes. Or quite how many departments, or customers, are involved. But today with Sir Douglas – it wasn't a one-off, that's for sure. And something like this could get Marlow's into serious trouble, as you appreciate.'

'Too right it could!'

Robert looked justifiably furious.

'Look, Jim, I can't thank you enough for telling me this. It's not what I expected to hear, not what this little chat was about at all, but I'm really glad we had it!'

'Good, well, I hope you'll be able to do something about it,' said Jim.

'Dead right I will! This is going to get my personal attention!'

With that, Robert Marlow got up, pinching the already perfect creases in his trousers back into shape and straightening his tie.

'I owe you one, Jim. Don't forget it.'

Chapter 7

Lily was in the middle of a dream when the sirens went off. She hadn't expected to be able to get to sleep at all, her head so full of what Beryl had told her, and now . . . well, was it a dream or a nightmare? It involved for some reason her old geography teacher, who was pointing at a map of British Bechuanaland and telling them that very shortly they wouldn't be able to get lipstick there, when a man with a moustache burst in waving an ashtray on a stand and said the Germans were coming. Lily awoke – mercifully – to find her mum standing over her, shaking her shoulder.

'Lily! Come on, love, shelter, now!'

It was a clear, starry night and perfect for an air

raid, Lily had time to notice as she squeezed through the gap in the fence and took her place in the shelter with her mum, Sid, Mrs Crosbie and Trevor and the dreaded bucket. Three long hours they were there, Lily propped between her mum and Sid, who had their arms round her, Trevor snivelling in his sleep, Mrs Crosbie knitting determinedly as the two-tone screams of the engines and the crumps and aftershocks reverberated. When the all-clear finally sounded, dawn was breaking salmon pink in the east. Through the side alley between the houses they ventured out into the street. The raid had sounded so close they couldn't believe their row of houses was still standing. In fact the whole street was, and what they could see of the next. There was no smoke hanging over Hinton at all.

'Must have been poor old Birmingham again,' Sid concluded. 'Or Wolverhampton, maybe. It was a big one, anyhow. And it's those damned twin engines. Don't sound that far away, do they?'

They never did to Lily. With every squeal and whistle of every plane something in her shrank a little bit more. She hated it: she hated spending her life cowering like this. And they'd all hoped the worst of the Blitz was over.

'This weather's got to break soon,' remarked her mum as they trooped back inside, trying as she always did to re-set their day back to 'normal'. 'The garden could do with it.'

Normal! Some hope.

It was hardly worth Lily going back to bed, so she concentrated on trying to tame her hair – she was getting more practised at it since she'd had to start looking smart for Marlow's every day. In the end, as so often when she had more time, she was late by the time she set out, and the bus with its woman driver was already wheezing round the corner a hundred yards away. Lily considered legging it to the next stop, but after the night she'd had and the lack of sleep both before and after the raid, she simply hadn't the energy. It would be more soothing to walk, anyway. It would mean taking the shortcut through the park, but it was daylight – her mother could hardly object to that. But the park brought it all flooding back. Only yesterday she'd sat here on a bench with Beryl and had heard so much to shock her. But as she walked round the pond with its shuttered boathouse and ever-hungry ducks – they didn't like the increasingly grey and gritty bread any more than the rest of the population – she saw someone she recognised.

'Jim!'

Lily had never been so glad to see anyone in her life. She'd been fretting as she walked about how she'd be able to get time with him on her own. Even if they managed to go to dinner together they couldn't be sure of not being overheard or being joined by other people. She'd have got in touch with him last night if she could, to tell him what she'd found out as soon as possible, but she had no idea where he lived – she hadn't known it was on her side of town.

'Lily! Is this your usual route?'

'Only when I'm late and miss the bus. What are you doing here?' Though as she asked the question she could see for herself. Jim had a box Brownie with him. 'I didn't know you were a photographer.'

'My landlady's such a misery and my room's so small and stuffy. It's such a beautiful morning, I couldn't bear to be indoors. Look at that tree!'

The horse chestnut – one of the few Lily could be sure of recognising – was certainly magnificent. Soon the five-fingered leaves would be crisping at the edges but for now, in this perfect clear summer – so-called 'Hitler weather', ideal for bombers – they still hung heavily green and the candles were a pure white.

'Not such a beautiful morning in Birmingham, I don't suppose. It's a wonder we can't see the dust from here,' Jim added grimly.

Lily had deliberately left the kitchen when the news came on. It had been Birmingham after all. Her mum and Sid were glued, but she was sick of hearing the reports. Only a month ago, with the Germans tied up on the Eastern Front, there'd been talk that the air raids would stop altogether. Some hope.

'Were they trying for Lucas and the BSA again?'

'Yep. Partial hit on one of them. And a complete

hit on a lot of people's homes. Again.' He paused, then: 'Anyway. Lucky meeting you.'

'You've got no idea how much!'

Jim tucked his camera away in its case.

'Come on then. What have you got to report? How did you get on?'

'You'll never believe it. I didn't at first!'

Jim's eyes gleamed behind his glasses.

'See! I knew you could do it!'

'You don't know what I had to go through to get it!' objected Lily.

'Never mind that. Come on, spill!'

'What? What? Oh, Jim!'

As she'd elaborated the full extent of what she'd learnt and how high up the management tree the scheme reached, Lily had wondered why Jim had gone quiet. His face, at first so animated and encouraging, had begun to look slightly wary, and then, when Lily began to name names, positively dismayed. Only then had he told her about his own conversation the previous evening with Robert Marlow. The final name that Beryl had whispered in Lily's ear.

'And you've gone and told him all you know? Oh, Jim! No! You can't have! What are you going to do?'

'Shush. Let me think.'

Lily had no time for that.

'You'll have to go to Mr Marlow – Mr Marlow Senior, I mean.'

'I can't.'

'Jim, don't be ridiculous. He has to know!'

'As if he's going to believe anything I say!' Jim was vehement. 'A mere employee – a nobody – slandering his own son – who's he going to believe?'

'But if you don't, Robert could tell him . . . well, Lord knows what! Make out you're in on the scheme rather than him . . . anything! You've got to get in first!'

'Lily, think about it! They live in the same house, for goodness' sake – it's probably already too late!'

'You can't think like that! Whatever Robert may or may not have said, you have to say your piece! Mr Marlow's a good man. Marlow's is a fair place to work – look how they treated me after – you know . . . '

Jim shook his head.

'No, Lily, It's no good. You did something sensible . . . I've done something stupid. And there's no way back from it.'

'Jim, I'm surprised at you – that's so . . . defeatist!'

Jim had the grace to laugh.

'This is so funny,' he said. 'Half my conversation with Robert – the first half, before we got on to Sir Douglas and his little set-up – was him asking me if I'd heard any insurrectionist talk on the shop floor.'

'Any what?'

She did wish he'd stop using words she didn't understand.

'Of course,' Jim went on – more to himself than Lily, almost – 'I don't know now if anything Robert said was genuine. The business about him being responsible for staff morale and so on . . .' He turned, seeming suddenly to remember that Lily was there. 'I mean, for all we know, Les had said something to him, whether casually or out of suspicion, and Robert was put on his guard. Decided to sound me out.' He shrugged. 'Anyway, it doesn't matter now.'

'It jolly well does! If he tricked you into telling him what you know – that makes him even more of a snake!'

'There you go again,' smiled Jim. 'Maybe he was right about that, anyway.'

'Jim, stop talking in riddles. What are you on about?' It was no good, she'd have to ask him outright. 'What does insurrectionist mean, for a start?'

He could see she was getting impatient.

'It means sort of . . . revolutionary. He was basically pumping me about anyone who didn't know their place. Who might stir up trouble or start a strike. Fix a walkout, agitate for better pay and conditions. And your name came up.'

'Me?'

'Yes – as a potential troublemaker.'

'Me? That's . . . me? I've only just started! I'm too young to join a union! I'm not sixteen yet!'

'Age has got nothing to do with it. How old were

the matchgirls in the Bryant and May's strike? And that was Victorian times.'

'What?' There he went again with stuff she didn't understand. 'Look, Jim, can we concentrate on you here, and not me? This isn't about making trouble! This is about what's right, what's wrong – and who's in the right! We've got to think how to stop Robert dropping you in it!'

'Lily, I've told you – it's already too late!'

'It isn't! It can't be!'

They'd left the park long ago and were now nearly at the staff entrance to Marlow's. Jim grabbed her by the elbow and pulled her into an alleyway between a tobacconist's and a bookshop.

'Listen to me,' he said. 'I've been a first-class idiot. I shouldn't have gone for a drink with Robert at all. I don't know why I did—'

'From what you said, he didn't give you much choice!'

'Listen, please. Don't interrupt. I shouldn't have done it, part of me was saying I shouldn't—'

'But he gave you a perfectly good reason – you mustn't blame yourself!'

'Lily, I'm trying to explain!'

Lily gave in.

'But I did it – I went. I don't know, maybe I was flattered that he'd suddenly taken an interest in me, maybe I was a bit intrigued, maybe I hoped it was a genuine overture of friendship.' He grimaced.

'Shows what I know. Anyhow it's too late, the damage is done. To me, I mean. Trust me. I know it.'

'Jim, please—'

'No. There's no more to say. Now drop it. And look. We mustn't be seen together. It'll only harm your reputation.'

'My reputation?'

'I tell you, there's no future for me at Marlow's. If you want one, you don't want to be seen associating with me. Thanks for trying to help and all that. But I'm damaged goods.'

There was obviously going to be no talking to him. With a shrug and a sorrowful squeeze of her arm, Jim turned and walked away. Lily stood in the alleyway and watched him go. She saw him take a deep breath and brace his shoulders as he stepped on to the pavement and into the light. The sun caught his glasses for a moment and made them flare. Then he was gone.

A skinny cat came and wrapped itself round her legs, mewing for attention, but Lily was too distracted to stroke it. She realised she was shaking, even more than she had been in the shelter the night before, and it was only when she heard Marlow's clock strike the quarter that she pulled herself together. She couldn't afford to be late.

She made it on to the department with seconds to spare and submitted to the daily fingernail check. Her hands were still trembling as she held them out in front of her. Miss Frobisher gave her a long look but said nothing. Lily hoped she assumed it was simply lack of sleep after the raid, which was the main talking point among the staff. Miss Thomas had a sister in Birmingham who lived near the Lucas and BSA factories in Sparkhill, and she was dreadfully worried about her.

Lily made the required noises of sympathy, but her mind was on more immediate things. The store wasn't busy. Most people must have been feeling too weary to come shopping except for essentials and apart from nappies and feeding bottles, not much of what they sold could be classed as that. On Household, a couple of women were contemplating a cork-topped bathroom stool with Mr Hooper hovering helpfully. Jim was nowhere to be seen.

By dinnertime he still hadn't appeared, nor by the time Lily and Gladys began to shroud the baby clothes and party dresses in their tissue covers and to robe the counters in their twill cloths against fluff rising from the carpets when the cleaners came in at night. Lily was by now seriously worried. Had Jim gone to see Mr Marlow after all, like she'd begged him to? If so, what was the upshot? He couldn't still be closeted with him – or maybe he was? And Robert too, as he wasn't on the sales floor either. She hadn't seen him all afternoon, come to think of it. Maybe everyone, from the delivery drivers up, was being carpeted, quizzed, cross-examined. Something was clearly going on.

What she couldn't understand, what had kept her withdrawn all day, and which she'd had to explain away to Gladys as simply tiredness, was why Robert Marlow would be involved in such a scheme. It was quite likely the Marlows and the Brimbles knew each other socially – surely it'd be far too embarrassing for him to accept money from Sir Douglas for bending the rules? Unlike a delivery driver or a salesman, he couldn't need it, anyway. So what was in it for him? However hard Lily thought about it, she couldn't come up with an answer.

It was that evening that Gladys was coming to tea. Lily's mum had really taken to her.

'Poor lamb, losing her parents like that. And it doesn't sound as if her gran's in much of a position to make a nice home for her,' Dora had clucked when Lily had first asked if Gladys could join them. 'She can come as often as she likes!'

Gladys had explained that her gran suffered with any number of ailments, and frequently took to her bed, so Gladys was left with shopping, cleaning, and basic cooking, which as far as Lily could gather meant that tea was usually bread and cheese or bread and dripping. No wonder Gladys loved it at Lily's, with something tasty, or as tasty as possible, on the table, the radio playing dance band music, and Sid, now almost back to full fitness and barely limping, in his usual bantering mood.

Lily had hoped that exposure to Sid would make Gladys more relaxed in male company, but Gladys still blushed scarlet whenever Sid addressed a comment to her and stuttered a reply – if she could make one at all. Tonight, whenever she surfaced from her preoccupation with Jim, Lily noticed it more than ever. Sid was off again.

'All right then Gladys, let's say your star potential has been recognised, you're running Marlow's as the leading ladies' fashion shop in town. So in the film of your life, who'd play you?'

Gladys's hand flew to her mouth. Sid was outrageous.

'Oh, I don't know!'

'Come on, I do – and so do you! Ann Sheridan? Ingrid Bergman? No, I know – it's got to be Vivien Leigh!'

Gladys turned beetroot and looked down at the tablecloth.

'Sid,' warned Dora, 'stop teasing the poor girl.' She passed Gladys a bowl of sago. 'Have a dollop of jam, love. If we get a bit more handy with the gardening and get hold of a few strawberry runners, we could be making it with our own fruit next year!'

Gladys took the bowl and immersed herself in spooning jam before pushing the pot over to Sid. She didn't dare pass it in case their fingers touched – that would have been too much for her.

'And who'd be your Rhett Butler, eh? Got your

eye on anyone? Some handsome chap on Gentleman's Outfitting? A sturdy warehouseman?'

Sid was swirling jam freely into his own pudding.

'Sid! That's enough! And I don't mean jam!'

Dora drummed his knuckles with her spoon. Unashamed, Sid turned his attention to his sister.

'You're very quiet tonight, Lil.'

'We're all hoping for a quiet night, Sid,' warned Dora. 'So don't you go stirring things up!'

Sid wasn't the only one to notice that Lily was quiet. As they washed up – Sid and Dora listening to a brass band tribute to the Merchant Navy – Gladys asked her friend what was up.

Lily scrubbed at a burnt bit of sago on the Pyrex dish. She didn't want to lie, but what could she say?

'I'm sorry, Gladys, I can't tell you. I would if I could,' she added quickly seeing her friend look hurt. 'It's nothing to do with you and me, I promise.'

'Really? So we're still friends?'

'Yes, of course, silly!' Lily handed her the dish to dry. 'It's . . . oh, look, it's someone else's problem, but I know about it, and it's bothering me.'

Gladys couldn't get any more out of her, and as she wiped a final fork, gave up and broached something that was bothering her.

'Lily, you know Sid . . .'

'He is my brother!'

'Yes, all right . . .' Gladys concentrated on the fork so that she didn't have to look at Lily. 'You don't think . . . do you think . . . well, you know how he talks . . . the way he talks to me, I mean . . . that is, the way he was talking at tea, about boyfriends and that . . .' There, she'd said it! 'You don't think, do you, it was a sort of, well, a hint, at all, to try to find out if I had got a sweetheart, because . . . well, because he likes me?'

'Of course he likes you, you chump!'

'Really?' Gladys's eyes brightened and she looked up. With a dreadful back-flip of her heart and somer-saulting of her stomach – neither a good sensation on its own, and together, almost tipping her back-wards into the sink – Lily suddenly saw what she'd done.

She hadn't meant it like that – that Sid had any romantic feelings for Gladys – but she now saw that was exactly what Gladys was hoping. If Lily hadn't been so preoccupied she'd have picked up the signals from Gladys's stumbling confession, but now she'd given her friend false hope. If Sid spoke to Gladys in a friendly, teasing way, it was only because it was how he spoke to Lily. He saw them both, Lily was sure, in the same light. He was kind to Gladys as Lily's friend, nothing more. His friendly manner was merely his way.

'So will you ask him?' Gladys breathed. 'If I could be his girl? 'Cos I think he's lovely.'

Lily wouldn't have credited that her day could get any worse. But she'd just managed it.

Well done, Lily, she thought.

All she wanted now was for it to be over, and for the last twenty-four hours – her session with Beryl, Jim's encounter with Robert Marlow, and now this embarrassing exchange with Gladys – to be wiped from the calendar. And for tomorrow truly to be another day.

Chapter 8

To Lily's amazement, she slept. Maybe it was the previous night's air raid, maybe it was the day's events. Either way, she was exhausted, but when she woke up she felt, if not ready for anything, at least ready for most. She slid out of bed and unpinned the blackout. The refracted sun warmed her face, but when she pushed up the sash and leaned out, the air was still fresh. The birds weren't singing as strongly in the early mornings now, too busy from dawn to dusk chivvying their young, but Lily had no need to hurry. It wasn't yet half past six; she could go back to bed. She could lie for a good long while as she tried to work out what might happen next. The trouble was, she didn't need a good long while. She didn't need any time at all, because she couldn't begin to know. She had to see Jim and find out what had gone on – where he'd been yesterday, what had been said, by whom and to whom. Her head started to fill with impossible-to-answer questions. She had to get going.

She crept downstairs, out to the privy, and back inside to wash her hands and face and brush her teeth at the scullery sink. She was worried the Ascot's rumbling and grumbling would wake her mother or Sid, but when she tiptoed upstairs, their doors were still firmly closed. She climbed into what was now her Marlow's uniform – a grey skirt which she'd pounced on at a Red Cross rummage sale, and one of her two blouses – both white – well, whiteish, but what could she expect from pass-ons from Renee across the street? One had a small dicky-bow at the neck; the other, which Lily preferred, was shirt-style with fancy revers and darts to the waist which at least gave it – and Lily – some shape.

She was doubly grateful to Renee. Everyone was hanging on to their clothes, even the shabbiest ones now, since clothes rationing had come in shortly before Lily had started at Marlow's. Just my luck, Lily had thought. The one consolation about having to leave school was the prospect of a bit of money to spend on herself and the chance to buy herself a few pretty things for the first time in her life. (After she'd splashed out on her mum and Sid, of course.)

But now everyone had a book of coupons, enough – thanks very much, Mr Churchill! – for one entire new outfit per person per year. For anything else, it was 'make do and mend' – more of the same, as far as Lily was concerned. But Renee, now she was eighteen, was leaving her job in the typing pool at the Municipal Council and joining the WAAF. She wanted to do her bit, she said.

Sid had been rather more cynical about her motives.

'Huh, you know what RAF stands for, don't you?' he'd remarked, with the casual contempt of the Senior Service for an upstart. 'Those fly-boys? Running After Fluff!'

Maybe he'd had hopes of Renee for himself, Lily thought. Still, good luck to her. Renee would be spending her working day in uniform now. She'd be given a mac and a greatcoat and shoes, plus stockings, so she could splash all her pay on nice clothes for outside work. And be paid well enough to buy better quality things that would last – the sort of things Marlow's Ladies' Fashion department sold – printed *crepe de chine* tea dresses and top-stitched linen costumes and taffeta evening gowns.

'How to Look Stylish in the Shelter,' Sid had mocked. 'What to Wear to a War!'

He could talk, Lily had replied, with his lusting after ties. But it was true – there was always a way round things if you had money. As Sir Douglas Brimble had proved.

Thinking about him brought last night's sick feeling back. Lily went downstairs, grabbed herself a piece of bread and marg to eat on the way and left her mum and Sid a note. They'd be amazed she'd gone already. 'No harm in being early for once,' she'd written. No harm. Let's hope, she thought.

He wasn't there. Jim wasn't there. Not at the start of the day, not when Lily went to morning break, not when she came back. Not when Gladys chuntered on about Hedy Lamarr – *I Take This Woman* was back at the Gaumont and Gladys had sat through the complete programme – twice – in a single night. Not when Miss Thomas twittered about 'That monster, Hitler,' but still worried that Britain was now fighting with the Commies against him; not when Miss Frobisher raised her eyebrows about the baby night-gowns that a distracted Lily had put away with the boys' hats and caps.

She pulled Lily to one side.

'Is something wrong?'

'No, Miss Frobisher,' lied Lily.

Nothing you can help me with, anyway, she thought.

Eileen Frobisher looked at her quizzically. She knew Lily by now.

'Don't take me for a fool, Lily,' she said, but gently. 'I can see something's bothering you. Now what is it?'

This was almost as bad as her mum and Sid being nice to her when she'd got home after the air raid on her first day at Marlow's and the incident with Violet that she'd had to keep from them. Lily bit her lip.

'I'm sorry, Miss Frobisher,' she said. 'You're right. I'm . . .' She struggled to put it in such a way that it wouldn't be a lie. 'I'm worried about someone. I haven't been able to get in touch with them, and I'm worried about how they are.'

'Oh, Lily. It's no good, you know. It's the war. We can't always get news of people we're concerned about when we want it.'

'I know, but – this is different.'

Eileen Frobisher considered. The store wasn't busy. The summer sales weren't starting for another week. She'd already liaised with signwriting about the show cards, and there was plenty of time for the salesgirls to mark down the individual price tickets and for the juniors to sort the 'Special Purchases' of bought-in goods.

'Then go home,' she said.

Lily gaped.

'Go on. You might as well. You're no use to me at all like this,' said Miss Frobisher. 'I'll write you a note. Take it to sick bay and give it to the nurse. Tell the timekeeper as you go. Clock out as normal; when you come in tomorrow go to the timekeeper first, then the nurse, before you come to the department.

And don't worry. The note will say you've got a sick headache – but I'll make sure it won't come out of your paid sick leave.'

Lily found her voice.

'Thank you, Miss Frobisher,' she whispered. 'Thank you.'

'I don't make a habit of this sort of thing, Lily, as you may have noticed. I didn't do it for Miss Thomas, did I, when she was worried about her sister?'

Lily omitted to point out that if Miss Frobisher did it every time Miss Thomas was worried about her sister Miss Thomas would never be there.

'No, Miss Frobisher,' she said. 'I really am very grateful.'

Eileen Frobisher shook her head.

'That's two of your lives you've used up already,' she observed. 'Even cats only have nine. You're getting through them fast, Lily.' But she was smiling. 'Go. Go on. Go!'

So Lily escaped – past an astonished Gladys, past the nurse, clocking out and into the warm summer air, scrambling into her jacket as she went, heading for the park and the street which – thank the Lord – Jim had pointed out as they'd walked yesterday – only yesterday – on their way to work. He'd pointed out the house, too – number 15, green door, not-very-well-scrubbed step; her mum would have certainly given it one of her famous 'looks'. Now Lily was lifting the knocker, only to have it drop from her hand and find herself nearly falling forwards as the door opened. Jim was standing there in the dim hallway, a suitcase at his feet.

'Lily!'

'Jim!'

'What are you doing here? Why aren't you at work?'

'Because you're not!'

Gabbling, she explained how Miss Frobisher had let her off, how she'd had to, because Lily was so distracted.

'It's good of you to worry about me.' Jim took off his glasses, looked at them, and put them back on again. 'But there's really no need.'

'No need?' squeaked Lily. 'You get me involved in your sleuthing, it all goes horribly wrong, you disappear, and then I'm supposed to forget all about it?'

'Probably too much to hope for. I obviously don't get rid of you that easily. Joke!' he added quickly as Lily looked indignant.

'Well, you're here now,' he mused. 'We can't stand on the step all day. Let's go.'

They had nowhere to go, so they went to the park, Jim carrying his case, with his camera slung round his neck.

'I'd like to think I look like a professional photographer,' he said as they made for a bench in the shade. 'I suspect I look more like a seedy commercial traveller-cum-Peeping-Tom hoping to sneak a photo of some girl innocently sunbathing.'

'How can you joke about it? And keep joking!' demanded Lily. 'When are you going to tell me what's going on? And why have you got all your things with you?'

They found a bench. Jim placed his case carefully on the ground and sat down. He didn't look at Lily. He spoke to the distance, to the denuded children's playground and the still-standing bandstand.

'I've resigned,' he said.

'What? Why?'

'Come on, better than the sack, don't you think? Bit of a blemish on your record.'

'I think,' said Lily firmly, 'you'd better start again. Maybe from when you left me yesterday morning?'

Jim conceded.

'OK. Here it is. Plain unvarnished truth. I didn't go to the department—'

'I know that!' cried Lily. 'I was there all day, remember, wondering what was going on!'

'Lily,' reproved Jim. 'Do you want to hear this or not?'

Lily nodded, mute.

'Thank you.' Jim resumed: 'There was a message for me at the staff entrance, you see. Would I go up to the third floor. Well, I knew then, if I didn't before, that the game was up.'

'Robert had spoken to his father,' breathed Lily.

113

'Like I said he would,' nodded Jim. 'So, I go in, Mr Marlow's there behind the desk, looking pretty serious. No sign of Robert. But he's thoughtfully taken the time to fill his father in on some of the . . . well, what were referred to as "surprising and unseemly goings-on". And which he'd pinned on me.'

'Robert blamed you for the racket?'

Jim nodded.

'Turns out I'm the biggest criminal mastermind since . . . well, you choose. Dick Turpin? Al Capone?'

'Oh, Jim! You didn't speak up for yourself, did you?'

'I don't know why we're having this conversation, Lily, because I told you I wasn't going to.'

'I know. But I sort of hoped – when you were actually there . . .'

'I'd have some kind of Road to Damascus moment? More like *Road to Zanzibar*. Or the road to nowhere. Sorry to disappoint.'

'I am disappointed, Jim.' Lily couldn't help herself. 'I thought you were . . .' she tailed off.

'No, go on.'

Jim was looking at her and he wasn't going to look away first.

'All right. I thought you were someone . . . I could trust. Who'd do the right thing. Who cared about justice and injustice. Who'd always tell the truth – and . . . and . . . stand up for yourself!'

Jim smiled.

'Lily, I really admire you, you know,' he said. 'You're wise beyond your years.'

'Don't say that!' cried Lily. 'It's so . . .'

What was the word, she'd heard it, it was in her head somewhere.

'Patronising?' offered Jim.

That was it!

'Look, I'm sorry,' he said. 'But it's complicated. One day you'll understand.'

That was even worse. He was making her feel four years old, not fourteen.

'Don't give me that!' She was cross, yes, and hurt, too. 'You sound like a bad film! I've had enough of that, with Gladys going on about Hedy Lamarr all morning!'

There was a pause. Then Jim took out his handkerchief.

'It's the best I can do for a white flag,' he said, waving it in her face. 'Don't worry, it is clean,' he added as she jerked back. 'Truce?'

Lily still looked mutinous but inside she was trying not to smile. He looked so ridiculous, flapping his handkerchief like that. But she wasn't going to let him see it. This was serious. Didn't he realise how serious? She folded her arms.

Jim got up and looked around. He wandered over to the shrubbery and found a snapped-off branch. Coming back, he offered it to Lily.

'No olive branches to be had,' he said ruefully. 'Will this do?'

Lily looked at him straight. He wasn't in his work suit, just some old drill trousers and a checked short-sleeved shirt. He had a scar on his forearm, not much more than an inch and a half long, but lumpy: it should have been stitched. Some boyhood accident? A nasty one; the wound must have been deep. She realised there was so much about him she didn't know.

'It's holly,' she said coldly. 'Hardly the best peace offering.'

'Cripes, Lily, you're a demanding woman!' cried Jim. He dropped the branch and fell to his knees. 'This is worse than seeing Mr Marlow! Is this what you want? Abject grovelling?'

'Get up!' hissed Lily.

A man walking his Yorkshire terrier was giving them a very suspicious look. Even the dog turned its head.

'Ooh, someone's looking! So you do care what people think!'

Jim got up and resumed his seat. He touched her hand briefly.

'Look, I'm sorry. I'm sorry I haven't lived up to your expectations. I'm sorry if I'm not the person you thought I was. All can say is one day I promise I'll explain.'

One day? Why not now? But, but . . . oh, what

was the point? It was like all the fruitless speculation about why that stray bomb had dropped on Hinton a few weeks ago.

Jim had said he was sorry. What was the point of pushing it? If she did, he might walk away and never tell her. Maybe the best thing was to do what the posters had been telling them since before the war had even begun: 'Keep Calm and Carry On'.

'All right,' she sighed. 'You win. I don't like it but . . . well, what can I do?' She looked at him and shook her head. 'I know a brick wall when I see one. So have you thought about what's next? You've got no job. You've obviously left your lodgings . . .'

'Luckily my rent was paid up till today,' said Jim. 'So it couldn't have come at a better time, really.'

Lily shot him a 'don't start that again' look which, if she'd only known it, she'd got straight from Dora.

'Look, my landlady was an old boot who hated me from the start, I don't know why. She was a one-woman Ministry of Misery. Rationing? The more the better – baths, food, light . . . said I left shavings in the basin – I didn't, by the way – complained I slammed the front door – you had to, or it stuck – moaned if I ever had the radio on . . . I couldn't wait to leave.'

Leave? But to go where? He didn't mean leave Hinton? He couldn't!

'Are you going back home then?' she faltered. 'To wherever it is – Worcestershire?'

117

'Don't say it like that! It's not the end of the earth!'

'So you are?'

'No. No, no, no. Don't be silly. I'll get some other work round here. And some other lodgings.'

Oh, she was silly now, was she, for even thinking it! Lily added mind-reading to the list of skills she was clearly going to need in adult life.

'And how are you going to live till you do? And where?'

Jim shrugged.

'I've got a bit of money put by. There's always the YMCA.'

'A hostel?'

'Again, don't say it like that. It's not the work-house!'

'Maybe not, but . . .'

Then she had a brainwave. Reg wasn't at home. Sid was going back to the Navy any day now. Jim could have the boys' room!

Chapter 9

They couldn't go straight back to Lily's, of course.
Sid, or her mum, or both, might be there, not unrea-
sonably wondering what Lily was doing home in the
middle of the day, and with a young man in tow.
There was nothing for it, explained Jim. Hard as it
would be, they'd have to enjoy themselves.

It was a wonderful afternoon. Jim put his case in
Left Luggage at the station, then treated them to
something to eat – a sort of down-payment on the
rent, he said. All the same, she thought she'd better
not have anything too expensive – her Welsh Rarebit
was 4d, though Jim splashed out with a meat pie
which he proclaimed not bad, even if its contents
had, he reckoned, been an outside chance in the 1935

Derby. Then he gave her the choice of the pictures or back to the park.

'Oh, the park!' said Lily at once. 'Far too nice a day to be inside!'

So they found the one lone park-keeper, a bent old man in a battered cap, and Jim persuaded him to unchain one of the boats and find them some oars. Then, with the boat a floating see-saw, Lily clambered in, helped by Jim, and seated herself towards the back – the stern, Jim advised her – while he took the other seat and grasped the oars. He pushed off confidently, with Lily steering, or trying to, and rowed them with surprising strength all the way round the pond and under the bridge into the shadier bit with the overhanging willows and the little island where the mallards and geese built their nests. There he lodged the oars and let the boat drift and lay back and looked at the sky.

'Is it going to be a better world?' he asked her. 'After the war? What do you think?'

'It had better be!' Lily was stirring the silky weeds with her hand. 'Else what on earth are we fighting for?'

'I wonder sometimes,' said Jim. 'Hitler had to be stopped, don't get me wrong, but the way things are going – there's going to be a lot more fighting to come, I reckon. Let's face it, this war's turned out to be no more "over by Christmas" than the last. And we've invented a lot more nasty weapons since 1918.'

'Can we not talk about it?' said Lily. 'It's such a beautiful day, and we're not at work, and . . . I know I'm ducking it, and we can't get away from it, and I hate it and get fed up with it sometimes, hanging over us like it does – but not today, Jim. Please not today!'

'There's not going to be much we can talk about soon, is there?' said Jim with a grin. 'I was trying to keep off controversial subjects. Like Marlow's.'

Lily looked at him, exasperated.

'Well, we know whose fault that is! But don't worry, I'm not going to go over it all again. Instead, why don't you teach me to row? Properly.'

So Jim did, crouching behind her as she sat and grasped the oars, showing her where to place her hands for the best control and how to dip just deep enough in the water to make progress without wasting too much energy. To Lily's pride – and not without some amazement – she got them safely back to the boathouse without tipping them both in. The old man looked pretty amazed too.

'Good on you, chick,' he said, as he leant to drag them into the side. 'Don't see many young lasses take the oars. Thinking of joining the Wrens, are you?'

It was a stark reminder of their conversation – the one Lily had cut short.

'I think she needs a bit more practice,' said Jim quickly, to spare her. He got out first and helped Lily out too.

121

They found a patch of scrubby grass that hadn't yet been ploughed up, and lay contentedly in the sun, revelling in their freedom almost as much as the children streaming noisily out of a nearby school. They'd all been evacuated at the start of the war, but a lot had come back within weeks, either the children or their mothers hating the separation so much that they'd decided to run the risk of any bombing, which hadn't materialised at that point anyway. But then the air raid warnings had started virtually every night, and some of the mothers had braced themselves and sent their children away again. But Lily could still see them, and hear them, these ghost children, surging out happily with the others. There was another ghost she remembered too. There'd used to be an old man with an ice-cream cart who'd wait outside at the end of the school day in summer, but he wasn't there this year, and he hadn't been last year either. He'd gone, and not because of sugar shortages. Gennaro was Italian; he was in an internment camp somewhere up north, Lily had heard. Ridiculous – what was he going to do? – conceal messages in a wafer-cone for sweet-toothed spies? Because obviously he was bound to hear important secrets in Hinton, from the children playing catch-me-if-you-can and their mothers swapping recipes for left-overs.

She must have fallen asleep then, because the next thing she knew, Jim was poking her in the ribs and pointing at his watch.

'Closing time soon at the shop,' he announced. 'Look sharp.'

Lily sat up and rubbed her eyes.

'I think I was properly asleep,' she said.

'I know you were,' said Jim. 'Snoring.'

'What rubbish! I do not snore! You . . . !'

She tugged up a meagre handful of grass and threw it at him.

'Hey!' Jim ducked. 'Play fair!'

'I could change my mind about that room, you know,' Lily warned.

Jim looked serious.

'Are you sure about it? Really? Your mum won't mind?'

'Of course not!'

Lily spoke with a confidence she wished she felt. She was counting on Dora's good nature – and if that failed, the rent Jim would pay, however small, however temporary, would surely be a sweetener. She stood up and brushed the tufts of grass from her skirt. It reminded her of the first day she'd met him, scrambling up and brushing carpet fluff off that awful dress of Cousin Ida's. Thank goodness she'd managed to ditch that vile thing! She glanced over at Jim, who was polishing his glasses on the tail of his shirt. They'd both come a long way in a short time.

'Let's get going, then!' she said.

* * *

'But who is he?'

Dora had left Sid chatting to Jim over a hastily brewed cup of tea while she interrogated Lily in the scullery.

'Mum, I told you, I know him from work,' explained Lily.

'Yes, yes, Furniture and Household, I got all that.'

Dora was chopping carrots. Up, down, up, down, went the knife.

'What I mean is, where's he come from, and what's he doing here? Most importantly, why's he been let go?'

As Lily had seen her do a thousand times, in one expert move she seized the saucepan with one hand, held it below the level of the table and swept the pile of carrots into it with the back of the knife.

'Well?'

But Lily wasn't daft. Knowing this was the first question they'd be asked, she and Jim had rehearsed their story on the way. The best thing, they'd decided, was to stick as closely as possible to the truth. Jim, she hoped, was relaying the same tale to Sid in the other room.

'Jim resigned, actually.'

It was gratifying, really. Her mother nearly dropped the pan she was filling with water.

'Who resigns from a job at Marlow's in this day and age? Why would he do that? He must think something of himself!'

'It's not like that, Mum. Jim's got principles. He didn't like the way his department was being run. So he took a stand.'

'Took a stand? For his principles? That's all very well! We all like a principle!' Dora slammed the saucepan on the stove. 'If you can afford them!'

'It's not a problem, Mum. He'll walk into another job.'

'And what about a reference? Marlow's aren't going to think much of someone who flounces out on a whim. Or even on a principle!'

Lily hadn't thought of that. Maybe nor had Jim. She'd have to improvise. While sticking as closely to the truth, etc. etc.

'There was never anything wrong with Jim's work. He's honest and punctual and well-presented . . .'

'Well-presented? I've seen smarter scarecrows.'

Lily preferred seeing Jim out of his work clothes, actually. It made her feel more relaxed. But she spoke up for the more formal Jim anyway.

'He looks quite different in a suit. He'd never have been taken on at Marlow's in the first place, would he, if he couldn't cut it?'

She made sure to keep her voice reasonable, not indignant, or whiny. Dora had to concede the point. But she thumped the lid on the carrots all the same.

'And you want me to feed and lodge him? Starting now?'

'Only till he gets himself sorted. He'll pay!'

Dora lit the gas under the pan and turned round.

'Lily,' she said, calmer now. 'You know that's not the point. How many times have I had Gladys over to tea, and your other friends, when you were at school. I never mind another mouth to feed, even these days. But . . .'

'What?' asked Lily. 'Sid'll be going any day now . . .'

Dora said nothing. She went through to the other room and came back with a letter, which she held out to Lily. Lily took it in surprise.

'Came by the second post.'

The gas pulsed in the silence as Lily read the letter.

'Oh, Mum! Why didn't you say?'

'Mind? Why would I? It's not as if you're letting out my room before my bed's had chance to get cold!'

Sid sounded genuinely upset.

'I didn't know!' protested Lily. 'How was I to know this would be your last night?'

'Look,' said Jim awkwardly. 'I'll go. It's fine. The YMCA . . .'

Sid collapsed in laughter.

'Your faces!' he chortled. 'I had you there!'

It was true, even Lily had been momentarily taken in. Jim still looked doubtful. It took a while to get used to Sid's sense of humour.

'So . . . ?' he began.

'Come off it, Jim, you can't leave me on my own with these two!' objected Sid. 'I'll have them fussing round me all night! And I'm only going back to training! What are they going to be like when I'm actually deployed?'

The letter had been from Sid's unit, recalling him to his base by 0900 hours the next morning. The first train of the day left Hinton at six – 'sparrow-fart' according to Sid, which Jim mildly pointed out was an impossibility: birds didn't build up air in their stomachs like other creatures. But ornithologically accurate or not, Sid stuck to his description. If it had been Lily, she'd have left that same night, to be on the safe side – trains were hardly reliable – but Sid was confident the six o'clock – the milk train – would definitely run. He was determined to have this evening – his 'last supper' as he called it – at home. His terminology wasn't exactly helpful to his mum's nerves, though he was far from being posted yet.

'You'd better not snore, that's all,' he warned Jim, but interrupted himself to smack his lips as Dora arrived with the treat she'd always planned for Sid's last night – a bacon joint. It might only be the size of a half-shoulder of hamster, but it was still a treat.

'Can one of you boys make yourselves useful and carve? Or is that too much to ask?'

Dora's earlier mood had dispersed and she was back to her usual cheery, if no-nonsense self, on the surface at least. It had been the shock, that was all, of Lily turning up with this strange young man on an evening when she was still trying to come to terms with Sid going. But given that he was – and it wasn't as if she hadn't known the day was coming, and soon – well, to have another man about the place could only be a good thing. He seemed polite and willing, this Jim, eager to help too, judging by the way he'd set the table and carried in the coke for the fire. Coming from the country – near Evesham, he'd said – he seemed keen on their bit of garden too, praising her runner beans and instinctively bending down and pulling out a bit of groundsel he'd noticed. But such a skinny lad, a real strip of wind! Never mind. Rationing was taxing everyone's ingenuity, but he'd already given Dora his ration book. She knew how to stretch things, and she was planning a few good meals to fill him out.

Tea over, Dora took herself off: Cousin Ida was having a knitting party for Allied Prisoners of War. She'd mithered about it as it was Sid's last night, but he said he fancied a drink down the pub with any of his schoolmates who might still be around, so Dora headed off with her maternal conscience clear. It was a good thing Jim was here, or Lily might have had to go too, helping her mum and Ida and Ida's wispy friends wind wool in Ida's stuffy front parlour. Instead, she and Jim were left to weed and water the veg plot. Their task completed, Jim had gone inside to fetch them a drink when Lily, pinching off side shoots on the tomatoes, heard the back gate creak open. She peered round the wigwam of runner beans and saw . . . Gladys.

Gladys's face broke into a smile. From behind her back she produced a small paper bag.

'You're up! Feeling better? Good – 'cos I brought you these!'

Sweets!

'Oh, Gladys! You shouldn't have!!'

'Chocolate caramels,' said Gladys triumphantly. 'I know you like them.'

'Like them? I love them! You'll have to help me eat them though!' said Lily, slavering already. The bacon joint seemed a very long time ago.

'You're going to eat them now?' Gladys was sounding doubtful. 'If you've had a sick headache I did wonder if you'd fancy them at all.'

Lily had forgotten she was supposed to have been laid low all afternoon. She'd better get a grip on herself.

'I'm ever so much better,' she reassured her friend. 'I just needed to get out and get some fresh air, really.'

Like Miss Frobisher, Gladys was assuming that it was all down to the other night's air raid, the warm weather, and sheer exhaustion, which Lily was happy to go along with.

'I thought you weren't yourself last evening,' she said. 'You picked the wrong day to go sick, though,' she added importantly, thrilled at having some information to impart. 'You know Jim Goodridge? Well, he's been—'

'Let go?'

At that moment, Lily had actual proof. Jaws really do drop, or Gladys's did, as Jim appeared in the doorway with two glasses of water.

Lily's face signalled 'Help!' but Jim, listening from the scullery, had obviously had time to get his thoughts in order and he met Lily's look with one which said 'Leave it to me!' So Lily did. She went inside to fetch Gladys a drink, while Jim, she could hear through the open window, told Gladys the same story they'd told her mum and Sid. That though Marlow's clearly had to be seen to have taken the decision, Jim had actually resigned. He simply repeated that he hadn't been happy on his department, and that he was on the lookout for a better job, in Hinton if possible, and was staying at Lily's for a while till he could get himself settled.

Jim had waved Gladys to the ancient kitchen chair which Lily had brought out earlier, while he perched on the side of the raised bed. Lily emerged in time to see Gladys's still open-mouthed reaction.

Dear Gladys, thought Lily, handing over her drink and dragging over her mum's canvas stool as a seat for herself. Dear, unsuspecting, never-step-out-of-line, don't-say-boo-to-a-goose Gladys! What Jim had done – what Lily had done in skiving off, if Gladys had but known it – was as unthinkable to her as doing the Dance of Seven Veils in the middle of the staff canteen. But even Gladys, dear, slow-witted, backward-in-coming-forward Gladys, was bound to have a few burning questions in her mind. Like – and fair enough – why, of all places, had Jim turned up at Lily's for shelter?

But Lily's time indoors hadn't been wasted.

'I'm glad you came over,' she said – and meaning it. 'You see, Sid's been recalled. So when Jim said he was leaving his lodgings . . .'

It worked. Gladys homed in on the only thing Lily had said which mattered. She didn't ask how Lily had come to hear Jim had nowhere to stay – especially as Lily was supposed to have been confined to bed all afternoon with a headache. Jim simply didn't exist for her any more. The only person that mattered was . . .

'Sid . . . ?'

'Back to his unit,' Lily confirmed. 'The letter only came today.'

She felt terrible, though. This was like pulling wings off butterflies or tying a tin can to a kitten's tail. But she had to do it – especially after she'd let Gladys down so badly by letting her get her hopes up about Sid in the first place.

'Hey up!'

The hinges on the back gate were working hard tonight. Jim raised a hand. Lily wheeled round and turned back to be rewarded by the sight of Gladys's jaw dropping for the second – or was it the third? – time that evening. But her face, Gladys's dear, plain, puddingy face was illuminated. She looked almost beautiful.

'So – he hasn't gone yet?' she breathed.

Lily could have kicked herself. The way she'd put it, Gladys had thought she'd missed Sid altogether. Now Gladys had been given a sudden, unexpected, wonderful gift!

Sid came to join them, perching on the side of the raised bed alongside Jim.

'No one interesting at the pub,' he shrugged.

So they sat there in the dusk sharing Gladys's caramels, Lily and Jim steering the conversation far away from Marlow's in case Lily's own afternoon of deception came to light, and Sid cracking jokes – only the clean ones, as there were ladies present, he said, which alone was enough to make Gladys blush. Finally, unwillingly, Gladys said she had to go – her gran would worry. Lily thought it was doubtful – the old girl went to bed as soon as she'd had her tea, but she could hardly say so. Both Sid and Jim offered to walk her home, but Gladys wouldn't hear of it. She'd be fine by herself, she said, and Lily realised that any more would have been too much. Gladys didn't expect much out of life – why would she, poor thing, after the experiences she'd had – and she had quite enough to treasure from the evening already.

An hour in the company of her idol was more than enough to be going on with, and Lily knew Gladys would replay Sid's every word and gesture as she made her way home, and that she'd fall asleep with a smile on her lips.

When Gladys had gone, Jim gallantly said he'd wash the glasses and put up the blackout, tactfully leaving brother and sister to themselves.

Sid grinned at Lily.

'He's not a bad sort, your Jim,' he observed, rolling a cigarette.

'He's not "my Jim", don't be ridiculous!'

Sid licked the cigarette paper.

'No? Methinks the lady doth . . . whatever it is.'

'Just because you've got all the girls falling over themselves for you, Sid Collins, you think we're all as bad! Though, actually . . . about that. I've got to talk to you.'

'Gladys, you mean?'

He'd noticed, then. How Gladys looked at him. How she hung on his every word.

'Bless her, she's a nice kid, but, come on, Sis. She's only your age. I could be locked up!'

'She's older than me,' said Lily. 'It'll all be legal soon.'

'Thanks for the warning! But look,' Sid patted her hand. 'Don't worry about Gladys. I'll drop her the odd postcard—'

'Sid, no!' Lily was horrified. 'That'll only make it

worse! You'll only have to write "weather is lovely" and she'll read it as "wish you were here"! You'll come back and find she's planning her bottom drawer!'

'Now that truly is scary!' Sid blew out a perfect circle of smoke. The attention he paid to all those Hollywood pictures was paying off. 'As usual, you didn't let me finish. I'll drop her a couple of postcards, and then I'll let her down gently.'

'How?'

'Don't worry about it, Sis. Leave it to me. You've got enough to think about. You've got your Jim to get settled.' Lily glared. He was doing it deliberately, to tease her. 'And your own job to keep hold of – don't you go putting your job on the line like him, will you?'

And he didn't even know about Violet – or this afternoon!

'You can't afford to.' Sid was serious for once. 'Mum's got enough worries with Reg and me away. You know what she's like. She covers it up, but she feels it all right.'

Lily nodded. She loved her mum to pieces – so did her brothers. Lily really would have to keep herself in check. Dora didn't deserve any more anxiety.

'I promise, Sid,' she said.

Sid gestured with his cigarette-free hand.

'C'mere.'

He crooked his arm and Lily settled into it. She

breathed deeply and happily. His shirt smelt of tobacco and washing soda and he smelt of coal tar soap – and the stuff he put on his hair to mask the smell of coal tar soap. Lily sighed. She'd made a promise. Now all she had to do was actually keep it.

Chapter 10

Lily didn't hear Sid leave. His kitbag had been ready by the front door the night before; he must have crept out with the dawn. Lily got up and eased open her bedroom door, wondering if Jim was still asleep: he'd chosen the sofa in the front parlour in the end over a camp bed in Sid's room. She listened for a while. There was no sound, but she didn't dare go downstairs to check. She could hardly risk running into him in her nightie, washed to near-transparency, the elastic gone in one of the sleeves and no hope of getting any to replace it. She slunk back into her room, tiptoeing over the uneven boards, but before she could start to get dressed, she heard from below the unmistakable sound of the Ascot. Jim must be up: maybe Sid leaving had woken him. She hurried on her skirt and blouse – it was the shirt-blouse today – and made her way downstairs.

'Morning!'

He wasn't just up, he'd laid the table, boiled the kettle, and cut some bread. He had also, he informed her, watered the veg (extravagant, but they needed a good soak, he reckoned, and early morning was the best time) and, by the way, had they thought of keeping chickens? Now eggs were rationed, if he could get hold of some wood, he was sure he could build a henhouse.

'Whoa, whoa,' said Lily. 'You only got here last night! What next, build our own anti-aircraft gun? Mum's got a couple of bent spoons you can start with.'

'Sorry, sorry!' Jim backed off. 'Only trying to show a bit of initiative.'

'Well, yes, and – thank you. That would be wonderful.' Lily marvelled at the idea. 'Chickens! I mean . . . eggs! We did think of trying, but none of us knows anything about keeping animals.'

'Strictly speaking, they're birds,' Jim corrected her.

'You know what I mean! Do you? Know about chickens, then?'

'Lily, I've been working on farms since I was about eight,' shrugged Jim. 'Egg washing, fruit picking, bird scaring, dehorning, dagging, dipping, rolling fleeces . . . you name it.'

Lily hadn't the first idea what half those things were, but she was impressed. More that she didn't know about him.

'All right then, ask Mum. But seriously, Jim. You won't have time. You'll be far too busy looking for another job. Won't you?' she added, so she didn't sound quite so bossy.

'This'd be as well as, not instead of. And of course I'd ask your mum.'

'Of course. I knew you would.' It was a generous offer, after all. It would make all the difference. 'Thank you.'

Jim grinned.

'Right then. We agree. Makes a change!' And before Lily could reply, he draped Dora's tea towel over his arm and, bowing like a proper waiter, asked: 'Tea and toast, madam?'

Jim's tea and toast set Lily up for the day. And she'd need it, she thought, as she did as Miss Frobisher had instructed, trudging from the timekeeper to the nurse before she arrived at the department.

Miss Frobisher simply asked if she was feeling better, but the others all made a huge fuss of her, Miss Thomas especially, sympathising about how the air raids got you down and preyed on your nerves. Lily didn't want to be cast in the same mould as Miss Thomas, so blamed her 'sick headache' on something she'd eaten, before realising that this made her scoffing of Gladys's caramels the night before even more suspect. What a tangled web we weave, as her mother would have been the first to say.

Gladys, luckily, didn't seem to notice. She was still all-aglow after her time in Sid's company, and pleased to hear he'd got off all right.

'You will tell me the minute you get any news, won't you?' she asked, eyes pleading.

Safe in the knowledge that Sid had his own plan for Gladys, Lily reassured her that she was sure they'd be hearing very soon. On her friend's contented sigh, Lily resolved to look out for a very large cup for Gladys. She'd need it to contain all her happiness when Sid's postcard arrived.

But as the morning wore on, Lily's own mood lowered. Robert Marlow was very much in evidence on the sales floor, and Lily saw him deep in conversation with Mr Hooper, the buyer on Furniture and Household, then with Maurice Bishop, now back from his Blackpool holiday, and then with Mr Hooper again. Beryl, she noticed, was watching Robert's every move.

It turned out she was watching Lily's too. Because when Lily emerged from a cubicle in the Ladies at dinnertime, Beryl was at the mirror, fluffing her hair. She wheeled round and pounced.

'What have you said?'

'What? Sorry?'

'Have you told anyone – anyone in the store – what

I told you about Les and all the rest of them? The delivery thing?'

Lily thought quickly. She'd told Jim, of course, but she hadn't told him 'in the store' – she'd told him in the park. And Jim wasn't 'anyone in the store' now, was he? He didn't work there any more.

Lily knew she was clutching at dandelions. The white lies she'd already had to tell her mum and Sid had made her uncomfortable enough: she hated lying, even if you called it a fib, even to someone like Beryl. But she had to protect Jim, as far as possible. And after her promise to Sid, she had to protect herself.

'I have not breathed a word to anyone in the store,' she said firmly. 'You have my word.'

Beryl didn't look satisfied, but then she rarely did. Her mouth was a perpetual pout, either from dissatisfaction with her lot or because she thought it made her look attractive. This time it was one of the more sullen ones.

'Well, there's a Fifth Columnist somewhere,' she said. 'Someone's blabbed. Mr Marlow Senior knows all about it!'

Lily tried to look suitably shocked.

'Is that why Robert Marlow was talking to them on Household?'

She'd suspected the worst. Now she knew for sure.

'Yes, well, that's the only good thing about it. It's Robert who's doing the investigating.'

Marvellous! thought Lily. And how clever. The

scheme's real mastermind was charged not with the crime, but with supposedly finding the culprits. Talk about 'it takes a thief to catch a thief' – another of her mum's sayings. Turns out it was true!

Beryl had turned back to the mirror and her hair.

'With any luck, he should be able to keep some people out of it altogether, and – well, it's all Les can hope for – put in a good word for anyone he does have to name. Make up some sob story about how they needed the little bit extra for their sick granny or something.'

'I see.'

So they were going to get away with it! And all because Jim hadn't stood up for himself and told Mr Marlow that Robert was the real villain! This was what happened when you didn't tell the truth, the whole truth, and nothing but the truth! (Gladys might go on about Hedy Lamarr, but Elizabeth Allan wrongly accused in *Inquest* was more to Lily's taste – especially now.) Oh, Jim, she thought, see what you've done!

Somehow she managed to turn an innocent face to Beryl, and her look of concern was genuine, though not for the reason that Beryl might think.

'So what do you reckon'll happen?'

'Like I said, with any luck, Robert can damp it all down. Oh, he'll have to pick out a few scapegoats, but most of it, the detail, Cedric Marlow need never know.'

Especially his own son's part it in, thought Lily wrathfully.

'That's the good bit. The worst of it's the kibosh it puts on me and Les.' Little Miss Sulky was back. 'He was going to take me to Blackpool for the weekend. And buy me some more stockings. I'll be lucky to get to Burton-on-Trent for a day out now. And it'll be gravy browning and eye pencil, same as everybody else.'

Lily had to bite back a smile. Typical Beryl. All she could think about was what it was going to do to her. No days out, no stockings, the cheap seats in the cinema and no boxes of chocolates. Dear oh dear, she might be reduced to ankle socks if she wasn't careful!

'I tell you one thing . . .' Beryl was leaning over the basins now and examining her severely plucked eyebrows. 'That Jim Goodridge. He's disappeared. Bit of a coincidence.'

'I heard he'd been let go,' Lily said innocently. 'I thought . . . overstaffing?'

'Huh. If you believe that! It's got to be him who's dropped everyone in it. Sneaking to Cedric Marlow.'

Lily could feel her insides clench as she longed to put the other girl right. No, it hadn't been like that – it was Robert who'd tricked Jim into his confidence, Robert who'd pointed the finger at Jim and forced him to leave, Robert who—

Only the shrilling of the wall-mounted bell saved

her from saying something she might regret. Both girls leapt to attention. It was the five-minute warning for those on early dinner to start making their way back.

'Back to the grind,' moaned Beryl. 'Some days I'd do anything to get out of this place.'

There'd been developments on Childrenswear though, as Lily learnt on her return. The bought-in sales stock had arrived, and once Gladys had had her dinner, she and Lily spent the afternoon in the stockroom, taking the pins out of shirts and shaking the worst creases out of baby dresses ready to be piled into big wooden 'Special Purchase' bins on temporary trestles. Miss Frobisher said that if things got busy, Lily and Gladys might even be allowed to stand behind them and answer any queries customers might have, just like proper salesgirls. On any other day Lily would have been delighted. Today it hardly registered.

Gladys, thankfully, was still in a world of her own. Sid had passed out of training top of the class, and had been posted to . . . here the details became a bit hazy; Gladys wasn't very well up on the difference between a frigate and a destroyer. But it didn't matter. Basically, Sid was the hero of the hour, on the bridge in foul weather, scanning the horizon with binoculars, through mist and rain somehow spotting a German U-boat, alerting the captain and thus saving not only his shipmates but the entire nation. He was mentioned

in despatches, garlanded with medals, promoted . . .
By the end of the day, Lily could tell, he'd be First
Sea Lord. But she let her friend ramble on. Luckily
all Gladys required was an occasional 'yes', 'probably'
or 'that sounds like Sid'. So while smiling inwardly
at Gladys's fantasies, she could indulge in more
serious thoughts of her own.

She still couldn't understand – and until he gave
her the promised explanation, she never would – why
Jim hadn't wanted to tell Cedric that Robert was
behind the racket. Of course it would have been
awkward – Mr Marlow's own son – but to get to
the truth . . . Instead, from what Beryl had said, there
was going to be a massive cover-up, saving face for
everyone. Meanwhile Jim was tramping the streets
– at least Lily hoped he was – looking for work!

It was a different Lily from the one who'd left that
morning who arrived home that night. Beryl's
cat-with-the-cream look after an earnest exchange
with Les as they left the store and the way Beryl had
linked her arm through his as they strolled off had
told her all she needed to know. Les had escaped
censure. Les and how many others? Lily scurried to
catch them up, then, as she overtook, turned round
to nod a quick goodnight. But a triumphant Beryl
detached herself from Les and pulled Lily confiden-
tially into a shop doorway.

'Robert's done it! They pulled about half a dozen

up to the management floor for a telling off – but Les wasn't one of them!'

Lily ungritted her teeth with difficulty.

'That's good news,' she said. 'But what about the ones who did get carpeted? Are they for the sack?'

Beryl shook her head.

'That's the best bit! What would it look like, see? Dreadful for staff morale, and it advertises there was something going on, doesn't it? And if this got out any further than Marlow's, well, you know . . .'

Lily did – she and Jim had realised that from the off. It was wartime. Falsification of transport records, not to mention the illegal acquiring and use of petrol, were serious offences. It would have led to prosecution and a court case – a disaster for the store's prized reputation.

'Robert's so clever. He's managed to close it right off.' Beryl sounded as if she could hardly believe it herself. 'And anyway, they can't afford to let even half a dozen people go. That Jim Goodridge is one thing. But not proper trained-up salesmen, under-managers, or experienced drivers. Try replacing them these days!'

'So, relief all round,' said Lily, sugar-coating the sourness she really felt. 'Is your trip to Blackpool back on, then?

'Could be!' Beryl smirked. 'Play your cards right and I might bring you back a stick of rock!'

* * *

Jim merely nodded when she told him, but Lily's indignation poured out like the stream from the watering can he was holding.

'I can't go on spoiling them like this,' he said. 'The water butt's nearly empty.'

'Would you shut up about the veg for a minute and listen!'

Jim put down the can.

'I'm not going to get any peace till I do, I suppose.'

'No, you're not,' said Lily. 'Look, I'm not going to ask you again why you didn't tell Mr Marlow that Robert was at the centre of the whole thing, because I know you won't tell me.'

'That's progress at least,' said Jim.

'I do listen, see?' retorted Lily. 'So let's move on. Les, Maurice, fair enough – they wanted the money. But Robert Marlow? Why was he involved? What was in it for him?'

'I agree. That's been puzzling me too.'

Thank goodness. They were back on the same side again.

'Well, any ideas?' demanded Lily.

'None whatsoever,' admitted Jim. 'And we may never know.'

There may have been many things that Lily didn't know about Jim, but he knew her even less if he thought she could let something like that lie. But she didn't press the point. She didn't want to start another argument.

'Did you collect your reference?' she asked. Jim
had been told it would be ready for him at the staff
entrance. He'd already had to hand in his name badge
and staff manual.

'Yup,' he replied.

He moved further away and crouched down, examining the potatoes for blight. Lily followed him.

'And what did it say?'

'As I thought, that I'd been let go owing to overstaffing. No blame attached.'

Lily was thankful – the last thing she wanted
was for Jim to have been given a bad reference. At
the same time, something irked her. Mr Marlow
was falling faster in her estimation than a German
incendiary. First he'd allowed Robert to look into
the racket instead of doing it himself, blithely
handing the investigation to the person who should
have been investigated. Now, although he believed
Jim was guilty of organising a serious fraud – a
crime – he'd given him a perfectly respectable reference. What if Jim really had been a criminal
mastermind?

'That should help with your job search, then,' she
said as evenly as she could manage.

'Oh, I've got a job,' said Jim airily.

'What? You might have said!'

'Yes,' remarked Jim, straightening. 'I might have
if you hadn't launched straight in.'

'So?' questioned Lily eagerly. 'What is it?'

'I thought I'd retrain,' he said. 'As a gentleman's barber.'

'What?!'

'Or a bomb disposal expert.'

'A bomb . . .'

Lily gaped and Jim let out a puff of laughter.

'You are so gullible! I could tell you anything!'

No, he wasn't as bad as Sid, he was worse!

'So?'

'Neither of the above. I thought it would make sense to build on the experience I've got.'

So he was staying with shop work. That was sensible, anyway.

'So, where? Burrell's? Stokes and Howard?'

She named Hinton's other department stores. Jim shook his head. Lily moved on to furniture shops.

'Walsh and Packer? Erm . . . Vellacott's?' She drew in her breath. 'Not Richard Gillespie?'

Richard Gillespie was very upmarket.

Jim made a gesture with his hand. It seemed to mean 'lower'.

Lower what? Her expectations?

'The Co-op? No? Oh, Jim, not Woolies?'

Jim frowned and shook his head.

'OK. Not Woolies. I give up, then. Where?'

'Tatchell's.'

Tatchell's? The speedometer place that was now churning out aircraft parts? How was that building on his Marlow's experience?

'Factory work?' Lily was aghast. 'Oh, Jim!'

'What's wrong with it? There was nothing doing in any of the shops. There's not much furniture to sell any more. Or much of anything. And anyway, it's got to be better for the war effort than flogging fancy ashtrays – while we can still get them – to the Sir Douglas Brimbles of this world.'

'Even so!'

Lily simply couldn't see Jim, bookish, bird-loving Jim, in a factory.

'I hope Marlow's isn't turning you into a snob, Lily,' he said severely. 'I start tomorrow.'

Lily said nothing.

'I thought you'd be pleased! You were the one nagging me to get another job!'

Lily shrugged.

'I am pleased, then. I suppose.'

'Thank you. But don't worry,' he went on. 'I haven't forgotten about the chickens. Your mum's dead keen. And it's shift work, so I'll have plenty of time to knock up the henhouse. I can start as soon as, if you'll come scavenging for wood with me later.'

Resigned, Lily nodded her agreement. She was the one who'd said they had to move on, after all: Jim seemed to be doing fine at it. She was also the one who'd promised Sid faithfully she'd look after their mum and not cause her any anxiety. That meant not stepping out of line again at Marlow's. But you can't change who you are with a promise, thought Lily, however sincerely you meant it at the time. And she knew in her heart of hearts she wouldn't rest till she'd got to the bottom of the whole wretched delivery business. Not till justice had been done.

Chapter 11

'Your promises are like pie crust, my girl! Easily broken!'

Previous scoldings from her mum echoed in Lily's head as she followed her feet up the staff staircase at Marlow's next day. She tried to remember which past misdemeanours had tended to provoke them. The time Lily had promised to wash up but had got engrossed in *Jane Eyre* instead? When as a child she'd promised to be careful with a new dress (new to her, anyway) only to rip it climbing a tree? Or the time when . . . there were far too many, so Lily gave up. The stairs wound on, past the second floor. Gypsum sparkled in the stone steps. Nearly there now . . .

* * *

'Come in!'

Lily took a deep breath and grasped the brass doorknob with its chased edging. She turned it and the door swung smoothly back. Cedric Marlow sat behind his desk across an expanse of carpet which suddenly looked mile-wide. Lily felt her knees start to tremble. What was she doing? Had she really ever thought this was a good idea?

'Well? Shut the door, please, Lily. And come and sit down.'

His tone was impossible to read. Not exactly welcoming, but not accusing either. But then he didn't know why she was there. He didn't know she was the one who'd be doing the accusing.

It was too late now. Lily did as she was told, blundering the door shut and walking jerkily across to the chair he'd indicated. She had time to notice its maroon Regency-striped seat before falling gratefully on to it.

'You wanted to see me?'

Did she? Not now she was here!

She had first thing, though, when she'd made the request to an astonished Miss Garner in the staff office. She'd come in especially early to catch her.

'Are you sure it's nothing I can help you with?' Miss Garner had asked.

'I'm sorry,' Lily had replied. 'It has to be Mr Marlow himself. He's the only person who'll do.'

Miss Garner was puzzled. After that first shelter

incident, she'd heard nothing but positive reports about Lily. According to Eileen Frobisher, whose judgement was impeccable, Lily was neat and tidy, quick to learn, polite with the customers in the little direct contact she had with them . . . in short, she had all the makings of becoming a valued member of the team and before too long a promising salesgirl herself.

'Lily, you're not unhappy here, are you? If you're thinking of leaving . . . ?'

'Oh no, Miss Garner, it's not that, I promise!' There I go again with my promises, thought Lily. Every time I open my mouth . . . 'I love it here! I don't want to leave at all! Ever! That's the last thing I want to do!'

It was only as she said it, though, that she realised how very true it was. Leave Gladys and Miss Frobisher, and the stock she lovingly unfolded and refolded, hung and re-hung, covered and uncovered every day? Leave the cheery porters and ware-housemen, who tipped their caps and, never letting her forget Violet, called her 'Knockout Lil'? Leave the customers who in the beginning had seemed so daunting, with their smart tailored clothes and accents to match, but who she was now beginning to know simply as anxious wives and mothers, just like the women in her own street? Leave Mrs MacRorie with her three boys, Mrs Powell with her four girls, and pretty Mrs Elliot, who'd come in during Lily's first week to complete her baby layette and had come back only the other day to show them dear little Clara?

A pity, then, that if Mr Marlow didn't like, or believe, what she intended telling him, that leaving was exactly what would happen. Except she'd be lucky to get off as lightly as Jim and be 'let go'. Most likely it'd be the sack. Immediately.

Miss Garner straightened her blotter, then her pen tray. The little japanned box was still there, on her right, near the telephone.

'Are you prepared to give me any reason at all? Mr Marlow's bound to ask.'

'I'm sorry, Miss Garner. I really can't. But it won't take long. I shan't take up much of his time.'

Miss Garner shook her head and edged the blotter minutely to the right. She said nothing, so Lily did.

'I know it's most irregular.'

'Not just irregular, Lily. Unheard of!' Miss Garner admonished. 'I am here to act as the conduit for all staff matters. Mr Marlow should not be bothered with them.'

'No, Miss Garner,' said Lily.

'But if you insist . . . I shall have to ask him. Though please don't think you can make a habit of this.'

'I have no intention of it, Miss Garner,' said Lily truthfully.

'Well. You'd better get to your department.' Miss

Garner looked at her watch. 'Come and see me at morning break. I'll have an answer for you by then.'

She'd only agreed to ask because she'd been confident the request would be turned down, and she presented it to Cedric Marlow in that light. Miss Garner didn't want every Tom, Dick and Lily thinking they could access him when they felt like it, and she didn't suppose he did either. She'd been absolutely stunned when instead of saying she would have to deal with it, he'd simply shrugged and agreed.

Miss Garner had gone back to her office in astonishment. But then Mr Marlow hadn't been quite himself lately. She thought back to his odd remark on the day of Lily's interview about the way ordinary people were suffering in the war. She hoped he wasn't getting . . . she gave a shudder . . . Socialist sympathies! He'd be allowing a union next!

So when at morning break, Lily re-presented herself, Miss Garner had told her that on this occasion, purely as a one-off, she could see Mr Marlow in her dinner hour.

'So?'

Brought sharply back to the present, Lily realised where she was. Cedric Marlow's office . . . and he was waiting. It was no good. She'd better get on with it.

'Thank you for seeing me, Mr Marlow,' she began. 'I know it's unusual. And I wouldn't have asked if it wasn't important. It's really hard for me to do this, and I think it'll be hard for you to hear. But I have to tell you. You have to know the truth.'

Cedric Marlow looked confused.

'I agreed to see you, Lily, because I was intrigued. Now I'm increasingly worried. You'd better say what you've come to say. The truth about what?'

So Lily told him. She told him the hard truth – that Jim had only stumbled on the delivery racket by accident, because Maurice Bishop was away. That Jim and Lily had managed to uncover how it worked, but that it had never even involved Jim, let alone been his idea. Instead, the person who'd started it all off, who'd thought up how it could work, who oversaw its running, and had recruited everyone who was mixed up in it from the under-managers who turned a blind eye to the salesmen who falsified sales dockets to the drivers who fiddled their records, altered their rounds and got hold of petrol by any manner of means, was in fact his own son.

There was a silence. A silence long, big and wide enough to drive a tank through and still have room for hand signals. In it, Lily could hear the pigeons yattering outside. She could hear the tick of the carriage clock on the desk. Most of all she could hear and feel her own heart thudding in her chest. She gripped the sides of the chair.

Why didn't he say something? He obviously didn't believe a word she'd said – and was trying to work out why on earth she'd have said it. Maybe she shouldn't have after all?

Lily thought of all the people she'd let down. Sid, of course, to whom she'd promised faithfully she wouldn't step out of line. Her mum next, because she was going to be so upset at the chance Lily had thrown away. And not just upset – angry, and ashamed – what would the neighbours say? How would they explain it away? First Jim and now Lily chucking away a good job, both of them under her roof in disgrace! Lily's head drooped at the thought of the scenes which would follow. And not only scenes with her mum. There'd be Jim to face, Jim who'd insisted that he was damaged goods, that she shouldn't associate with him, and who'd specifically told her not to get involved.

And then, and then . . . what about Gladys, who'd become such a good friend, and who'd now be on her own again to face Beryl's sarcastic remarks. Beryl, who'd be crowing when Lily was sacked for telling malicious lies, while she and Les stuffed themselves with chocolate caramels and capered around in Blackpool.

What about the other salesladies, Miss Thomas and Miss Temple, who'd been nothing but kind . . . most of all Miss Frobisher, who'd placed such faith in her after the incident with Violet, who'd explained the workings of the department so patiently, who'd kindly let her off sick only yesterday . . .

Still Cedric Marlow said nothing.

And then, and then . . . what about Miss Norris, who'd put in a good word for her with Marlow's in the beginning? Lily didn't know it, but she and Miss Garner were friends: they had to stick together, the surplus women left without a man after the Great War. Lily even felt she'd let down Mrs Tunnicliffe, who'd taken the trouble to ring up and praise her for her actions with Violet. What would she think of Lily's 'quick thinking' now?

Lily squirmed in her seat and drove herself further into despair. Why had she ever thought this was a good idea? She knew from what Jim had said that Robert already had her down as a potential trouble-maker and future shop steward. What if Cedric Marlow saw her in the same light? He might think her outburst was merely because she had it in for the boss class. She was for the sack, and no mistake.

She swallowed hard and, by an enormous effort of concentration, managed to lever herself off the chair. Somehow she managed to stop her voice from wobbling as much as her legs.

'I'm sorry if I've spoken out of turn, Mr Marlow,' she said. 'I really didn't want to.'

'Then why did you?' Cedric Marlow snapped back into life. 'Why on earth would you slander my own son? It's impossible! Why on earth would Robert want to dream up such a scheme? Robbing his own father? Risking our name and reputation?'

'I don't know,' said Lily. 'I can't answer that. That's what I can't work out.'

'And if there's a shred of truth in it, why didn't Jim Goodridge tell me all this for himself the other day?'

'I can't answer that either,' said Lily sadly. 'He won't tell me. Maybe he's more sensible than me.'

'Maybe because he realised I'm unlikely to take the word of an . . . an employee against that of my own son!'

'Maybe. I'm not sure I ever expected you to, Mr Marlow. And I'm truly so sorry to have had to be the one to tell you.'

'Then for pity's sake, again, why did you?'

'Because,' said Lily simply, 'my mum's always brought me up to face the truth. And to tell the truth. My mum. It's as simple as that.'

Cedric Marlow looked down at his desk, then looked up again. He stood up.

'I think you'd better leave,' he said. 'Now.'

When the door had closed behind her, Cedric Marlow sat staring at it for a long time. He didn't see the fine grain of the wood or the beaded panels. He looked through it down the long vista of Robert's childhood and adolescence.

They'd been so happy, he and Elsie, in the summer of 1920. As they waited for their baby's birth in the autumn, they'd existed in their own private paradise.

He used to pinch himself, he felt so blessed. Individually, they'd come through the War and then the Spanish flu. Now they were together as a couple, he knew they could survive anything.

As a young man, he'd had no time for a personal life, let alone romance. After a year at commercial college, he'd joined the shop his father had set up. Twenty-year-old Cedric had worked twelve hours a day, six and a half days a week, the same as the assistants: the only difference was that he lived at home, rather than living in. But he might as well have lived over the shop, or in it. After it shut, he walked the sales floor – they only had one floor then – tweaking the displays or tidying drawers. On other nights, he stayed behind in the cash office, poring over the takings, fretting over profit margins, working out ways of squeezing bigger discounts out of suppliers without giving them bigger orders.

Things were moving fast in shopkeeping. In London, Selfridges and Harrods were leading the way, aping concepts imported from America. Cedric wasn't slow to catch on, and, overcoming his father's caution, he transformed Marlow's from a staid Victorian drapery into a plush Edwardian emporium, acquiring larger premises, expanding the staff, widening their range of goods and coining the slogan 'Nothing but the best'. He personally made sure it applied in all parts of the business – in quality, value, and service, tirelessly touring suppliers with the buyers he'd appointed, travelling to shows and exhibitions, visiting manufacturers to check their working practices and to strike the best deals.

What didn't show on the balance sheet was the price he paid – his private life. His twenties passed in the stroke of pen every time he signed off the annual accounts. 1901 . . . 1902 . . . 1903 . . . It was only his father's retirement and the dawn of a new age with the coronation of George V that made him realise that his thirties were passing too. If he wanted a son to succeed him, he'd better put his mind to it. But he discovered he couldn't buy romance to order like a consignment of numdah rugs or a delivery of top hats. The suitable young women that the young Cedric might have met at balls or tennis parties had long been married off. They were matrons with children now. And if anyone was still unclaimed, well, there was always a reason. Plainness or dullness in a future wife wouldn't have deterred Cedric, but insanity in the family? A dowry of debts? He wasn't going to gamble Marlow's future on those.

Winter followed summer and year followed year – and before he knew it, there came the War. Like all young men of his type, Cedric was a captain in the Territorials; he marched off at the head of his unit, his father's peaceful retirement interrupted to take back the helm at the shop. But Captain Marlow didn't have much time to distinguish himself. Wounded by shrapnel in the First Battle of Ypres, he was operated on in the field then shipped home to be nursed in the hospital set up in the requisitioned Great Hall of Birmingham University. His left arm had been pretty useless after that, but the Army made one of its more sensible decisions when it assigned him a desk job in the Ministry of Supply in London. Cedric's practised negotiating skills and experience in dealing with manufacturers might at least have eased the lot of the poor devils at the Front by a few degrees, he consoled himself, as he signed off supplies of puttees and delousing powder.

Fellow officers made the most of their leisure time, going to dinners and music halls, and seeking female company of both a reputable and disreputable kind. Not Cedric. He lived in a serviced flat and worked as hard at his war work as he had at Marlow's. He'd seen enough in his brief time as a soldier to know that the reports of conditions and casualties weren't the half of it. Hard work, insanely hard work, was the only way he could ease his conscience for having what he felt was a cushy war.

When in early 1919 he was finally demobbed, he was ready to resume full responsibility at the store, and, at forty, resigned to the fact that he might never marry. And then, into his life, impossibly, like a vision, came Elsie. How had he never noticed her? She'd started at Marlow's, he learnt, shortly before the War, but had left, as did all the female assistants, on her marriage. She'd only come back during the War to replace the salesgirls who'd left to go nursing or conduct buses or make machine gun parts. Now she was chief *vendeuse* on Ladies' Fashions, Miss Garner, returned from her nursing, explained – they still used the fancy French term then; it sounded so much more refined. But – tactfully lowering her voice – Miss Garner also told him that Elsie – Miss, not Mrs, Cartwright, in the shop – needed to keep on working because her husband had been killed at Passchendaele.

'Luckily, there were no children,' she added.

We'll soon change that, thought Cedric.

He courted her assiduously. Elsie was tentative; the staff manual warned against 'undue intimacy' with other staff members, let alone the son of the store's owner. But Cedric was utterly proper in his attentions. He began by asking her advice on the New Season stock; fashions were changing, he said, which was true, and he wasn't sure he could entirely trust the buyer, who belonged more to the era of wasp waists and picture hats than to wrap coats and a flash of ankle.

Thanks to Elsie, Marlow's stole a march on Burrell's that autumn with a new Sportswear department – their customers were playing golf and going hiking, she told him. Thanks to her, Fashions had a more casual, relaxed look too: sweater coats with funnel necks; skirts with wider, deeper waistbands and, crucially, pockets. So useful, said Elsie. Cedric, who like all men had always taken pockets for granted, was amazed. Something so simple – who'd have thought it? Yet women had been deprived of them for all these years!

It was only natural for him to ask her if she'd do him the honour of joining him for dinner when the September sales figures reached a new high. A proper courtship began.

Elsie had taken some time to feel comfortable with Cedric, so she was understandably nervous when she was first invited to the Marlows' home. His parents hadn't been too sure when he'd explained who she was: her father was a railway ticketing clerk; she was definitely Not Of Their Class. But Cedric reminded them, and not too gently, that they'd both started out as drapers' assistants; it was no good giving themselves airs. Any status the Marlows had in Hinton had been only lately acquired and thanks to her work at the shop, Elsie was refined and well-spoken. Most of all, she understood their world and loved it almost as much as they did. Even at that first meeting, his father had to be impressed by her grasp of the business and his mother could see she would be a wonderful support to her son. By Christmas they were quietly married and when shortly afterwards she announced that she was expecting, Cedric could have wept for joy.

On the morning of 11 November 1920, at the eleventh hour of the eleventh day of the eleventh month, the King laid a wreath of poppies at the newly unveiled Portland stone Cenotaph on Whitehall. It was a sombre day anyway, in Hinton and all over the country, but Cedric was hardly aware of what was happening outside the bedroom where he and Elsie had belatedly known such joy. She had given birth to their son only the week before, and now lay dead of puerperal fever.

The weeks, months, and years after that had had a nightmarish feel to them. Cedric's mother had had to take charge, finding first a wet nurse, then a succession of nannies and governesses for the boy. Cedric had done the only thing he knew – thrown himself into work, struggling to keep himself and Marlow's going.

It was exhausting for everyone, and it was a relief when, at seven, Robert was old enough to be sent away to school. There was nothing unusual in it – he'd be getting a good education in a secure environment, with boys his own age for company. It was clearly the best thing.

At first it seemed so, and he settled in well. Some of the other boys were far worse off – with parents in the colonies or the services, they had no choice but to stay at school over the vacations. Others, who did have homes to go to, invited Robert to stay, their mothers taking pity on a poor motherless boy. Cedric was too relieved and preoccupied to notice that the invitations tended to dry up after one or two visits, or that over the years Robert's school reports said that he was able but failed to apply himself; that the admiration of his classmates was more important to him than the approval of his teachers. In other words, he was the clown of the class, something astutely detected by the mothers during those holiday visits. As mothers do, they swiftly expunged a potential bad influence.

When it came to Common Entrance, though, Robert's lack of application became a serious problem. He was clearly not going to make it to Eton or Harrow, but even second-ranked public schools were, the headmaster advised, not a viable option. He suggested a small establishment in Berkshire, a school with a simple if strict regime: it might help Robert finally to 'knuckle down'.

Cedric knew nothing of the workings of English public schools. He'd had a grammar-school education in Hinton, and been grateful for it, but the family's improved circumstances and standing meant that a public school for Robert seemed the 'right thing' to do. Cedric went along with the suggestion.

It was a fatal mistake. Unknown to Cedric, the school had become a repository for boys that prep school heads didn't quite know what to do with. Robert's fellow pupils didn't need much leading astray and Robert was happy to be their leader. Soon he and his little gang were being sent out of lessons, smoking with cigarettes bought off the servants, brewing poteen from potatoes dug up by moonlight in the school's kitchen garden. Punishments had no effect. The group was regularly caned and threatened with suspension, but they were hollow threats – the school was struggling and couldn't risk losing several sets of fees. As Robert's power grew, so did his ambitions. Teachers were taunted and younger boys found their tuck boxes raided. Sent on cross-country runs as punishment, Robert and his cohorts hid their day clothes en route, changed into them, and sloped off to the pub.

Cedric knew none of this. Wall Street had crashed; the heavy industries of coal and steel were in decline; millions were unemployed. Admittedly coal miners and steelworkers hadn't been Marlow's customers in the first place, but the Midland mine owners and steel magnates had. Hit with reduced income and higher taxes, they were – relatively – worse off too. While local spending power was falling like a stone, Germany was rearming. The atmosphere was febrile.

By the time Robert finished school he was qualified for nothing except a continuation of the feckless life he'd managed for the past seven years. The school simply reported that 'While academic work may not be his strong point, Robert's many other abilities and his easy charm will doubtless take him far in life.' He'd got away with it.

Cedric had always imagined that Robert would join him and, in time, be trained up to take the reins at Marlow's, as he himself had done. But Robert wasn't having that – bury himself in Hinton? Not likely – not straight away, anyhow. Cleverly he persuaded his father that a tour of foreign capitals would give him an insight into shopkeeping and provide some innovative ideas. By now it was the summer of 1939. Cedric was worried about the situation in Europe but didn't want to dampen the boy's enthusiasm. So he made arrangements with his agents abroad to introduce Robert to the Galeries Lafayette in Paris and the Kaufhaus N. Israel in Berlin – which, the way things were looking in Germany, might not be there much longer.

Setting off on his own in late July, Robert intended to make the most of his Grand Tour. By day he traipsed up and down the *grands boulevards* with Cedric's Paris contacts and marvelled dutifully at the *grands magasins*. But free to roam at night, he also made sure to lose his virginity in several novel ways in less reputable areas of the city before moving on to Berlin. There, Cedric's agent was less forthcoming. Berlin in August 1939 was no place for an Englishman who, however much he might now think himself a man of the world, was still an innocent abroad. The agent cabled Cedric, who cabled Robert and summoned him home. At once.

It was a disgruntled Robert who arrived back in Hinton: hardly the best frame of mind in which to begin his career at Marlow's. Compared with the glamour of Paris and the frustratingly little he'd seen of Berlin, Hinton was backward and provincial, and Marlow's, for all its aspirations to style and class, epitomised both. When the lights went out all over Europe – again – in September, Robert's own outlook, he felt, could not have looked more bleak. In the six months of the phoney war, however, as restrictions and regulations poured into the management offices, Robert began to see a way out. He'd spent his entire school career bucking the system – that's what it was there for, in his view. Wartime was going to provide him with some rich pickings, he could see. It was only a matter of choosing which to pursue.

At school, he'd held the other boys in thrall through hero-worship and adolescent hormones. Now he had status as well. And when Sir Douglas Brimble, of all people, had expressed dissatisfaction with wartime delivery arrangements, well . . . it was exactly the sort of challenge for which Robert's brain was perfectly wired.

Seated at his desk that summer's afternoon, with the sleepy clock and the scuttering pigeons, Cedric couldn't know any of this. Or could he? Of course he could.

For all Robert's school career, he admitted now, he'd known perfectly well what lay between the lines of his school reports and behind the falling-off of invitations to stay at friends' homes. Robert was trouble. There'd been yet more evidence once he'd left school. He'd wanted a motor, of course, and there were the prangs and the visits from the local police, gentle reprimands about Robert needing to take greater care 'for his own safety, you understand, Mr Marlow'. There were the betting slips which their housekeeper had accidentally-on-purpose – she was most apologetic – left on the hall table, having turned out Robert's pockets to send a suit for repair.

Cedric had closed his mind to it because the truth was too hard to face; not just how different it could have been had Elsie been at his side to be a proper mother to the boy, but his own abject failure to fill the void. And when he had involved himself . . .

The war could have changed it. It could have been the making of Robert; but Cedric had lost his wife; he couldn't risk losing his only son as well. So when the prospect of call-up loomed, Cedric had contacted the Chief Medical Officer at the Army Medical Board; they went back to the days of the yeomanry together. It was a small matter to ask him to find that Robert's childhood rheumatic fever, which genuinely had left him with a weak heart, had left him with a heart far weaker than it was. It was only a matter of time before Robert would be forced into some kind of war work, but Cedric knew he'd use his influence again, and swing him a soft number, like the desk job he'd had, though at least his own cushy war had been earned.

He stood up and stretched his back. He knew that

what Lily Collins had told him – such a bright little thing, and how brave – he had to admire her – was likely to be all too true. Robert had organised the racket. But this wasn't something that could be explained away by boyish high jinks, a cheeky desire to buck the system. He knew Robert didn't share his passion for shopkeeping, but he surely couldn't have so hated life at Marlow's that he was prepared to undermine the whole operation, get them prosecuted and convicted? Cedric came back to the same question he'd posed to Lily and which she'd been unable to answer – why? Why would Robert do such a thing?

He'd have to face it. After all these years, they needed an honest conversation. He'd have to tackle Robert and ask him. Tonight.

Chapter 12

But Robert wasn't at home that evening.

He was at Holmwood, the Victorian Gothic mansion – some might say monstrosity – which was home to Sir Douglas Brimble.

They were in what Sir Douglas called his library – though it said something about him that the books he used most were *Who's Who* and *Kelly's Trade Directory* while Scott and Dickens gathered dust.

'You'd think it's a misspelling of "home", wouldn't you?' Sir Douglas pontificated. 'But in fact "holm" is old Norse! Means an islet – or land prone to flooding. It certainly gets very boggy down beyond the stream in the winter.' He waved the hand which wasn't holding his whisky and soda. 'The stream in the paddock, I mean. I've got four and a half acres here in total, you know.'

Robert did know. He sipped his own whisky and nodded politely.

'I think you have mentioned it.'

About a dozen times.

'On the other hand,' continued Sir Douglas, 'holm is also an old word for holly. And we're not short of that!'

It was true, the place bristled with the stuff.

There'd been holly around, lots of it, decorating the house on the night Robert had first met Evelyn Brimble; met her properly, that is. He hadn't taken much notice of her before the war. He'd only seen her at the odd tennis party or hunt ball, where she'd been a lumpy thing in her teens, chaperoned by her mother or giggling with her friends, and he the relative sophisticate. But when the threat of the war put paid to any idea of her being 'finished' in Switzerland, Sir Douglas had smartly despatched his wife and daughter to America, where Evelyn was entered in Miss Kelly's school in Boston. In the eighteen months she was away, the duckling became a swan.

When she reappeared at the opening meet of the hunt in November 1940, she was a stunning figure in her immaculate new riding habit. Robert looked on, mesmerised, as she chatted with the master and whipper-in with equal poise and was equally taken when he saw her in action on the field, her riding veil streaming behind her. At the Brimbles' annual Christmas party, she was even more stunning in white tulle spangled with silver – she'd brought her entire wardrobe back with her from the States – and Robert could see he wasn't the only one who was captivated. 'Lucky' Mickey O'Rourke, Roger Framlingham, Johnny Massey – in their Army or RAF uniforms, damn them – clustered round her. Ducking military service had seemed like such a good idea at the time – God knows, Robert didn't want to fight – but now he cursed the day he'd let his father 'put in a word'. With that lot – and no doubt others – banging on about their exploits in Bomber Command or the Coldstream Guards, how was he ever going to make an impression?

So it was a gift from the gods when, at the buffet table, Sir Douglas starting muttering about how inconvenient the war was proving to shoppers.

'This "Account and Take" business,' he grumbled, spooning salmon mayonnaise – no sign of rationing here – 'I've been talking to some of the other chaps I know about it. Have you any idea how tiresome it is to leave Marlow's with fifty Havana cigars and have to cart them around to a business meeting? Or our wives, having to go to lunch lugging a lampshade? Damned irritating, I call it.'

Robert had tried to explain about wartime restrictions – delivery was allowed for bulky, heavy items only. They were down on vans as it was – the two smallest had been requisitioned by the military at the start of the war and a larger one, only last month, had gone to Birmingham as an ambulance. Then there was the ten-mile limit . . .

'At least Holmwood falls within that for any large purchases,' he soothed.

'Precisely.' Sir Douglas gave him a crafty look. 'So who's to know if one of your chaps makes a slight detour with something a bit smaller?'

Robert saw his chance. If he could oblige Sir Douglas, and a few of his cronies, maybe, by adding their purchases on to vans delivering larger items . . . well, Evelyn Brimble was a daddy's girl, he knew that much, and if Sir Douglas looked on him kindly . . . all's fair in love and war, he thought.

'Leave it with me, Sir Douglas,' he said. 'I'll see what I can do.'

After that it was easy enough to get Sir Douglas to specify a list of departments and to find a willing salesman on each who'd go along with the nod-and-wink set-up, and then a couple of drivers to do the same. Robert had never asked any of the customers like Sir Douglas to pay for the service, of course – he'd tipped the staff out of his own pocket and paid up for any bootleg petrol. He saw it as an investment, a down-payment on his future with Evelyn. He had never in his life been denied anything he wanted, and if a few deliveries could smooth the way . . . And if it was bending the law, well . . .

It had all been fine, of course, for the past six months, until Maurice Bishop had gone off on his holiday and Jim Goodridge had served Sir Douglas. Thank God Les Bulpitt had happened to mention the requested delay on delivering the ashtray, and his conversation with Jim. It meant Robert had been able to get to Jim with that fabricated story about possible strikes – and then get to his father first when Jim had obligingly coughed up what he knew about the scheme without Robert even having to lead up to it. The next step had been to stop Cedric looking into it himself by applying the rule Robert had learnt as a senior boy at school – if you're likely to come under investigation, make sure you're the one to do the investigating. He'd had to take a chance that Jim, when questioned, would do the decent thing, hide the truth and fall on his sword, but his hunch, thank God again, had proved right.

Yes, it had all worked fine till now – there'd been beaming smiles and a warm welcome from Sir Douglas, his wife, and their circle; it was Robert, not Mickey or Roger or Johnny invited to go beagling or make up the tennis four, and of course to take Evelyn out to the pictures or a country pub. They – and others – appeared on their occasional leaves, but they had plenty of other opportunities with their ATS girls and WAAFs – after all, who needed a girlfriend pining away back home? One by one they fell away anyhow – Johnny's plane went down near

Hamburg and Mickey's luck ran out when he was shot by a sniper.

Confident of success in the end, Robert had been playing the long game. He wanted Sir Douglas to appreciate how useful he could be, so he hadn't pushed things with Evelyn further than a goodnight kiss. He hadn't dared, because he knew any more would get him too carried away and, despite her surface sophistication, he could tell she was inexperienced. He'd choose his moment to up the stakes. But now, for all his clever planning and execution, the whole thing was a mess. He wished he'd acted sooner with her, because all his preparation was going to come to nothing. He daren't carry on with the scheme. Now Cedric knew, it had come much too close to home. Robert would have to tell Sir Douglas their little arrangement couldn't go on, Sir Douglas would take it as a personal affront, and would erupt. Robert would be banished, never to darken their doors again. Sir Douglas might even take his custom to Burrell's and as a big spender, Marlow's would notice the loss. But it had to be faced, tonight, and sooner rather than later, so he could make his escape before Evelyn got home.

She'd volunteered for war work – mostly clerical duties helping the harassed billeting officer in the village with runaway evacuees and discontented displaced persons. It was hardly thrilling, but Robert admired her for doing something at least. Plenty of girls in her position didn't bother. Oh, Evelyn . . . but no, he couldn't face her once he'd told Sir Douglas. It would be easiest if he simply disappeared, and quickly. The last thing he wanted was for her to see him slinking out of the door, humiliated. He took a deep breath.

'I've got something for you in the car, Sir Douglas,' he began. 'The ashtray you bought the other day.'

'Ah, I was wondering what had happened to that! You do realise it's not for me personally? Hideous thing! It's a wedding present for the housemaid!'

What?! Robert was outraged. After all that . . . the scheme exposed and losing his chance with Evelyn . . . all over a housemaid's bottom drawer?

'Really? Well, I hope she and her new husband enjoy it.' He could hardly get the words out through his fury. 'But I'm sorry, Sir Douglas, but I have to tell you . . . I'm afraid there's been a slight hitch and the arrangement that we've had will have to—'

'What are you two doing shut up in here on such a lovely evening?'

The door had opened – it was Evelyn. She was back early! Robert hadn't heard the front door, but as Sir Douglas was fond of pointing out, Holmwood was a sizeable house, with its four reception rooms and . . . how many bedrooms was it again? The only one that mattered to Robert was Evelyn's.

Now she swished across towards them. She must have been home for some time, long enough to change into an emerald shantung dress, her blonde hair loose on her shoulders.

Sir Douglas glowed as she kissed him, then she offered a formal cheek to Robert, who'd leapt to his feet.

'Mummy and I are starving! You will stay for dinner, won't you, Robert?'

Lily wasn't sure how she'd got through the rest of the afternoon. She made it back to the department on jelly legs and busied herself, under Miss Frobisher's instructions, in moving fitments around and then, with Gladys holding the steps, climbing up to fix 'Sale!' and 'Grand Reductions!' banners to the wall. Luckily the jelly-legs had more or less set by then, or she'd have been off to see the nurse for real this time. But every nerve-end was jangling, and every time she caught sight of someone new on the sales floor, she was convinced it was a messenger come to escort her off the premises. She didn't know, of course, that in his office, Cedric Marlow was feeling, if possible, even worse.

She listened with a quarter of an ear as Miss Frobisher explained that in the general frenzy of the sales, if the salesgirls weren't available, customers still confused about how to use their coupons might ask Lily and Gladys for advice. She therefore gave them a complete run-down on the procedure. Words wafted over Lily's head. 'Never accept loose coupons' . . .

'Cut, never tear, coupons from the book . . . ' She'd have to ask Gladys later what it had all been about.

'This is all so important,' said Miss Frobisher in conclusion. 'You – and Marlow's – could be prosecuted if you sell anything without the correct number of coupons or before the date for which they've been issued . . . Lily, are you listening?'

'Yes, Miss Frobisher,' said Lily automatically. She only hoped Gladys had been taking it all in.

As she found out later, sadly not.

Gladys had been given a dispensation to go home during her dinner hour as her gran had taken to her bed again. There'd been no chance for the girls to chat during the afternoon with Miss Frobisher standing over them, telling them 'Right hand side up a bit' or 'A little higher,' but in the staff cloakroom at the end of the day, Gladys was smug as she opened her locker.

'You'll never guess what I've got in here!'

Glumly getting her things out of her own locker and thinking, not for the first time, that this might be the last time, Lily was in no mood for parlour games. In her present state, a pistol or a cyanide pill would have been welcome. Fortunately, before she had time to make any suggestion, Gladys, unable to contain herself, had given her the answer.

'Look what was waiting for me at home! Oh, Lily!'

Lily looked dumbly at the card Gladys was holding out to her.

'Go on, you can read it! I don't mind!'

Lily took it. It was the standard HMSO-issue services postcard, no picture on the front, simply Gladys's address – and in very familiar handwriting.

Lily thought her heart had already sunk as far as it could go, but she felt it swoop further as she turned the card over.

Dear Gladys,

How are you doing? Had a merry journey back, cancelled trains and an air raid holding us up, good job our mum had packed me enough sandwiches to last till Christmas! Stay well.

Sid

It was completely innocuous. It said nothing and promised even less, but Lily could see that to Gladys, it might as well have been garlanded with hearts and dripping with diamonds. She also knew that an identical postcard would be waiting for her at home, bright, breezy – brotherly.

'I didn't hear a word of what Miss Frobisher was saying, you'll have to tell me,' Gladys breathed, taking the card back off Lily and studying it lovingly. 'All I could think about was . . . oh, you know. I can't believe he's written already! And hasn't he got lovely handwriting?'

She held the postcard against her heart.

'Shall we go?' said Lily, feeling sick. 'I could do with some air.'

'Not another headache?' asked Gladys, concerned. 'If you keep getting them, you'll have to go to the nurse.'

When they got out into the welcome fresh air, Gladys tripped happily off towards home, Sid's post-card safe in her pocket. Lily trudged to the bus stop. After a good twenty minutes, no bus had arrived, but that wasn't unusual. There was no explanation, but that wasn't unusual either. At first the bus company had blamed 'operational reasons', which could cover anything. Now they'd found they didn't even have to bother with that. Like everything else, in the end, people merely shrugged and accepted it, blamed 'the war' and plodded off home, Lily included.

At least it meant she wouldn't have to face Jim, she thought, as she watched her feet, one in front of the other, just as she had up the stone stairs at Marlow's earlier in the day.

Jim's first week at Tatchell's, it turned out, was to be on the night shift. He'd have left by the time she got in, so at least, for now anyway, she'd be spared the awfulness of telling him what she'd done – and how badly it had turned out.

But then, what had she expected? Cedric Marlow to jump up and tell her she was saying what he'd always wanted to hear – that his son was a cheat and a liar and couldn't be trusted? The more she thought about it, the more she cringed. That was effectively what she'd said. So what had she expected? In a horrible moment, Lily realised she hadn't thought beyond the telling – the getting it off her chest. She thought she'd been doing it for Jim, but had she actually done it to make herself feel better? What a mess – and all her own doing.

At home, Dora had had a bad day as well. She'd burnt a huge hole in a tea towel and dropped one cup and chipped another while trying to rescue it. Though Lily appreciated the difficulty and cost of replacing anything, relative to her own situation, this slight domestic annoyance didn't loom large, but she could see it was a serious blow to her mother, who prided herself on her housekeeping.

'I don't know what got into me!' Dora fretted. 'Leaving the tea towel that close to the gas! I can't have been thinking straight!'

You and me both, thought Lily. But at least in Dora's disaster only a tea towel had suffered. Lily had lit the gas under her entire future.

'So there it is, Sir Douglas,' concluded Robert.

He'd had to wait till after dinner to make his full confession, which had made for a very strangulated conversation at the table. Evelyn had looked at him most oddly as he'd blabbered on about Marlow's forthcoming sale, sounding as if he was touting for business, before veering wildly into a pointless story about a pre-war cricket match. Thankfully she'd weighed in about the irony of sorting gas masks on the village hall stage with a backdrop of a beautiful sylvan glade – the local amateur dramatic society was holding a musical evening in aid of St John Ambulance.

'Not *Tales from the Vienna Woods*, I hope!' Sir Douglas chortled at his mordant wit while his wife and daughter looked on fondly. Robert took another gulp of wine. After dinner, the men had returned to the library while Evelyn and her mother went off into the drawing room to chat about womanly things: it was that sort of household. Now, having fabricated a story about the 'national good' and explained that the tightening of regulations meant that petrol usage was even more closely monitored, Robert was gulping again as he waited for his dismissal.

'Well, that's a pity,' said Sir Douglas.

He was obviously going to work up slowly to the full lambasting.

'But maybe, in the end, it'll be for the best.'

This had to be a joke. Or some kind of mind-game; playing with him, cat-and-mouse.

'The best . . . ? You're not . . . disappointed?'

'It's a shame, of course,' said Sir Douglas. 'But we've had a jolly good run.'

'I see! Well, it's extremely good of you to take it like that, sir.'

'The thing is,' confided Sir Douglas, 'between you and me, there's talk of me being made an alderman on the council. And,' he added meaningfully, 'president of the local Board of Trade.'

'Sir Douglas, what an honour! Both of them! Congratulations!'

'Well, it hasn't happened yet,' said Sir Douglas, coming as close as he ever got to modesty. 'But I can't afford a whiff of scandal. So best all round, I think, if we drop the whole thing. I'll square it with the other chaps. I'm sure they'll understand. War effort, got to pull together, all the rest of it.'

Robert simply couldn't believe it. All that worry, all the machinations to keep the truth from his father and set up Jim Goodridge while protecting the others who'd really been in on the scheme? And tonight, giving himself indigestion at dinner thinking about the blasted housemaid sitting by her fireside with her new husband tapping his pipe into the fateful ashtray while any hopes of sitting opposite Evelyn at their own fireside one day had been dashed? All that worry – for nothing! Nothing! He'd got off scot-free!

'I appreciate all you've done, Robert, I really do,' said Sir Douglas. 'It's been good doing business with you, as our American friends say!'

'My pleasure, sir.' Robert paused. The relief was dizzying. 'Would you mind awfully if I changed my mind and had that cigar?'

'Help yourself!' Sir Douglas gestured at the box beside him. 'In fact, I've got a proposition to put to you. Do you play golf?'

Chapter 13

Cedric waited up late into the night, but when by midnight there was still no sign of Robert, he had no option but to go to bed. He didn't sleep well; in fact he hardly slept at all, though he must have dropped off at some point because he was unaware of Robert coming in.

The next morning, he was looking jadedly at a boiled egg when, much to his surprise, Robert appeared in the dining room. Though a place was always laid for him, he never usually joined his father for breakfast. By contrast, he seemed in very good spirits.

'Morning!'

He sat down, removed his napkin from its silver ring and flicked it open like a Morris dancer at a

May Day merry-making. He reached for the coffee pot.

'Good morning. You were late last night,' said Cedric evenly.

'I was,' said Robert smugly.

High on his whisky, wine, and cigar-fuelled conversation with Sir Douglas, he'd dared to suggest that he and Evelyn pop down to the local pub for a nightcap and an indulgent Sir Douglas had agreed. There'd been a most agreeable smooching session in the car with Evelyn afterwards. With the relief and exhilaration which had flooded him, he was starting to feel he might actually be able to move things on with her.

'You didn't want me home for some reason, did you?' Robert poured himself some coffee.

'I did, actually,' said Cedric. 'But we'll have to have the conversation now instead.'

Robert listened, watching grains of sugar fall from his spoon as Cedric explained about the visit from Lily, the contradictory story he'd been told of the delivery scheme, and who was actually behind it.

'What do you want me to say?' Robert said when Cedric had finished. He spread his hands in a gesture of . . . knowing Robert as Cedric was beginning to, neither innocence nor supplication. 'I've been rumbled. Copped. Bang to rights.'

'It's nothing to joke about, Robert!' Did he still not realise? 'You could have landed us in court!'

'But it didn't come to that, did it?' Robert swigged his coffee. Thank God it was one thing they hadn't rationed yet. 'Trust it to be that little minx though.'

Robert had never shown it before, but this time, just this once, given the gravity of the situation, Cedric had really hoped for contrition. He could see now he was never going to get it. It was hopeless. Robert would never value Marlow's in the way Cedric did. All his father's and grandfather's hard work could have been undone at the drop of a sales docket, and Robert wouldn't have cared a jot. Cedric was beginning to suspect he might actually have been glad.

'I know there's no point in my lecturing you, Robert,' he said wearily. 'I've had a long time to think about this, and I'm not without blame myself. I've let you go your own way for far too long. I closed my eyes to all the signs. I helped you out of scrapes; I stretched a point to keep you out of the war. I've connived in making you what you are, so if you're guilty of anything, then so am I.'

'Oh, come on, Dad, don't be so hard on yourself! Nature and nurture, don't they say? It's just the way I am. Is that toast still warm? If so, I'll have some, please.'

Cedric passed the rack and Robert took two pieces, put them on his plate, and began buttering. As they both had a midday meal at the store, and often dined out, their rations went further at home.

'Which relative was it,' Robert went on, 'that

went off to Canada to seek his fortune and never came back? Your wicked Uncle Oliver, wasn't it? Married a French Canadian who was a quarter Red Indian or something? Maybe I've got some of him in me!'

Cedric almost had to laugh. Robert was incorrigible. And there was something refreshing in the way he refused to be cowed. He could quite see why his son was so popular and found people easy to get along with – not something Cedric could claim. He'd always been serious, even at Robert's age; Elsie had been the same. It was certainly hard to see where Robert had got it from, unless it was some kind of genetic throwback.

He had one more try.

'Whatever, you must acknowledge the seriousness of the situation, Robert,' he said. 'You've broken the law; Marlow's has broken the law.'

'Yes, yes, and the only people in the know aren't going to do anything about it!'

'How do you know?'

'It's in no one's interest, is it? And this is why I wanted to see you.' Robert was munching his heavily marmaladed toast. 'I've got some good news.'

'Oh?'

This interview was hardly going the way Cedric had planned. Somehow, Robert seemed to have the initiative, the upper hand, even. He picked up his spoon and tapped at his egg.

'I wasn't in last night because I was at the Brimbles',' Robert explained. 'Breaking it to Sir Douglas that our little scheme had got to stop.'

'I see!'

'I couldn't really risk it any more,' shrugged Robert. 'We'd had a good run, as he was the first to say.'

Cedric couldn't help but notice that 'I' – not 'we', not Marlow's. It said everything about the feeling Robert had for the store, or lack of it. 'We' only came when Robert was talking about his little conspiracy with Sir Douglas.

'He didn't mind?'

'He'd come to pretty much the same conclusion himself for, well . . . various reasons,' said Robert. 'We both agreed we're going to draw a line. He'll square it with his pals, end of story.'

So they wouldn't be losing Sir Douglas's custom after all . . . Hating himself for even now thinking about the store's profit and loss account, but unable to help himself, Cedric pushed a pile of shell tidily to the side of his plate.

'Not quite,' he said firmly. 'There's the little question of Jim Goodridge, who you decided to set up as your stooge and who very decently resigned rather than drop you in it. Perhaps you'd like to explain what you thought you were doing there?'

Robert had the grace to look slightly regretful.

'I know, poor old Jim. Sorry about that. But he found out about the whole thing, you see, and . . .

well, he was sort of collateral damage,' he agreed.
'Look, of course it wasn't very gentlemanly.'

'It was a bit more than that!' objected Cedric.

'I'm sure you can put it right.'

'Oh no. For once I'm not going to bail you out.
You're the one who needs to put it right, Robert!'

'Yes, yes you're right. And I can. I know how to
do it, too. Let's level the score. Why don't I resign
instead?'

'Robert! That's not what I meant! Is that really
necessary?'

'There you go again, Dad, trying to protect me!'
said Robert. 'You should sack me, by rights, you
know you should.'

Cedric sighed. In the dark watches of the night,
he'd come to the same conclusion.

'You're as hopeless as I am, in your way.' Robert
smiled ruefully. 'I don't think you'd do it, you see,
because of how it would look. But I can save you
the embarrassment anyway. I've got another job.'

'A job . . . ?' The yolk of Cedric's egg was
congealing on the spoon. Robert took another sip of
coffee.

'Sir Douglas has offered me a position in his firm.
As a junior stockbroker.'

'No!' It was astonishment, not refusal.

'Yup,' said Robert. 'Said he thought the scheme
I'd come up with was ingenious. Said I had an eye
for the main chance, not afraid to take a risk, plus

I must have a pretty good feel for the consumer market, thanks to Marlow's. There'll be plenty of opportunities to get in on the ground floor of some exciting new industries after the war, Dad – not that there aren't now. He thinks I'd be perfect.'

Precious as it was, Cedric gave up on his egg.

'How do you do it?' he marvelled. 'Things always work out for you – you get away with it every time, with or without my help. It's not good for you, you know.'

'It probably isn't, but I'm not going to turn down an opportunity like that, am I?' said Robert reasonably. 'Come on, Dad, this is the best and most honest conversation we've ever had, so let's get it all out in the open. I'm not cut out for life as a floor walker. All those hours cooped up in the shop, worrying about fiddling little things like display tickets and damages and have the cabinets been properly dusted? Have the salesmen got their ties straight and their name badges on? I couldn't care less!'

Cedric replaced his napkin in its ring. It was hard to hear, but again, it was only what he'd always known.

'I'm sorry if that's hurtful to you,' Robert went on. 'But honestly, we're both better off with me out of it. It's been brilliant training, if only to teach me what I don't want to do for the rest of my life. And this way – well, if I'm properly in business with Sir

Douglas I'll have every excuse to see more of Evelyn.'

Cedric stared. If he'd been a man to show emotion, he'd have been open-mouthed. Evelyn Brimble? Robert had mentioned her once or twice since the start of the year, but surely . . . had she been the reason all along? Robert had fallen for her, simply wanted to get closer to her, and had seen a way to do it?

Suddenly he saw his son in a different light – a light which might seem forgiving, but which was anything but. It was more pitying. Robert was just a young man, not the confident swaggerer he seemed, but in fact not at all sure of himself. He'd only been trying to make headway with a girl – in the wrong way, of course, because he was Robert – but trying all the same. It almost made sense. Cedric knew from the way he'd felt about Elsie what love did to you – at any age.

'Oh, Robert,' he said. 'Why didn't I try to get to know you better? Why didn't we have this kind of conversation years ago?'

'Come on, Dad, you didn't have it easy, did you?' said Robert. 'Left with a baby and a business to run. Don't go blaming yourself. I know I'm not perfect, and I must have been – am – a sorry disappointment to you. But you never know. Maybe this can be something of a new start for the pair of us?'

And the start of something for Robert and Evelyn? thought Cedric. Well, well. All that, for the love of a good woman. At least, he hoped Evelyn was a good woman. But that was for Robert to find out.

It was breakfast time at Lily's too, but Lily had no appetite. She too had had a sleepless night, thinking back over the happy few weeks when she'd actively looked forward to going to work at Marlow's, when there was so much to learn, and so much to enjoy – her friendship with Gladys, and Jim, getting to know the other staff and the store itself. For the last few days, though, she'd been filled with nothing but dread. Her mother had gone out early – there was a rumour that the grocer might have some tins now the Americans had started sending food over and Dora wanted to secure her place in the queue – so Lily had the house to herself.

As she'd expected, Jim had left for work by the time she'd got in last evening and Lily had been relieved. Things were supposed to look better in the morning, her mum was always saying, but now it was here, Lily wasn't convinced. Should she hang on to see Jim when he came in? And tell him that, thanks to her blundering, like him, she might be 'let go'?

But it was already too late to choose. As she dithered, she heard the gate open and footsteps crossing the yard. She went to the back door and opened it.

Jim looked exhausted, pale yet dark-eyed. He was in filthy blue overalls which Tatchell's must have given him, far too big for his skinny frame. Round his hand he had a grubby bit of cloth with a rusty stain on it.

'Jim!' she cried. 'What happened?'

'I think this is where I say, "You should see the other bloke", isn't it?' he said, coming inside. Lily closed the door.

'You haven't been in a fight? Not on your first shift?'

'No, of course I haven't!' Jim put down his gas mask. 'And please don't fuss. It was an accident. A bit of a nick, that's all.'

'Come here, sit down.' Lily led him to a chair. 'It looks like more than a nick to me.'

Jim didn't argue but sat down and let her unwind the clumsy bandage. She winced as much as he did as she peeled it away where it had stuck and saw a nasty ragged gash across the heel of his hand.

'It might hold up work on the henhouse a bit, I'm afraid.'

'It should hope it's going to hold you up from ever going back to that place!'

'Don't be daft. Of course I'll go back,' he said.

'Well, you're an idiot!' said Lily before she could stop herself. 'You mustn't! How did you do it?'

'It was my own fault.' Jim was trying to sound casual, but he just sounded weary. 'I was adjusting a clamp on the workbench, so I had my gloves off. A lad came by with a trolley of metal sheets. The top one started to slip and I stupidly went to catch it and—'

'All right, all right, I get the idea.' Lily winced as she pictured the sharp edge meeting the soft flesh. 'But you should have had stitches. Haven't they got a nurse? They must have!'

'She was busy,' explained Jim. 'One of the women went into labour on the factory floor. Well, not quite literally,' he added. 'They got her to the rest room. She shouldn't still have been working, but she needed the money, apparently.'

'She didn't have the baby there?'

'Oh yes,' said Jim. 'And back at her bench within the hour . . . No, of course she didn't! It was all clanging bells and they carted her off to the hospital. I was hardly going to bother the nurse after that lot with a little scratch.'

'It's not a scratch, and you should have!' Lily threw the stained bandage in the bin. A shocking waste of cloth – but it was one thing to make do and mend. She didn't fancy washing that nasty thing out.

'It's the real world, Lily. These things happen. It's not all refined and quiet like Marlow's!'

Jim wasn't very refined or quiet either as Lily dabbed his hand with antiseptic.

'I'm sorry, I'm sorry!' she cried as he gritted his teeth. She held his hand as gently as she could and dried it carefully. 'Hold still.'

She reached for a new bit of rag – Dora kept strips in a bag on the back of the pantry door – and started

196

to wrap it round. Unlike yesterday's lesson in coupon-handling, Lily had paid close attention in Marlow's first aid classes.

'I'll learn,' said Jim. 'I shouldn't have tried to catch it, but it's all against the clock, rush jobs, urgent supplies, do it yesterday. Like I say, it's not Marlow's.'

'Oh, Jim, it sounds awful! It's not for you! Please, please, you must be able to find something else!'

'Lily, I'm tired and I need to get to bed. We've had this conversation. I don't want to re-rehearse it if you don't mind.'

Lily answered by tearing the end of the rag down in two as she'd been taught, wrapping the strips around and tying a knot. It wasn't the neatest bandage ever, but it was clean, at least. Jim held up his hand and looked at it.

'Not bad for a first go,' he said, managing a half-smile. 'Thanks, nurse.'

It was completely the wrong moment, she knew it was. He'd given her as clear a signal as he could that he didn't want to talk about anything and certainly nothing to do with jobs, wherever or whatever they were. But Lily couldn't tell anyone else, and it was killing her. She busied herself screwing the top back on the bottle of antiseptic so that she didn't have to look at him.

'I've got something to tell you.'

'I hate it when people say that. It's never good news, is it?' he observed.

He couldn't have been more right, but it was too late – she'd have to do it now. She took a breath.

'I went to see Mr Marlow yesterday. And I told him the truth about the delivery thing. I told him Robert was the one behind it, not you.'

Jim stared at her in disbelief. When he spoke, he didn't sound like the Jim she knew.

'And you call me an idiot! Well, you're the worst kind of fool! Why did you do it, Lily? What for? What good could it possibly do?'

Lily said nothing. Yesterday she'd been convinced it was the only thing she could do, but that conviction had been waning ever since she'd entered Cedric Marlow's office, and she certainly wasn't convinced now.

'So what did he say?' This was a harsher Jim than she'd ever have imagined.

'He didn't say anything. He listened, then he asked me to leave.'

'What? Leave his office? Or leave Marlow's? You too?'

'I don't know. I suppose when I go in today I'll find out.'

Jim threw up his hands, then dropped them into his lap.

'So it's achieved less than nothing. You haven't got my job back and you've maybe lost yours as well. Terrific. What a marvellous result.'

Lily hung her head.

'Lily – what am I going to do with you?' At least he only sounded sad now, and not so angry. 'After all I said . . . why? Why? Me having to leave is one thing, you've gone and thrown away the best chance in life you're ever likely to have!'

'Well, I don't want it!' flared Lily. 'Not if it means working for a place where no one can say what's what, and the truth has to be covered up because it's too hard to face, and it's easier to let people get away with things! They can keep their stinking job!'

She felt her lip wobble. How could they be arguing like this when they were both on the same side and when she'd only done it for him?

'Oh, this is crazy!' Jim jumped up. 'Lily . . . oh, why? I told you not to interfere . . . you've no idea! You've made things so much worse!'

'I'm sorry. I didn't mean to . . . What are we going to do?'

'Do? Well, I suppose I'll have to go and see Mr Marlow myself now and explain how I never asked you to do it! And I can't do it today, I'm due back at Tatchell's!'

'What? You've only this minute got in!'

'I told you, rush job, they wanted volunteers for overtime, and since I didn't know you were going to fling a huge great spanner in the works, I said yes!'

Lily gaped.

'They've sent me home for a couple of hours' sleep, then I'm going back there.'

'Right,' said Lily. 'So that's instead of your shift tonight?'

'No.' Jim looked puzzled. 'It's overtime. As well as.'

'Jim! That's crazy!' cried Lily. She wasn't sure how they'd got to arguing again, but they were. 'You need a proper rest!'

'And you think Bomber Command are getting much rest, do you? The Tank Corps in North Africa? The Atlantic convoys?'

'No, but—'

'No, no buts, Lily! What are we never allowed to say at Marlow's if a customer starts complaining?'

'"Don't you know there's a war on?"' muttered Lily.

'Well? Don't you? You never forget it if you work in a factory, I can tell you! So please don't try to tell me what I should and shouldn't do, and when!'

'Oy! What's going on here? I can hear you two in the entry!'

The back door had opened without them seeing or hearing. Jim sat down again as Lily spun round. The only good thing was that it wasn't Dora, but Freda, the girl who'd been delivering the letters since their postman had been called up. She always came round the back. She liked delivering to their house because Sid had been home when she started and, of course, hadn't been able to resist shooting her a line, asking her name, then telling her it should be Penny – Penny Black.

But there was no Sid today, as Lily explained, and a disappointed Freda handed over the letters. The personal service would probably stop now, Lily thought, as she sifted through them. Her postcard from Sid hadn't been waiting for her last night as she'd expected, but it was here now, along with the gas bill – that'd be popular – yet more 'Instructions for Householders' from the Government – even more so – and a letter for Jim, re-addressed from his old lodgings.

She held the envelope out to him and saw him go even paler. He obviously recognised the writing.

'Marvellous,' he said. 'That's all I need.'

Chapter 14

Lily let Jim read his letter while she tried to concentrate on her postcard, though it seemed meaningless now.

> *Hi Lil!*
>
> *How's my favourite sister? Sorry, forgot, I've only got the one! All well here. Hope you're being good. I am – worse luck! Lots of PT but the foot's holding up well. See you again soon I hope.*
> *Love*
> *Sid x*

At least he'd had the sense not to put 'Love, Sid' on Gladys's. Lily put her card to one side and watched

Jim's face as he read. Whatever was in the letter, he didn't seem very pleased about it. He refolded it and replaced it carefully in the envelope.

'Jim . . . ? It's obviously something . . . who's it from?'

Jim stuffed the letter in the pocket of his overalls. He met her eyes.

'It's from my mother,' he said.

'Oh! Is there something wrong . . . at home?'

'No. Both my parents are fine.'

'Good. So what's the problem?'

'Ach.' Jim rubbed his forehead with the back of his uninjured hand. 'I suppose I'm going to have to tell you. I'd have had to tell you anyway, in the end.'

'Jim? What?'

'All right. You'd better sit down.'

That was another thing people said which only ever meant bad news. Lily sat.

'The thing is . . . well, I'm sort of related to the Marlows, you see.'

Lily stared at him. Of all the things she might have imagined . . .

'Sort of? How do you mean? Either you are or you aren't!'

'Don't start with your questions, please, Lily,' pleaded Jim. 'Don't say anything, hear me out, all right? Please, try to listen for once.'

Lily gave a nod.

'All right. Here it is. My mother's younger sister

Elsie was married to Cedric Marlow. So Robert is my cousin.'

'Mr Marlow's your uncle?!'

She'd naturally forgotten the sworn vow of silence.

'I can tell what you're thinking,' said Jim. 'I know what you're going to say. You'll have some crazy, cock-eyed idea that I should be sleeping on silk sheets and eating off gold plate or something. It's not like that. We had nothing to do with them when I was growing up. My mother never got on with her sister – she'd left home and moved away by the time Elsie and Cedric met. Elsie was a salesgirl. My mother was a housemaid. My family are just like yours – my home is just like yours.'

He could see her disbelief, but he ignored it.

'We're the country cousins, country mice, not town mice, call it what you like. My mother left Hinton for a job at a country house – the local squire, don't you know – and that's how she met my dad. He worked on the estate – on the farm. They got married, but the War came and the squire's son raised a battalion. Farming was a reserved occupation then, like it is now, but my dad went off to fight with the rest of them anyway.' He paused. 'I don't know the details, he doesn't talk about it. None of them do, do they? All I know is that he was gassed. So that got him out of the fighting, but his health was done for. His chest. No good for farm work, or any kind of heavy work after that. The old squire, who might have been a bit sympathetic, had died by then, and his son, well, he'd been killed by a sniper the year before. Oh, the estate manager did it all by the book – that was the trouble. There was a small settlement, but the tied cottage had to go – and the little extras – well, quite big extras really, the sacks of flour and potatoes and the turkey at Christmas. So the family fortunes, such as they were, took a bit of a hit.'

For once Lily had no need to say anything. Now she understood. She understood perfectly. As her mother must so often think but rarely said, their own family situation would have been vastly different if Lily's father had still been there and able to support his family.

'So my dad became a sort of village odd-job man, still is, when he's up to it – nothing too heavy, all his strength has gone, but with his bit of a war pension, it's a living. Of sorts.'

Jim sighed.

'Anyway,' he went on, 'in happier news, they had me, and somehow with scrimping and saving and not having any more children they managed to keep me at school to get my school cert. My teachers wanted me to carry on, but . . . that was never going to happen.'

This, too, sounded very familiar.

'I love the country. I love the life, but when I finished school, my mother wouldn't hear of me starting out at the bottom as a farm labourer like my dad. She wanted better for me than that. But with no money to send me to the Agricultural Institute . . . Like I say, we'd had nothing to do with the Marlows, ever. No reason why we should – my Aunt Elsie died soon after Robert was born, and Cedric sort of shut himself off. My mother's parents were too overawed by the marriage in the first place and then too stunned by Elsie dying to expect anything from him. But now, my mother thought . . . why not see if Cedric would give me a helping hand? So she wrote him a letter. She didn't like to ask outright, but at the back of her mind, she was hoping – we all were – that he'd offer to support me while I studied and got a farming qualification. Instead he offered me a job at Marlow's. Not what was expected, but I didn't have much choice but to take it. It would have been too embarrassing to refuse. And . . . the rest you know.'

Lily did indeed.

'From the day I started, Robert treated me like any other employee,' Jim went on. 'I didn't want anything different – I was all for keeping the connection quiet. But when he approached me . . . I didn't know what he was like. I didn't know I couldn't trust him. I don't know why I did – stupidly I felt flattered, I suppose, thought it was an overture – family feeling or something. And when it all fell apart and I got called in and questioned about the delivery thing . . .' He sighed. 'Robert had dropped me in it good and proper, but I felt I could hardly start badmouthing him after the big favour Cedric had done me and my mother. I thought it was better to let it go, leave, find another job, and in time tell my mother that Marlow's had been good experience, but I'd moved on.'

'And now? The letter?'

Jim pulled a face.

'Turns out a friend of a friend of hers came into the shop. To look at blinking bathroom stools, of all things. This woman asked about me, did I still work there, how I was getting on, and she was told I'd been "let go". My mother's asking if it's true, and why.'

'Oh, Jim. Oh, no. What bad luck! I'm so sorry.'

'Me too. It's all a mess. Even more of a mess, I mean.'

'What are we going to do?'

Jim rubbed his forehead again.

'I don't know. I've been working all night and I've got to go back in a couple of hours. I can't think straight.'

'No, of course. You must get to bed.'

'I think I'd better. And hadn't you better get to work yourself?'

Oh no – the time!

'I'll be late! I have to go!'

She ran. She had to. She ran all the way to the bus stop, grabbed the rail and jumped on the few free square inches of platform just as the bus was pulling away, to a finger-wagging from the conductress. She ran again, from the stop in town to the staff entrance and reached the timekeeper as the minute hand of the clock clunked into position. She'd made it, just. The timekeeper raised his eyebrows and reached for the late book as Lily signed the register. The next person after her wouldn't be so lucky.

But she had more eyebrows to face, and maybe more finger-wagging too, thought Lily, when she saw Miss Garner waiting in the corridor on the way to the staff cloakroom.

'Come with me, please, Lily,' she said. 'Mr Marlow would like to see you. Now. You can bring your things with you.'

It was as she'd expected. The sack. There was obviously no point in her putting her things away because she'd be going straight out of the door again.

Miss Garner didn't say any more on the way up in the service lift, and when they got to the management floor, she simply indicated Mr Marlow's door and disappeared into her own partitioned office.

With a horrible feeling of familiarity, Lily tapped on the door, heard the request to come in and turned the handle. Oh well. It had been nice at Marlow's while it lasted. Most of the time.

* * *

'A most unusual girl, that,' Cedric Marlow said to Miss Garner later. 'It was your friend Miss Norris, I think, who sent her our way?'

'That's right.'

'Thank her for me the next time you see her, will you? I know you had your doubts, but I think Lily Collins, with a few of the rough edges you were worried about rubbed off, could be a big asset. A buyer perhaps, in time.' He smiled to himself. 'I'd like to see her deal with our suppliers if the men's vests had faulty seams or the bath brushes started losing their bristles.'

Miss Garner accepted the compliment on behalf of Miss Norris but wasn't sure that thanks would be the first words on her lips when they next met over the consignment of oiled wool that their WVS Knitting Group was busy turning into seamen's socks. Frankly, Lily Collins was taking up far too much of her time. This was the second time that something Lily had done hadn't had the expected outcome, and Miss Garner didn't like the unexpected. But if Mr Marlow thought she was a good thing . . .

'She certainly seems to have spirit,' she said.

She hadn't asked what had gone on between Mr Marlow and Lily either yesterday or today, but Lily had been sent off to her department, so it had obviously been resolved somehow. Mr Marlow appeared to be happy with how things had turned out. He seemed happier in himself, too, than she'd seen him for a long time, and with the single woman's devotion to her employer – and that covered not just the shop but the man himself – that mattered a lot to Miss Garner.

And Lily? Lily was on Cloud Nine and a half. Or maybe even Ten. She'd walked on air back down to the lockers and then up to the department, hugging to herself all Mr Marlow had said. He hadn't divulged exactly what, if anything, had gone on between himself and Robert – she'd hardly have expected him to – but something must have, and the truth must have come out, because he'd asked about Jim. He said he'd established that Jim's resigning had been premature, and did Lily know where he was and what he was doing? It seemed his secretary had phoned Jim's lodgings and been told he'd left there without a forwarding address.

'I assume from your speaking up for him that you might be friends,' Mr Marlow had said. 'Would I be right?'

Lily had been happy to tell him that she did know where Jim was, and could certainly get a message to him.

'Good,' said Cedric. 'And do you happen to know if he's found another job? Because I'd like to reinstate him. If he'd like to come back, that is.'

'Oh, I'm sure he would!' cried Lily. 'He's gone to Tatchell's, but it's not right for Jim.'

'Goodness, no, not at all!'

'He's having to work nights – and overtime – and it's horrible work – he's already hurt himself and—'

'No, no. This won't do. We must sort this out.'

Knowing what she now did about Jim's family connections, Lily could see why Mr Marlow sounded concerned. He'd brought him to Hinton as a favour to Jim's mother, to a job that was safe and secure, not to work in some dangerous factory. It also explained why, though at the time, thanks to Robert, he'd had doubts about Jim's honesty, he'd given him a decent reference.

'What have you got to look so pleased about?' hissed Beryl as Lily passed the Toy department later on her way to the stockroom. Mrs Powell's youngest girl was shooting up in height, and there wasn't a sun suit in the right size on the display. 'You've had that Cheshire cat grin on all day.'

'Maybe I'm one step closer to buying that lipstick,' said Lily blithely. 'Payday again soon, isn't it?'

Maybe she would buy it, one day. After all, against the odds, she still had a job!

Then she bowled away across the dove-grey carpet, up the stone stairs, past the taped-up windows and the 'Shh! You Don't Know Who's Listening' and the 'Let Us Go Forward Together' posters. Mr Marlow had listened, and he wanted Jim to come back. 'Let Us Go Forward Together' indeed!

Upstairs, Lily pushed through the double doors into the stockroom. What had she come for? She'd almost forgotten. Ah, yes, sun suit. Gingham, pink. And age six . . . She found the sun suits in their section and selected an age six. But little Eleanor Powell really had grown . . . It looked to her as though an age six might not be long enough in the body. She picked up an age seven as well.

'And I was right – she was an age seven!' Lily reported triumphantly at tea.

Dora's foray to the grocer's that morning had been a waste of time – the rumour of tins as empty as the shelves – but in the queue, she'd heard that the butcher might be making sausages, so she'd traipsed there and had triumphantly come away with half a dozen.

Lily had rushed home from work, bursting with her news and desperate to give Jim Mr Marlow's – his Uncle Cedric's – message. But he was asleep when she got in and Dora, as outraged as Lily about the double shift he'd agreed to, forbade her from waking him until tea was on the table.

'He's his own worst enemy,' she said, pricking the sausages and putting them under the grill. 'I don't want him having another accident. Mind you, you didn't do a bad job of dressing his hand, Lily.'

If she hadn't been so frustrated at not being able to tell Jim the news, Lily would have glowed at this rare praise. Instead she had to get on with laying the table, while her mum clucked, understandably, about the gas bill.

'Mostly filler and water, of course, but what can you expect?' said Dora later as they sat down at the table. She'd given herself and Lily one and a half sausages each, and three to Jim along with a huge pile of potatoes. He'd protested and tried to push some on to their plates, but Dora was having none of it. He was doing a man's job, he needed a man's meal.

'You do at least get a break, I hope?' she asked him, pouring him some more tea. 'And they give you something to eat?'

'Oh, yes, there's a canteen,' said Jim. He still looked bleary after his sleep and his hair was sticking up all over the place – almost as bad as Lily's when she got out of bed. He was also, she noted, still putting a brave face on the job. 'It isn't your cooking, Mrs Collins, but it's – well, better than nothing.'

Dora tutted.

'Mucks your system right up, I should think, having to eat in the middle of the night. Not that you must know what meal it's supposed to be. Do any of us, these days, there's so little about. Still, what can't be cured . . .'

Lily glanced at Jim. Usually they'd have exchanged a smile – he'd been quick to note that Dora had a pithy saying for every occasion – but tonight he kept his eyes fixed on his plate. He hadn't even tried to get her on one side to ask if she'd still got her job. He couldn't still be cross with her, could he?

Chapter 15

'I'll walk with you,' she said as he got his things together – a knapsack with his overalls in it, his gas mask and, forced on him by Dora, a packet of sandwiches and a bit of cake – the last slice, Lily noted enviously, made with hoarded sugar and eggs which Dora had acquired by swapping a sudden glut of garden produce. Why did men always get the favourable treatment?

'Right,' Lily began as they emerged into the relative privacy of the back alley. 'No, I listened to you this morning,' she warned as he opened his mouth. 'I've been desperate to tell you since I got in – I've been desperate to tell you all day! You can listen to me this time!'

'Do I have a choice?'

'You'll like it!'

'By which I suppose you mean you do,' said Jim. He still wasn't smiling. 'Go on then. What have you gone and done now?'

Lily shook back her hair. She was much better at dealing with it these days and tonight it was held off her face with a periwinkle blue ribbon – Haberdashery at Marlow's had become one of her favourite hunting-grounds for short lengths they couldn't sell and let go to staff for pennies or sometimes for free.

'It's a message from Mr Marlow. He wants you back.'

And so she told him. She didn't spare the detail: all about how she'd been summoned to see Cedric Marlow and, while he hadn't explained the whys and wherefores, he'd told her that he'd established the truth of the matter in the delivery racket, that Jim was – what was the word he'd used? – exonerated, that was it – and he wanted him to come in as soon as possible to clear things up.

'He was horrified you'd gone to Tatchell's!' concluded Lily in triumph. 'Of course he was, with your mother thinking you had a nice, safe, clean job in a shop!'

'Is that it?' said Jim. 'You've finished now, have you? 'Cos when you said I'd got to listen, I didn't think you meant all the way to work!'

It was true, they were nearly at Tatchell's gates.

215

Lily had been so intent on telling her tale, she hadn't noticed.

'Don't go in, Jim, please.' Lily stopped and impulsively clutched at his hand – luckily not the bandaged one. 'You're not going to be all high and mighty and keep saying making aircraft parts is more important than flogging ashtrays, are you?'

For the first time that day, Jim smiled his funny smile, the one that crinkled up his eyes.

'The Germans are wasting their time with Lord Haw-Haw, you know. Wind you up, let you go and you'd do a far better propaganda job.'

'You know what I mean! You are coming back to Marlow's, aren't you?'

'You are incredible,' marvelled Jim. 'Do you realise that you've been going on and on about me and my job and you haven't mentioned the most important thing of all?'

'What?'

'That you've still got your job, you idiot, after putting it on the line for me.'

'Oh, that,' said Lily. 'Well, yes, that too.'

Jim laughed. It was so good to see.

'I dunno . . . you're a funny one,' he said. 'There's something . . . just something about you, Lily.'

They stood there on the grimy street. The factory hooter had gone. The full day-shift at Tatchell's was over and the workers pushed past them, some jostling and chatting, some worn out and simply relieved to be out in the fresh air. Women with scarves wound turban-like round their heads and wrap-around pinnies; men young and old, in overalls, in work shirts with braces; boys not much older than Lily, laughing and shoving each other, rudely raucous despite a day spent doing a man's work.

'Well? Are you going in?'

'Yes,' said Jim. 'I must. I owe it to them, and I'll have to work my notice. It's only fair.'

'Then it's back to flogging ashtrays? Promise? You won't let Tatchell's bully you into changing your mind?'

'That's rich, coming from you – you're the biggest bully of the lot!' Jim grinned. Then he swooped down and planted a quick kiss on her cheek. 'But thank you,' he said.

It was enough.

Jim saw through his shift at Tatchell's. His interview with Mr Deakin, the works manager, wasn't the most comfortable ten minutes of his life, and the 'Don't you know there's a war on?' mantra which he'd used to rebuke Lily was turned against him now. But Jim stood his ground.

'I'm sorry,' he said. 'Maybe I never should have started looking for another job in the first place. I . . . ' he stopped. The truth was 'I might have known Lily wouldn't let things lie' but that was hardly going to make any sense to Mr Deakin. 'I should have given it a bit more time. But my old boss wants me back, and that's where my loyalties lie.'

'You'll work your notice!' said Deakin. It wasn't a question.

'Of course,' said Jim. 'But no more overtime, I'm afraid.'

He could give Lily that.

Next day, washed, brushed and with a smaller, neater dressing on his hand – Dora had seen to it this time – he went to see Cedric Marlow, or 'Uncle Cedric' as Lily now teased Jim she was going to call him. It was their private joke. He'd made her promise not to say anything to her mum or anyone about his family link with the store.

In the office where Jim had gone through so much humiliation and Lily such agonies, Cedric Marlow apologised. But he pointed out that Jim wasn't without fault, either.

'Why didn't you speak up for yourself, you silly boy?!' he asked. 'I know you said when you started here you didn't want to exploit the connection, but surely . . .'

Jim pulled a face.

'That was the reason, sir,' he said. 'I felt I couldn't. You'd done so much for me as a favour to my mother when you didn't have to . . . I couldn't bring myself to . . .'

'To drop my son in it,' said Cedric. 'Though he hadn't hesitated to do the same to you?'

Jim shrugged.

'Not my style, sir.'

And there lay the difference between the two boys. But Cedric let it pass.

'No, well, you're not the only one who hasn't been entirely honest.' Cedric wasn't only thinking about Robert, but his own stubborn refusal to see the obvious about his son. 'The whole episode has given me a lot to think about. Robert too, as it turns out.'

'Really, sir?'

'Yes. In fact, you may as well know . . . Robert's going to be leaving. He's been offered another opportunity, and he's taking it.'

'I see!'

'And someone else has handed in their notice, too. Maurice Bishop. Blackpool, it seems, has exerted a strange pull over him.'

'Blackpool has?'

Cedric nodded.

'I don't know the place myself, but he enjoyed his holiday so much he went into the Co-op and asked if they had any openings. They've got a huge store up there, the Jubilee Emporium. Do you know it?'

Jim smiled inwardly. All the upheavals of the last twenty-four hours, which had caused such ructions between himself and Lily, between himself and Tatchell's, between, presumably, Cedric and Robert before things were peaceably settled, yet Cedric was

219

as interested in Maurice Bishop's move to a compet-
itor as in any personal drama. Once a shopkeeper,
always a shopkeeper, it seemed – business came first.
Jim had a sudden stab of sympathy – and under-
standing – for Robert.

'I can't say I do, sir.'

'No? There was an article about it in the *Drapers'
Record* . . . They've even got a theatre, you know,
on the top floor . . . quite fantastic.'

'Something you're thinking of doing here, sir?' Jim
ventured, tongue-in-cheek.

Cedric Marlow took him seriously, of course.

'Hardly! Not at the moment, with the Air Ministry's
demands. Anyway . . . Bishop's been taken on up
there. So, um . . . well . . .'

Cedric Marlow stood up. Jim stood up too.

'Here's your staff manual again, Jim. And your
name badge. Though not quite the same badge as
before.'

Jim took the booklet and the badge. It read: *Mr
J. Goodridge. Second Sales Assistant.*

'Congratulations.' Cedric allowed one of his rare
smiles. 'You'll get an official letter in due course. And
a small pay rise. In line with regulations.'

'Thank you, sir. Thank you! But you do understand
I can't start back straight away. I've got to work my
notice at Tatchell's.'

'I'd expect no less of you.' Cedric was all smiles
now. 'As long as you're back for the Sale.'

Jim grinned. The cunning old bird. With customers desperate to get their hands on anything while it was still available, the Summer Sale would be pandemonium. And he'd tried to tell Lily that Marlow's was civilised!

'Your mother will be pleased to hear you're doing so well, I'm sure,' Cedric added as the two men moved to the door.

'She'll be thrilled.' Doubly thrilled, thought Jim, given she was under the impression he'd been sacked. 'I can't wait to tell her!'

Cedric Marlow, though, had one last card up his sleeve. He'd instinctively gone along with Robert's suggestion that he should investigate the delivery racket and had come to regret it. Well, the least Robert could do in return was to deliver the news of Jim's reinstatement to the first-floor staff.

That evening, after the main doors had finally been locked after the last customers, Robert assembled them at the bottom of the staircase leading up to the second floor. He mounted a few steps and turned around to face them.

'I'll only keep you a minute,' he promised. The crowd was mute, keeping their grievances at being kept late to themselves. 'You all work damned hard and I know you want to get off home, or on to your war duties. You're an amazing bunch of folk and I want to thank you for all your hard work. I also wanted to let you know in person about a few

221

comings and goings. I'm sure you'll all want to congratulate Mr Bishop who, on his holidays, found, as the song has it, that he really does like to be beside the seaside. So much so, he's off to work in Blackpool.'

Those who didn't know swivelled to look at Maurice Bishop, who managed to look both proud and bashful. Those who did, knew that he'd fallen for the girl who worked in the cigarette kiosk on the Prom and that that, rather than career advancement, was the real reason for his move. But Robert was still speaking.

'In his place, we're going to welcome back Jim Goodridge.' Gladys goggled and nudged Lily, who beamed and nodded. 'And finally, I need to tell you that I'm going to be moving on myself.'

That got everyone's attention – Lily's too. This was a turn-up! Gladys goggled at her again, but Lily wanted to listen.

'I've been offered the chance of an opening in business,' Robert went on. 'And with my father's agreement I'm going to take it. I've learnt a lot working here, from all of you.'

He looked directly at Lily. They both knew what he meant.

'I'm very grateful to you for putting up with me. You've been very patient and kind as I learned the ropes. I'll be here for a couple of months yet. But you won't have to indulge me for much longer.' It was meant as a joke and there was polite laughter and demurring. Lily looked at the floor. 'Well, that's all I have to say. My replacement will be announced in due course. Thank you for your time.'

No one sang 'For He's a Jolly Good Fellow' – perhaps that could wait till the day Robert actually left – though Lily wasn't sure she'd be joining in if it happened, after all Robert had put her and Jim through. Instead, there was a faltering round of applause, led, Lily noted, by a couple of the buyers. Of course! They wanted his job! As the staff dispersed, some made their way to Maurice to pat him on the back, while a couple of the more pushy departmental under-managers and buyers hurried towards Robert to shake him by the hand.

'How about that?' squeaked Gladys when she and Lily finally got outside. It was a humid evening, typical of that summer, with a heavy white sky. 'Did you know?'

'Not about Robert!' said Lily. 'Though, yes, I've got to admit, I did know about Jim.' She wasn't going to lie to Gladys, or keep anything from her, not any more. 'I'm sorry. I couldn't say anything till it was official. It's wonderful, isn't it?'

'Of course.'

But Lily could see Gladys was upset not to have been taken into her confidence.

'I really am sorry, Gladys.' She knew she owed her friend an apology. 'But I had to wait till Marlow's announced it publicly.'

'Oh . . . that's all right.' Hopeless at bearing any kind of a grudge, or putting up with any kind of disagreement, Gladys wound her arm through Lily's. 'As long as it's all sorted out – I know you didn't like him working at that horrible factory.'

'No, I did not. And I told him so.'

'I bet you did! And how! Poor Jim!'

'Don't you dare take his side!'

'All right. But listen. In return, you can do something for me!'

'Go on then. What?' Lily certainly felt she owed Gladys something.

'Let me be the one to tell Sid!'

Lily had to laugh. She might have known. But she was happy to oblige.

Chapter 16

For Jim there was the added satisfaction, when he told her that evening about his promotion, of seeing Lily completely speechless.

'Well, that's marvellous,' she said when she'd found her voice. 'I'm thrilled for you, Jim, I really am! I mean, I do all the hard work and you get the reward!'

'You'll get your crown in Heaven,' replied Jim, knowing not to take her seriously. He'd anticipated she might have something to say about it and her reaction was perfectly fair. 'In the meantime . . . would chocolate caramels go some way to consoling you?'

He dangled a paper bag enticingly in front of her

and in relief that everything had worked out so well – and some amusement at being so transparently bribeable – Lily accepted them – and shared them – with good grace.

'I could never understand why you left Marlow's in the first place,' Dora remarked a couple of evenings later. 'But it's all cleared up now, is it? The things you weren't happy about in your department?'

'Absolutely, Mrs Collins,' Jim assured her. Still taking care of his bandaged hand, he was carefully sawing a piece of wood to size.

He was working his notice at Tatchell's by night but before he went each evening he was determined to 'crack on' with the henhouse. He and Lily were having a competition for the most wince-inducing egg-related puns.

Together they'd scoured the neighbourhood for discarded bits of timber. Anything decent had long since gone for props and battens, but they'd managed to find a few planks which weren't too rotten. Along with a three-legged table which they'd found tipped half in a storm drain, a few more odd pieces begged from various places, and some plywood, only slightly warped, Jim thought they could add up to something serviceable.

'Well, I'm pleased to hear it,' said Dora. 'Now you watch yourself with that saw. I don't want you cutting your other hand!'

'Don't worry, Mrs Collins. I'll take care. And when

you next take a look, we'll be on the way to a positive Poultry Palace.'

Dora tutted and tossed her head, but she went off into the house with a smile. He was a caution, that Jim. Him and Sid together were a right pair.

'I can't believe you've got away with saying so little about it,' said Lily enviously. 'It's only because she doesn't know you that well that she can't give you a proper grilling. If it was me who'd upped and left, I'd never have heard the end of it!'

'It nearly was you upping and leaving, if I can remind you,' grinned Jim. 'Anyway, I deserve a break, don't you think? With you nagging like you do.'

'Charming! After I got you your job back! And a promotion!'

'I should think Cedric Marlow gave me that out of sympathy!' Jim retorted. 'He had one single conversation with you and caved in. He must have realised I have to put up with you going on at me all the time!'

'You've got a nerve! If you weren't already injured . . .' Even as she said it, Lily remembered saying something very similar to Sid when he'd been cheeky.

The end section of the piece Jim had been sawing fell away.

'Right, that's enough messing about,' he said. 'Let's get down to business.'

He bent down and started to sort through the skimpy collection of nails, most of them bent, rusty, or both, which they'd also managed to scavenge. Selecting one he judged to be the right length, he arranged the two bits of wood together at right angles, placed the nail in position, and turned to Lily.

'Do you want to hold it or hit it?'

Lily didn't really fancy either, but she thought Jim was probably more practised with a hammer than she was – and they couldn't afford to waste any nails.

'Hold it, I suppose,' she agreed. She bent down too and assumed her position. 'Right, ready.'

Jim raised the hammer.

'And what about your mum?' she asked.

'You'll have to hold that nail a bit straighter if you don't want your thumb bashed off.'

Lily adjusted her grip.

'Have you written to tell her the good news?'

'Of course. Told her it had all been a misunderstanding, and far from being asked to leave, I'd been promoted, and if her friend's friend wanted to come back in, I'd serve her personally – and by the way, our bathroom stools were a very good buy at a keen price. She should get one while we've still got them.'

There was a pause while Jim wielded the hammer. Lily tried not to flinch every time it came down.

'You don't trust me, do you?' Jim gave the nail a few more sharp taps. Luckily his aim was true.

'Yes, I do!' lied Lily unconvincingly. 'So has she written back?'

She hadn't noticed a letter arrive. But as she'd

predicted, Freda wasn't bringing their post round the back any more, not to a household minus Sid. She shoved it through the front door like she did for the rest of the street.

'Nope.'

'That's a shame. I wonder why.'

'There's no hurry. Anyway, she doesn't need to, she'll be seeing me soon enough.'

'Seeing you?'

'Yes,' said Jim. 'Now hold this one.' He gave her another nail and repeated the operation. Lily was flinching a bit less now.

'But . . . how? Is she coming here?'

'No. I'm going there. Or rather, we are.'

'We are?'

'And I call myself a birdwatcher,' said Jim. He looked around. 'There's a parrot round here somewhere.'

'A parrot?'

Then she got it; he was joking.

'Why, don't you want to come?'

Was he serious? A day out in the country? Meeting Jim's parents? Of course she did!

'But – when? When are we going? And how are we going to get there?'

'It's Worcestershire, Lily, not the Western Desert. There are roads, and trains, and buses.'

'Really?' said Lily. 'Still?'

'Well,' he admitted. 'OK, that may be duff gen.

There used to be. I don't know. I haven't worked it out yet. But once I have, we'll go, on a Sunday. We'll get there, trust me – you've just said you do, haven't you?'

Lily nodded. She did trust him. Jim smiled again.

'How else did you think we were going to get these chickens? That they'd fly here?'

With her job and Jim's secure at Marlow's, and a day in the country to look forward to when the henhouse was finished, there was only one thing left to bother Lily. Miss Frobisher hadn't been in the crowd of acolytes pressing round to congratulate Robert Marlow, but that might not mean anything. Miss Frobisher never let her feelings show. Was she one of the ones who might put herself forward for his job?

'What, and leave some other poor soul the task of trying to keep you in line?' she said when Lily dared to voice her fears. 'I don't think anyone deserves that, do you?'

It was only when Miss Frobisher smiled that Lily realised she was joking.

'I've got quite a big enough job already, what with running the department and taking care of my son,' said Miss Frobisher. 'You have to be so careful with boys.'

Lily nodded. She was beginning to appreciate just how much.

And that should have been the end of it, but not as far as some people were concerned.

'Jim Goodridge suddenly back, and promoted into the bargain? Maurice Bishop and Robert Marlow going? Bit of a funny business if you ask me!'

A shark-eyed Beryl had trapped Lily in the Ladies again – literally trapped her in the corner between the sinks and the roller towel.

'But no one is asking me, are they?' she went on. 'I'm asking you. You know more about this than you're letting on, don't you, Lily Collins?'

'No!'

The tiles were cold against Lily's back.

'Oh, come on!' scoffed Beryl. 'All that back and forth of yours lately? Frobisher letting you off for the afternoon? A sick headache? A likely story! And disappearing off up to the management floor in your dinner hour – don't think I didn't see you! This is all still to do with the delivery thing, isn't it? Have you been telling tales?'

'Have you been following me? Watching me?'

'More to the point, have you been watching us?'

Beryl's face came closer. Lily could smell her perfume. Only the salesgirls on cosmetics were actually allowed to wear perfume, but a simple rule was never going to stop Beryl, and benign Mr Bunting did nothing to stop her either. It was Soir de Paris, Lily knew, because Beryl had bragged at the lockers about the bottle Les had bought her. More like 'Sewer de Paris' on her, thought Lily uncharitably. But charitable was hardly her overriding feeling at that moment. She tried to draw back but her head was already pressed hard against the wall. She twisted her face away, but Beryl caught her by the chin and yanked her head round.

'Are you some kind of spy? Have management put you on our floor to rat on the rest of us?'

Lily tried to sound more nonchalant than she felt.

'A spy? Honestly, Beryl. You spend too much time at the pictures.'

She wasn't enjoying this. She hadn't been so scared of another girl, actually, since she was about five and a gang of bigger girls had barged into the French skipping game Lily had been playing with two friends on some waste ground. The gang had pinched their elastic, and then tied them up with it, along with some rope they'd found lying about. Lily and her friends had cried for their mothers while the bigger girls had stood around and laughed but it had been no use; there was no one to hear. It was only when a couple of women with pushchairs had come by that the bigger girls had run off and Lily and her friends had been released. But that had been ten years ago. Lily wasn't a kid any more. She had to remember that.

'I'm not a spy,' she said as firmly as she could. 'I don't know any more than you do or have any more

contacts that you do in the management. I just want
to get on with my job, thank you.'

'Very noble.'

But Beryl took a step back and Lily's heartbeat
slowed a little. As it did, she felt some of her usual
pluck return.

'I don't suppose it'll make much difference to you,
Beryl. You've obviously got Les where you want him.
He can always treat you out of his wages.'

Beryl tossed her head.

'Les Bulpitt? Don't make me laugh. He's a dead
duck!'

'It's over between you?'

'I'll say!'

Poor Les. He'd obviously served his purpose.

Beryl checked her appearance in the mirror; heaven
forbid she had a hair out of place. But she kept one
eye on Lily too.

'I still don't believe you,' she said, wetting a finger
and smoothing her eyebrows. 'It's the last time I ever
tell you anything, mark my words!'

'Suits me,' said Lily. 'You don't ever have to speak
to me again if you don't want to!'

Beryl sniffed and flounced off, her heels pattering
on the tiles. Lily splashed her face with cold water
– not much of it, and she put the plug in the basin,
she didn't let the tap run. The Government's endless
'Don't Waste Water' warnings had entered deep in
her soul, even at moments like this.

But the encounter had shaken her more than she'd ever have admitted, and she didn't say a word about it to Gladys, or Jim, or anyone. She knew it wasn't helpful to have made an enemy of someone like Beryl and she knew this wasn't the end of it. She'd have to watch her back because Beryl would be watching her every move.

But with lucky timing, and on the day Jim started back, Marlow's Grand Summer Sale began. It had always passed Lily by, but it was, she now understood, a big event in the town, for both staff and customers. Even in wartime, in fact especially because it was wartime, the bargain-hunters were out in force. Children were allocated more coupons than adults to allow for growth, so Childrenswear was especially busy as customers pored over the reductions and pondered the 'Special Purchases' that Miss Frobisher had ordered while they were still available. Lily and Gladys had spent their dinner breaks over the previous few days swotting up on coupon etiquette, so that if a customer asked for guidance, they were able to give it, but mostly they spent their time crawling under the trestles to pick up the garments which customers rooting through the bins had tossed aside, rehanging, refolding, bringing yet more out from the stockroom, or wrapping things up. The pneumatic tubes hummed as money and sales dockets whizzed back and forth to the cash office and when the sales figures for the previous day were distributed each morning, Miss

Frobisher praised everyone's efforts – and told them to keep it up.

'It's our own front line!' she insisted. 'And however tired we are, we must never surrender!'

If Childrenswear was busy, Toys seemed under siege, though it wasn't as bad as the first Christmas of the war, Miss Thomas said, when the shelves had been virtually stripped bare. But no one knew when things like Meccano or train sets might disappear altogether, and those who could afford it were snapping up what they could. Nowadays nobody thought the war would be over by Christmas, and customers were planning ahead to birthdays and Christmases to come. Lily noted sadly that the toys on offer were increasingly warlike – 'Help the Spitfire Fund' model planes and jigsaws showing dogfights over the Channel, while the books of cut-out dolls that Lily had loved as a child now gave dolly a ravishing selection of outfits – the uniforms of the WRNS, WAAF, ATS or Land Army. It all meant, though, that Beryl was busy. She ignored Gladys and Lily in the canteen and staff room, easing her feet out of their unsuitable shoes, the heel a good half-inch higher than Marlow's staff manual instructed. Miss Frobisher had noticed, of course, and had pointed out the aberration to Gladys and Lily as a warning, so Beryl needn't think she'd get away with it for ever. But the demands of the Sale took precedence over strict adherence to the rules – for these few weeks the usual slogan was reversed, and it really was 'profit before people'.

Furniture and Household, when Lily looked across, was less busy, but nonetheless doing a steady trade in essentials – tea towels, slop pails, coconut matting. Though it was a good time to buy a new wireless if you could afford it, Jim had told Dora, taking his new Second Sales role seriously. Despite things dragging on, and the reports not being encouraging, Mr Churchill wouldn't brook any talk of giving in; there was fighting in Europe, the Mediterranean, Greece, the Middle East, North Africa, Russia, Scandinavia, the Atlantic . . . who could afford to risk missing the news? But Jim's sales patter went nowhere ('Since when did I have that kind of money to splash about? Sorry, Jim, you've come to the wrong house!') so they had to carry on crouching round the ancient set, straining to hear the latest developments over the snapping and popping of static. But sometimes Lily didn't mind if the signal went off altogether. Sometimes the world was too big for her to think about; it made her head hurt.

As the Sale frenzy quietened a little in the second week – it would stay that way till the 'Further Reductions!' advertisements went into the local newspapers – Lily and Gladys had a bit of time to draw breath. But Gladys only used hers to ask Lily the inevitable question, the one Lily had been bracing herself for.

'I don't suppose . . . when do you think Sid might be home again?'

If and when he did get some leave, Lily hoped her brother had a plan and that he was going to say or do something to deal with Gladys. Because, as kind as his gesture might have been in the beginning, as useful as it had been in keeping Gladys occupied through all the business with Jim, and much as she loved her friend, Lily couldn't stand much more of this.

Chapter 17

As it turned out, Lily didn't have long to wait. When she got home a couple of days later – Jim was staying late at the shop to help take in a delivery of the second-hand furniture that Marlow's were increasingly reduced to selling – Dora was getting her baking tins out.

'Those hens can't come soon enough!' her mum declared from the kitchen stool as she clattered pans about on the top shelf. 'This cake's going to use up all our egg ration for the week!'

'Cake! What's that in aid of?' asked Lily.

Dora got down, holding the largest tin she owned. She glanced in it, tutted, moved to the back door and shook it out.

'Spider,' she said enigmatically, and as Lily pulled a disgusted face, 'Don't look like that, they're perfectly clean, spiders.'

Lily knew it was no use contradicting her.

'Looks like you're planning a nice big one, anyway!' She'd save the 'egg-stra large' joke for Jim; her mum wouldn't appreciate it.

'It'll need to be! I doubt you and me'll get a look-in once Jim sees it, let alone Sid!'

'Sid? Sid's coming home?'

'Saturday. Letter's on the side.'

Lily knew her mum. Dora might sound abrupt, but it was only because she never let her real feelings show. Her baby boy coming home! Of course she was pleased! And if Dora was pleased, Lily was delighted and as for Gladys – she'd be ecstatic!

'Have a read of it,' said Dora, shaking drops of water from the tin. 'Then if you want to make yourself useful, you can start creaming some marg for me.'

Sid, the letter said, had passed his basic training ('flying colours' he claimed) and had been granted forty-eight hours' leave before he moved on to the next stage. Typical Sid, thought Lily. If he was that pleased with himself on paper, what would he be like when he got here, basking in the full glow of Gladys's admiration?

Lily, Gladys and Jim were all at work on the Saturday, of course. It was still the lull before the next big mark-downs, so, Lily realised with a slightly sinking heart – as she'd be on the receiving end – Gladys would have the whole day to fantasise about her hero's return. Jim, manoeuvring a tea trolley behind a nest of tables to show them both to best advantage, raised his eyebrows at Lily and nodded his head towards her fellow junior.

Gladys was pairing little plaid slippers which had become divorced from their partners, but she had a distant look in her eyes and Lily knew she was thinking of another – rather less achievable – union. She knew because Gladys had already described it to her in minute detail. A church wedding . . . White slipper satin with a Brussels lace veil . . . Bouquet of roses, Sid in the uniform he was wearing in the photograph on Dora's mantelpiece, the crisp sailor collar and the little hat – 'oh, and you as bridesmaid, of course, Lily!' Lily smiled back at Jim. He wasn't daft. He'd twigged for himself how besotted Gladys was.

Gladys's idyll was short-lived, however, because a minute later, Mr Bunting came over and conferred with Miss Frobisher and a minute after that, she called Lily and Gladys over.

'Miss Salter's not in work today,' Miss Frobisher explained. 'A sick headache, apparently.'

A likely story, thought Lily, remembering what Beryl had said about hers. Miss Frobisher didn't sound as though she believed it, either, but when Lily remembered her stolen afternoon with Jim, she couldn't really blame Beryl. Maybe she had a brother coming home on leave and felt she could justify skiving off. Maybe she fancied a day doing nothing, idling in the sunshine while everyone else was at work. Maybe she had a new boyfriend who'd surprised her with the longed-for outing to Blackpool. They could walk on the Prom, have tea on the pier and, knowing Beryl's cheek, seek out Maurice Bishop and talk him into buying them a drink. Maybe . . . oh, who knew? Since their encounter in the Ladies, they'd been avoiding each other: Beryl could have had any number of reasons for sneaking a day off. Lily dragged her attention back to Miss Frobisher.

'It's left Toys very short-handed. Some of the Christmas stock has arrived – yes, Lily, I can see what you're thinking, Christmas in August! – and needs attending to. So, Gladys, if you'd go to the stockroom with Mr Bunting, he'll show you what needs to be done.'

Gladys looked terrified – anything new and different always threw her – but she had no option but to trot off after Mr Bunting, who had a funny sort of penguin walk, Lily always thought. But he was a kindly man, and courteously held the door open for Gladys as they went through to the back stairs. Lily felt guiltily grateful. At least she'd be spared Gladys looking at the clock every five minutes and willing it to defy the laws of space and time.

But at the end of the day it was Gladys who slowed things down, and Jim looked pointedly at his watch when they finally joined him outside the staff entrance.

'I can't move. I've grown roots!' he said, peeling himself off the 'Walls Have Ears' poster he'd been leaning on. 'What were you doing in there? Actually, don't answer that, I can see. Gladys, you're transformed!'

That was what had taken the time, of course: Gladys had laid her plans carefully. It was a pity the sadistically tight curl papers she'd slept in the night before had left her looking, frankly, like a rather mangy spaniel, but Gladys seemed thrilled with the effect, so Lily had nodded enthusiastically. At least she'd persuaded her to grow out her bowl-cut fringe. But on top of that, it turned out, Gladys had asked for special permission to bring in her home clothes so that she could change out of her work ones at the end of the day. Lily had to admit she was impressed – she'd never seen Gladys show so much gumption. Gladys had warned her she was in for a surprise, and when she showed off her proposed outfit, Lily found she hadn't exaggerated.

'Red Cross Jumble Sale!' Gladys announced delightedly, holding up a dusty-pink crepe dress as she stood in her slip in the staff cloakroom. Like everything else these days, or what was available on their budget, it was far from its best. It had been let down, taken up and let down again as well as given not-very-expert darts by at least one of its many previous owners. It was also far too old – in the sense of grown-up – for Gladys. So Lily said the only thing she truthfully could, which was that it was a pretty colour. Well, it had been once.

'You haven't seen the best!'

From her locker, Gladys flourished a pair of white court shoes, the scuffed toes and heels lovingly Blanco'ed. With a fresh pair of white ankle socks – which were actually new – and a gash of puce lipstick, evidently once her gran's, the final effect was like a child who'd been at the dressing-up box, but Lily was hardly going to tell her friend that.

Nor was Jim, who gallantly offered them both an arm and walked between them as they set off for home, though Gladys kept having to stop and lean on him to ease her toes in her shoes. She hadn't tried them with the new socks before, and they made them rather tight.

As they came down the entry, Gladys clattering on her rickety heels, they heard Sid before they saw him.

'Hens? What next! A pig-pen?'

They filed through the gate to see Sid and Dora standing by the henhouse – now almost complete, and just waiting for a small chicken-wire run to be added. That was if they could ever get any chicken wire.

Lily couldn't help herself: she launched herself

forward, arms outstretched. Sid picked her up and swung her round, beaming.

'Blimey, you've grown! Been digging into that Woolton pie, I bet! Oof, I'll have to put you down, Lil! Talk about Ten-Ton Tessie!'

Lily punched him on the arm. Not quite the 'Knockout Lil' the warehousemen called her, but he was asking for it.

'Huh! Flying colours for fitness and you can't pick me up! Not exactly Popeye, are you?'

Sid would normally have come back at her with a jibe of his own, if not an actual jab, but he knew what was expected of him today.

'And who's this – not Gladys? I wouldn't have known you!'

Dear old Sid, thought Lily with relief. Not 'a vision of loveliness' or 'you look a million dollars'; not the kind of fancy chat he'd have tried with Renee or Freda. He was sticking to the truth, bless him. Gladys certainly looked different.

She edged forward shyly, flushed an unfortunate shade somewhere between the dress and the lipstick.

'Hello, Sid. Thanks for all the postcards.'

All! There'd been precisely two!

'My pleasure. C'm here.'

He took her by the shoulders and gave her a chaste kiss on the cheek.

'Nice to see you. And Jimbo! The master-builder!'

He and Jim shook hands as Lily smiled. Sid could

never call anyone by their given name – he always had to shorten it, lengthen it, or, like Freda the post girl, change it altogether.

'You've got plans for an egg empire, then? Oh – and congratulations. On your promotion and that. I dunno, I go away for five minutes and it's all been happening!'

Jim grimaced, and Lily looked away. Something of an understatement.

'Yes, well, nothing'll happen round here if I don't get on with tea!' Dora chipped in. 'Lily, get yourself changed and you can give me a hand.'

Lily ran upstairs. It was all very well to think mean things about Gladys's get-up; her own single summer frock was getting embarrassingly tight. She'd already moved the buttons, but she was still, as Sid would be sure to point out, busting out all over. But there was nothing to be done. It was all she had. After she'd handed over her weekly keep to her mum, what was left of her wages went in the old Fry's chocolate box under her bed towards the presents she'd sworn to buy for her mum and Sid. Only then could she justify spending any money on herself. Stockings . . . Tangee Uniform lipstick . . . a decent dress . . . a little jacket . . . and shoes, new shoes . . . her list was getting longer by the day.

Lily sighed and picked up her hairbrush, rasping it through her curls till they crackled, brushing the pointless thoughts out of her head. That wasn't the

Joanna Toye

kind of thinking that was going to win the war, was it? She pushed her hair behind her ears and pulled her dress down. Judging by what Gladys was wearing, there wasn't much better to be had, anyway.

Lily might not have felt she was dressed for the big occasion but Dora, regardless, had pushed out not just the boat, but the whole fleet. On Reg's last leave, she'd produced a hoarded tin of salmon between the four of them: now, suddenly, on the side in the scullery were two tins between five! Lily didn't dare ask. Her mother had obviously broken her own unwritten code of conduct as well as the actual law and chanced an under-the-counter transaction. Salmon, though! Pink salmon all the way from Alaska! Lily's mouth watered. If Dora hadn't been holding out their lethal tin opener (worse than a bayonet, Sid always said) Lily might have risked giving her a hug.

Everyone had a job. Lily was put to opening the salmon, then removing the skin to the pig pail, before mashing down the rest with vinegar, bones and all: the calcium was good for them, Dora claimed. Gladys, worried about her dress, was given a pinny and put in charge of assembling the salad. Jim was put in charge of laying the table, while Sid was instructed to make a pot of tea.

'Tea? Tea?' Sid's face was a mask of horror. 'Mum, I know you think it's "Tea for Victory" not "V", but this is a bit of a celebration, isn't it?' Bending down, he tugged open the drawstring of his kitbag and brought out a couple of bottles of lemonade and four of beer. When Dora opened her mouth – there was never any alcohol allowed in the house – Sid as usual turned the whole thing into a joke.

'I know, I know – you were hoping for my rum ration. Or port. Sailor . . . port . . . get it?' They all groaned dutifully. Sid shook his head. 'Hopeless, you lot. Pearls before swine.'

As he was talking, he was fetching the glasses from the sideboard. He poured beer for himself and Jim, persuaded Dora into a shandy, and put the case for very weak ones for the girls. ('I'll just show it the beer!') Glasses handed round, Lily and Gladys sipped cautiously. Neither of them had ever tried alcohol before, but they could hardly tell it was there under the blissful sweetness of the lemonade – nectar and ambrosia when they were used to nothing but boring old tap water.

With Gladys listening adoringly and the others listening with varying degrees of scepticism, Sid held forth as they sat down to tea. Yes, of course he slept in a hammock, not a bunk! (Did they believe him? No one knew.) No, he couldn't dance the hornpipe, but his jitterbug was coming along nicely, thank you, and if they wanted some sea shanties, the repeatable ones of course, he was their man! Only when he claimed part of the drill was having to shin up a mast did they shout him down, but Sid swore on Nelson's grave it was true, even if it did sound more like the training for a midshipman on Nelson's own HMS *Victory* than a rating in the modern Navy.

When there was still some pattern left on the plates, despite everyone's determination not to miss a scrap, Dora proposed a short break before the famous cake. Lily stacked the plates and took them to the scullery. Sid followed with the dish of cucumber in vinegar and the salad cream – the very last of a precious jar.

'Sid,' said Lily, turning. 'I've got to talk to you—'

'I know, I know,' said Sid. 'About Gladys. Don't worry, Sis. I told you I'd sort it, and I will. By the end of the weekend, you won't have to worry any more.'

Lily would have liked to know how, exactly, he proposed to sort it, but Gladys came out to put the kettle on. Dora couldn't last any longer without a cup of tea, apparently. Lily stayed to help her put the cups on the tray, and when they went back through, Sid was standing, glass in hand.

'Before we all sober up,' he said, 'I want us to raise our glasses – we've all got something to celebrate. First of all, Mum, you've done us a tea fit for kings – thank you!' They all chinked glasses and looked towards Dora, who tutted and tried to bat the praise away. 'Jim's got his job back,' Sid went on, 'and somehow seems to have wangled a promotion as well. Jimbo – here's to you!' Now it was Jim's turn to look bashful as they chinked their glasses towards him. 'Me, I've passed my training, so watch out, Adolf, I'm on my way!' Though Lily privately prayed the war would be over before Sid ever got near a foreign posting, they all chinked glasses again. 'And finally – big drum roll, bring on the dancing girls – Lily and Gladys. Two gorgeous girls with a long way to go in life. Long life and happiness, you two!'

'Long life and happiness!'

They all took up the chant. Gladys's blush was even deeper, the same colour as her lipstick this time and Lily had just taken another small sip of her drink when there was a knock at the front door. Dora went white. In slow motion, everyone put their glasses down. No one ever came to the front door except the rent man and he wasn't due. No one came to anyone's front door in their street except the telegram boys. No. It couldn't be. Not when they were all so happy. Not . . . surely not Reg? He hadn't left the country yet; he wasn't on active service. But he wasn't the best at keeping in touch. For all they knew, he might have been sent on further training, and something could have gone wrong. Accidents did happen, especially when young men were being turned into fighting men. Jim pushed his chair back at the same time as Sid got up, but Lily was on her feet too.

'Let me,' she said. 'Please. I'll go.'

Chapter 18

'Beryl!'

It wasn't the telegram boy – thank God, thank God – but Lily's first swamping wave of relief quickly ebbed away through amazement into concern.

Beryl was leaning against the door frame. She had on a cherry-red dress, limp and creased, not her usual style at all, with a shabby brown jacket over it. Black shoes – winter shoes, not summer – no stockings, and a grubby white handbag. Lily had never seen her look so mismatched. Her usually luminous hair was lank and dull and her face, bare of make-up, was clammy. She looked properly done-in.

'Hello, kid.'

'Beryl – what's happened?'

'Can I come in?'

Lily stood back and let Beryl into the tiny hall. She couldn't take her through to the back: what was she going to do with her? Helplessly she opened the door to the front room – the room they hardly used.

The room was dark – there was no point taking the blackout down – so Lily switched on the light. A dim bulb in a frosted glass bowl hanging from a triple chain on the ceiling, it didn't make a vast difference, but Beryl managed to fumble her way to the settee. She sat down and Lily joined her. She could feel the scratchy moquette through her dress, but Beryl didn't seem to notice. The room felt stuffy to Lily – the blackout, so useful against draughts in winter, made any room stifling in summer – but Beryl was hugging her jacket round her as if she was cold.

'You don't look very well,' said Lily. 'Is your head that bad?'

She felt horribly guilty now for thinking the headache had been a ploy.

'I wish it was my head.'

'What is it then?'

'Can't you guess?'

Lily looked at her, literally and in every other way in the dark.

'No, course you can't. Not you. I'm up the duff, Lily. In the club. Pregnant.'

'Oh, Beryl!'

Lily had heard – again from other women's

low-toned conversations – about girls who were 'in the family way', usually followed by the judgement that the girl under discussion was 'no better than she should be'. She knew that the proper reaction was to be scandalised. But all she felt was sympathy.

'What are you going to do?'

Beryl gave a short laugh.

'Well, I was hoping you might tell me that. You're the one with the magic wand that gets you and certain other people out of trouble.'

'But not . . . I haven't a clue – not something like this—'

'No? No. Well, I didn't really think so. Dunno why I said it, really.'

Lily was starting to realise that, perhaps, Beryl didn't mean a lot of what she said. Maybe not even the nasty things.

'I've tried pretty much everything they tell you to,' Beryl went on. What did they tell you? wondered Lily, but Beryl was about to tell her. 'I lugged my chest of drawers this way and that for the best part of forty minutes, but my dad just yelled at me to stop making so much noise, said I'd come through the floorboards, and it didn't do anything anyway. Not a twinge. I thought about bleach . . .'

Bleach? What were you supposed to do with that, wondered Lily – then thought she'd rather not know.

'But I didn't dare. I sat and looked at my coat hangers – I even straightened one of them out to . . . well . . . you know. I didn't dare do that either.'

Again, Lily didn't know, though she could imagine.

'I went out and got some gin,' Beryl continued bleakly, 'but I couldn't run a hot bath to drink it in, 'cos Dad hasn't paid the bill and there isn't any hot water. So I drank it on its own, but it only made me sick.'

All this was revelatory to Lily, but she let Beryl carry on.

'He was at the pub by then, of course, but he came back wanting his dinner and when I said I'd been too sick to do it, he started effing and blinding and asking why. So like a fool I went and told him, didn't I, and he went mad. Said I was a tart and a trollop and told me to pack my things.'

'Oh, Beryl! Surely he can't have meant it!'

'He meant it all right.'

'Well, maybe . . . at the time . . . he must have been shocked. And in the heat of the moment . . . but . . . perhaps when he . . .' Lily wanted to say 'sobers up' but ended lamely, 'When he calms down . . .'

'You don't know him,' said Beryl. 'He's never been calm in his life. But he's only really nasty with those that can't fight back. He's a coward like that, so you needn't think he'll go and defend my honour. He'd never stand up to anyone that might hit him back. And he'd never stand up for me anyway.'

Lily's heart and her hand went out to Beryl at the same time. She touched her arm.

'What about your mum?'

'I haven't got a mum,' said Beryl. 'Not one I remember, anyway. Died, didn't she. Probably because my dad hit her once too often.'

That explained a lot.

'Lily.' Beryl looked at her pleadingly. 'I've got nowhere to go. And no one else to turn to. I thought maybe your mum, you know, might know someone? I've heard you talk about her, and she sounds . . . Please, Lily. I haven't got anyone else to ask.'

Lily's throat felt dry. All the time, all day, when she'd been imagining Beryl in Blackpool, she'd been going through this. While they'd been eating their salmon and sipping their drinks and listening to Sid's tall tales, Beryl had been glugging gin and being sick.

'I'll go and get her,' she said.

In the ear-straining silence that had fallen on the little tea party, they'd obviously been able to hear voices in the hall, so at least the fear about a telegram had subsided. But a caller who didn't come round the back was very unusual, and the atmosphere was still muted when Lily went back in and signalled to her mother that she needed her. Dora, who'd been savouring her precious cup of tea, put down her cup and stood up.

'This had better be good,' her eyebrows signalled

as she joined Lily in the hall. Lily leant past her mother and closed the door to the back room. She told her everything.

Lily had sometimes – quite often, actually – wished her mum would unbend a bit, and be a bit more, well, motherly, but at that moment she wouldn't have exchanged her for another, ever. Dora listened in silence, then, still without saying a word, moved to the door of the front parlour and went in. Lily followed.

'Beryl, isn't it?' said Dora.

'Mrs Collins?' Beryl stood up shakily. 'Can you help me?'

'I hope I can, love. But not in the way you're thinking.'

Love! It was a word Dora hardly ever used to her own daughter, and here she was lavishing it on Beryl. But Lily didn't feel resentment or even envy. If ever anyone deserved a bit of coddling . . . Beryl dropped down on to the settee again and Dora sat beside her. Lily perched on the arm.

'Now look here,' began Dora. 'I won't have any more nonsense about getting rid of this baby.' Beryl went to object, but Dora stopped her with a look. 'No, I said no and I mean it. It's dangerous and it's criminal. No baby asks to be born, but once it's inside you, that's where it should stay. You're quite sure you're expecting?'

Beryl nodded.

'I'm as regular as anything. And I just know. I've seen it in other people. My skin's gone off and I'm dog-tired all the time.'

'Well, count your stars you're not suffering with morning sickness, at least,' said Dora briskly. 'Now, here's your options. You can have the baby, and have it adopted—'

'Mrs Collins, how can I? Round here? You know what people are like!'

'I do,' said Dora curtly. 'You'd have to go away as soon as you started to show, find somewhere to stay, have the baby there, and then—'

'I can't do that!' said Beryl again. 'I've got nothing! What would I live on? How would I keep myself? And anyway, I've got nowhere to go! That's why I'm here!'

'Well, then, you do the most obvious thing, and I'm wondering why you haven't done it already. You tell your young man – you do know whose it is, I hope?'

'Yes! I'm not that bad! Les – it's his!'

'All right, all right,' soothed Dora. 'I had to ask. And he didn't . . .' Lily could see her mother nerving herself to ask something else. 'He didn't force himself on you? Or get you drunk? You knew what you were doing?'

Beryl looked down into her lap.

'I knew all right. I won't pretend.'

Lily stared hard at the rag rug in front of the grate.

She wondered where Les and Beryl had done it. On a rug like this in front of someone else's grate? On a rug in the park, behind the bandstand, or in the bushes near where she'd lain on the grass that day with Jim? Lily went all hot, but with a funny shivery feeling at the same time. She swallowed hard. She didn't know how she'd ever look Beryl in the eye again.

'Well, that's one good thing.' For Dora, it was obvious. 'You must tell this Les and we'll have to make sure he'll do right by you.'

'Mrs Collins, I can't! You don't understand! I wouldn't be here if I could tell him!'

'Why can't you?'

Lily spoke for the first time. She didn't know Les at all. On the surface, he looked a flashy type – in that way, he and Beryl seemed made for each other – and he had been involved in the delivery racket . . . But at the same time, whenever she'd seen them together, he'd also seemed genuinely fond of Beryl, almost dazzled by her, in fact.

'You know why,' flared Beryl. 'I told you – me and Les are finished!'

'Yes, but only because you ditched him! This changes everything!'

'I didn't ditch him!' cried Beryl. 'I never said that! Don't you get it? He dumped me!'

Lily tried to process this astonishing information. Les dumping Beryl – it didn't make sense! Logic decreed that she'd finish with him once the delivery scheme had been exposed and he couldn't stump up extra for cinema seats and caramels, not the other way round!

'But of course you don't get it.' Beryl shook her head. 'Innocent, aren't you? Look, the first time we did it – the only time – was the night we found out about the . . . it was the night we found out Les was going to keep his job.'

She looked meaningfully at Lily, who remembered all too well. Beryl meant the night Lily had caught up with the pair of them outside the store and had learnt that Robert had cleverly managed to smooth everything over. No wonder Les and Beryl had felt they had something to celebrate.

'Well, after that, it all changed. First he seemed to be avoiding me, then he told me we were through. That's men for you! I thought he was a decent bloke underneath, but it turns out they're all the same. Give them what they want, then they don't want to know. And he won't want to know now. Like my dad said, why buy the cow when you can drink the milk?'

'That's quite enough, thank you,' said Dora sharply. 'Not in front of Lily. She's younger than you.'

'I'm sorry, Mrs Collins.' Now it was Beryl who put out a hand to Lily. 'Sorry.'

Lily shrugged as if to say 'it doesn't matter'.

'Look, Beryl,' said Dora, as gently as Lily had ever heard her. 'It seems to me you haven't got the highest opinion of men, and if your father's anything like what Lily's told me, that's no great surprise. But you mustn't judge everyone by his standards. Whatever's gone on between you and this Les since, you've got to tell him about the baby. However things stand between you, he's got a right to know, and it at least gives him a chance to put things straight.'

'That's right,' urged Lily. 'Truly, Beryl. Tell him! What have you got to lose?'

Her mother's glare told her that perhaps that hadn't been the best way of expressing it. Beryl said nothing. To give her – to give them all, perhaps, time Dora stood up.

'I'm going to put the kettle on,' she said. 'You have a think about it.'

The two girls were left together. Lily felt an overwhelming sadness. It had all been for show, all of it. Just Beryl trying to put her horrible home life behind her and determined that she wasn't going to be beaten down like her mum; not by men, not by the world, not by anyone. But as well as being sad for Beryl, she was disappointed in herself that she'd got Beryl so wrong, had judged her without knowing anything about her, or trying to find much out. And she was saddest of all for the baby that was caught up in all this.

'You have to try telling Les the truth, Beryl,' she urged. 'You really don't know how people are going to react till you do.' She'd had more than enough experience of that in the past few weeks. 'People can surprise you.'

Beryl put her face in her hands.

'No. No. I can't face him. Go round his house, in front of his mum and dad? Or hoik him out of the pub, in front of his mates, feeling like this and looking like this? Hardly likely to make him want to stand by me, is it?'

Poor Beryl, thought Lily – something she'd never have believed she could feel. She had so little confidence in herself. Underneath it all she was as scared of things as everyone else. Maybe more so.

'Well, look,' she began, 'how about this? You stay here. Have a wash and a bit of a rest and something to eat. You'll feel better, I promise. And while you're doing that, I'll go and find Les. I'll say you want to see him and it's really important. If he agrees to come, then will you talk to him?'

There was a long pause, then Beryl lifted her head. She gave Lily a feeble smile.

'You're a one, you are, Lily Collins,' she said. 'You're going to do it, aren't you, whatever I say?'

Chapter 19

Between them, thank goodness, Dora and Sid took charge.

Dora bustled Beryl off to the scullery to wash her face, instructing Gladys to go too and feed her tea and toast. Then, with Beryl out of earshot, she said Beryl was to have a lie-down in Lily's room: she was obviously exhausted. She could get up and talk to Les – assuming they could persuade him to come round – but whatever Les did or didn't do, said or didn't say, Dora was adamant – Beryl was not getting rid of the baby. Come what may, they'd talk sense into her. And, of course, she'd be staying with them for the moment. Lily would have to give up her bed, but could sleep in with her mum.

Sid also decreed, quite rightly, that there was no question of Lily going on her own to seek out 'this Les'. He therefore set to work briefing his reconnaissance party – Jim and Lily. Beryl had given Lily the address, as well as the name of Les's local pub, and the hall where he might be playing billiards.

'So here's the plan,' Sid began. The table had been cleared of their tea things, and now it might as well have been Admiralty HQ and Les a skulking German U-boat. 'It's still quite early, so we'll try the house, but a pound to a penny he'll be down the pub or at this billiard hall. No self-respecting bloke's going to be at home in the bosom of his family on a Saturday night. Well, I am, of course, but that's different.'

'It's going to look a bit odd if we turn up on the doorstep mob-handed,' objected Jim.

'At the house, that's just you and Lily, 'cos Les knows you,' said Sid. 'I'll hang back, I'm only there for backup. But if it comes to the pub or the hall, I'm not having Lily going in those kinds of places, so you and me'll go in, Jim. And in case this Les turns nasty, or his mates do, well, no offence, but I think I'll be handier in a bar brawl than you are.'

'Fine by me!'

What a good thing Sid was home, thought Lily. Jim's hand had healed, but she never, ever, wanted to have to bandage him up again. And she was confident that Sid, fresh from his naval fitness test – he'd shown them his biceps, to Gladys's embarrassment and delight – would pulverise Les Bulpitt – and his mates.

When Dora had shepherded Beryl upstairs, and with Sid showing Jim how to take on two attackers at once ('You never know . . .'), Lily finally had a chance to speak to Gladys. If Beryl thought Lily was a kid, Gladys was a babe in arms. As the only child of doting parents, her eyes had brimmed over when she heard how Beryl's father treated her and had treated her mother. But like Lily, after the initial shock, her instinctive reaction was concern – for Beryl and the baby. She also had the tact to say she'd leave them all to it and go home.

'No, don't do that,' urged Lily. It wasn't her fault, but she felt dreadful that the evening hadn't worked out as Gladys had hoped – the non-stop Sid Collins show, with a walk-on part for Gladys. 'Mum'd like the company. Stay and help her sort her knitting patterns. She's bound to start fretting about baby clothes – Beryl's hardly going to be getting them from Marlow's!'

It wasn't quite eight o'clock when the trio set off, to a not-very-salubrious part of town said Sid, though why or how he should know was anyone's guess. They passed down a shabby street of shops, some boarded up, past a scrubby park, now allotments, and some run-down sheds and workshops. Off Balaclava Road into Inkerman Street, a pub, houses and a former corset factory which now, of course, was making bandages, parachute harnesses and webbing. Finally into Alma Terrace, with a tatty café on the corner, pinched little houses that made Lily's modest home look like a palace, and the blank brick wall of the factory yard at the end. A couple of boys were kicking a half-deflated football at a goal they'd chalked up.

At least number 26, the address Beryl had scribbled down, looked a bit less sorry for itself than the rest. The blackout wasn't up yet; there was a cream lace café curtain in the window and the brown front door wasn't peeling too badly. The step had even been whitened. There was no knocker, so Sid rapped on the door. All was quiet.

'Out, like we thought.'

But he rapped again to make sure.

'All right! Hang on! I'm coming!'

'That sounds like Les,' said Jim. 'So he is here.'

'Right, that's me gone, then.' Sid looked around. 'I'll go and have a kickabout with the lads. But I'll be watching. If Les asks you in, go. But the first sign of any trouble, Lily, you come and get me.'

'What do you think is going to happen? He's going to go for us with a bread knife?' asked Lily. 'We're not telling him Beryl's pregnant – only that she wants to see him!'

'We don't know the real ins and outs of why they split up, do we? Les might not be at all pleased to see you come pleading on her behalf,' Sid pointed out reasonably. 'Don't forget, we've only heard her side of the story.'

'Oh, but, Sid,' Lily began. 'You saw her, she was in such a state—'

'Sid's right, though,' Jim put in. 'All this time you've not had any reason to trust Beryl, and now—'

'Exactly. It takes two to tangle,' pronounced Sid enigmatically.

But they could hear footsteps approaching and with a thumbs-up, Sid was gone. A moment later the door opened.

'What the heck . . . ?'

Les was standing in front of them. He looked different from how he looked at work – very different. No Brylcreem, for a start, which was, Lily thought, an improvement, old khaki trousers and a stained blue shirt. Well, they'd obviously surprised him: he hadn't yet got ready for his evening out. Then Lily noticed something else. Les had a book in his free hand, the hand that wasn't holding the door open. He was marking his place with his finger. The book was *The Tale of Jemima Puddle-Duck*.

Lily looked at Jim, knowing he wouldn't have missed it. He hadn't. Then, from inside the house, a little voice called. Over and over the same.

'Uuhh. Uuhh. Where you gone? Where you gone? Uuhh!'

It was getting more agitated. Les turned and called over his shoulder.

'All right, Susan! It's all right, darling.' He turned back to them. 'I can't leave her. Whatever you want, you'll have to come in.'

He vanished into the house.

Lily looked at Jim again. He opened his hands in a gesture of helplessness. They'd all assumed Les lived at home with his parents. What if this was his home? What if he was the parent? And if he had a baby already, what would that mean for his and Beryl's?

Nothing could have prepared Lily for what she saw when, with Jim behind her, she stepped cautiously inside and straight into the dim front room, then on through a draped velveteen curtain into the back.

There was an old-fashioned range on one wall, and either side of it, two chairs. Beside one was a footstool, and Les was sitting on it, tenderly wiping a long skein of dribble from the mouth of the girl in the chair. But she wasn't a baby and she wasn't a child, or not a small child anyway. She must have been about twelve, but in a puffed-sleeve blouse and loose pinafore, with a tea towel as a bib, she could have been a two-year-old. Her face was somehow flat but fat as well, her eyes were round behind thick glasses and her rosy mouth hung open.

'This is Susan,' said Les. 'My sister. Excuse the mess, she's not the tidiest eater. Splutters a bit.'

A half-full bowl of what was perhaps oxtail soup was on the side, with bits of soggy bread floating in it. The stains on the shirt . . .

'Say hello, Susan,' Les encouraged her. 'This is Lily and Jim. Nice of them to come and see us, isn't it?'

Susan looked at them. She pointed first at Lily and then at Jim and her face broke into a huge smile.

'Lo,' she chanted. 'Lo, lo, lo!'

Lily sat in the chair opposite and Jim stood while Les finished giving Susan her tea, then Jim said he'd sit with her while Les and Lily talked.

'She likes what she knows,' Les explained as he rinsed the bowl out under the scullery tap. 'She can be funny with visitors, but it looks like she's taken to you two.'

'Les,' said Lily. 'I'm so sorry. I had no idea.'

'No, well, why would you?' replied Les. 'I'm not going to broadcast it at work, am I? You don't exactly parade someone like our Susan.'

'What happened?' asked Lily. 'Do you know why . . . why she's like she is?'

'No. She was born like it. Just – backward, you know. Well, that's the kindest way of putting it. But people aren't always kind, that's the trouble.'

He was wiping the dish now, on a green checked cloth with scorch marks, identical to the one Dora had.

'It's one of those things . . . we've learnt to live with it. But – well, Mum blames herself, always has done. She won't let Susan out of her sight, won't hear of her going in a home. She's determined to keep her here. So I try and do my bit, help her out.'

'And your dad? Is he . . .'

'Well, yeah – when he's here,' said Les. 'He worked in an ironmongers when Susan was born, but it didn't pay enough. She's got a weak heart, a lot of them like her have, so if she gets ill . . . and she does – sore throats, ear infections, if she gets a cold it goes to her chest – we're always having the doctor out.'

Lily knew that wouldn't come cheap, and what Les said next confirmed it.

'It costs a fortune, what with the doctor and the chemist's. So Dad signed up for the Merchant Navy . . . probably five, six years ago. He's away a lot – more so since the war. He had some home leave earlier in the summer, but he's away again now.'

'That must be really hard. For all of you.'

'Yeah, well . . . it's how it is. Mum's got a couple of cleaning jobs in the evenings – that's where she is tonight. So I'm baby-sitting – well, Susan-sitting.'

'I see.'

Lily felt humbled. What had she said to Beryl? You really didn't know people . . .

'But you've never told anyone at work?'

'No!' Les sounded scornful. 'They wouldn't under-stand.'

'Not even Beryl?'

'Beryl? Not likely! But what's she got to do with it? Or is she why you're here?'

'Let's go back through,' said Lily. 'And see how Jim and Susan are getting on.'

They were getting on famously. Jim had taken Les's place on the stool, and Susan's head was bent to his as Jim read her *Cinderella*. Susan was pointing at the picture of Cinderella and the glass coach, crooning away. They didn't even notice the other two come back in.

'Pretty!' said Susan.

'Isn't she?' agreed Jim. 'Quite a cracker now she's smartened herself up a bit.'

'Sorry to interrupt!' said Lily. Honestly! What a way to talk to the girl!

But at the same time, she was touched. Jim had no reserve with Susan – he behaved with her like he'd behave with anyone – not shy, not constrained, not making any allowances. Not treating Susan any differently. How rare that must be for her.

After a bit, leaving Jim and Les to it, Lily went out to tell Sid: they couldn't leave him out in the street wondering what was going on. Not that he was: far from looking out for them, worried about Les wielding the suspected bread knife, Sid was lounging against the wall smoking and telling his two protégés jokes.

Ignoring the boys' sulky mutterings, Lily pulled him away and started to tell him what they'd found out. For once, Sid listened.

'Blimey. Didn't see that coming, did we?' he said when she'd finished. 'What a life. Poor bloke.'

'Yes,' said Lily. 'I know.'

'Still, on the plus side . . .' Sid could never be downbeat for long. 'He's hardly the evil swine we thought he was, is he?

'He certainly isn't. He looks different, sounds different and everything. A much nicer person.'

'So why'd he dump Beryl then?'

'I can't ask him that!'

'Maybe not. But have you told him about her? What did he say?'

'We just told him she isn't very well, and she'd like to see him. He sounded quite concerned,' Lily explained. 'But he can't come round tonight, 'cos of looking after Susan. Look, Sid. We're going to stay on a bit. Jim's reading her a story.'

'Oh yeah?' Sid grinned. 'Hidden talents, eh?'

'Well, Les deserves a break. It's hard for them all. When Susan goes out, people stare and children call her names and even throw things at her sometimes. You wouldn't believe it, Sid.'

'Oh, I would.' Sid took a last long drag on his cigarette. 'Anyone a bit different doesn't stand a chance round here.'

He threw the cigarette down and stamped it out.

'All right then,' he went on. 'Since you haven't fallen into the hands of a cad or an axe murderer, I'll skip off home, and tell Mum we won't be getting a visitor tonight. Beryl's probably sparked out anyway. But you take care, Lil. Even with Jim with you, you'll be home before dark, won't you?'

'Promise.'

There she went again with her promises. But this one should be easy to keep.

Not as easy as it should have been, as it happened. While she arranged with Les that he'd call round in the morning, and gave him the address, Jim was working through Susan's entire library. When Lily signalled that they should get going, and Jim closed the worn copy of *Milly Molly Mandy* he'd been reading to her, Susan's lip wobbled and her eyes filled with tears. Hanging on to his sleeve, she didn't want to let him go, and Jim only extricated himself by making a promise of his own – that they'd come and see her again very soon.

'Well, you made a hit there,' laughed Lily as they turned the corner of the street. Their progress had been slow because Susan had clamoured to stand on the step and wave till they were out of sight, so they'd had to keep turning round to wave back.

'There's a lad in our village like her,' said Jim. 'It's horrible, really. The farmers give him odd jobs, bird-scaring and that, but he gets more stones thrown at him by the other kids than he ever lobs at crows.'

He gestured to his arm.

'I had to step in to save him once; I think they'd

have killed him if I hadn't. It's how I got this. A sharp flint.'

So that's where his scar had come from.

'Oh, Jim!' said Lily. 'That's awful.'

'Far worse for him than for me,' shrugged Jim.

'I suppose so,' Lily agreed. 'But that's so cruel. It's not their fault, is it, his or Susan's.'

'Of course not, but people are idiots. And too quick to judge, aren't they?'

Lily bit her lip. It was exactly what she'd concluded about herself and Beryl a few hours earlier. And they'd misjudged Les too, by the look of things – all of them, Beryl included.

'The more I think about it,' she considered, 'maybe . . . If Les's dad was home on leave earlier this year, well, he was around in the evenings so Les could go out with Beryl. But if the delivery thing coming to a full stop coincided with him going back to sea, Les was suddenly short of all that spare cash to splash about—'

'And he wasn't free in the evenings anyway,' added Jim. 'Yes, I'd come to the same conclusion. And if Les was determined not to tell Beryl anything about his home life, he couldn't tell her why – so instead he told her they were through.'

'Yes,' reflected Lily. 'But what a pair, Jim. Both of them covering up, putting on a front, and really just trying to escape from everything they had to put up with at home.'

'It doesn't change where they are now, though, does it?' said Jim. 'Which isn't so much an escape as – well, I won't call it a prison – but a baby's a bit of a tie, isn't it?'

Lily had to agree.

'I know. But if Les is so tied up with Susan already – well . . .'

She tailed off as they turned on to more familiar streets. Halfway home now.

'You can't sort everything, Lily,' warned Jim. 'That's for them to work out when she tells him. At least we know Les has had some practice looking after a kid.'

'And so have you now!' she teased. 'Another skill I didn't know you had. You'll be teaching Beryl what to do when the baby comes!'

'Well, I've bottle-fed enough lambs . . .' Jim shrugged. 'What's the difference, really?'

Lily had to laugh. She might not have much ex-perience of babies, but one thing she knew.

'Lambs don't need nappies, for a start,' she said. 'Perhaps you'd better stick to your hens after all.'

When she and Jim got back, just as Lily had predicted, Dora was making up a ball of baby wool from various odd lengths she'd amassed. Lily assumed Sid was walking Gladys home – that would more than make up for the interrupted teatime – but Dora explained she'd left before he'd got back. Not knowing when they'd return, Dora wasn't having her walk home on her own in the dusk, let alone the blackout, but had promised she could come back tomorrow to carry on where they'd left off – cake and all. She knew full well how much Gladys idolised Sid. Well, as she'd often said when Lily had tried to get something past her, she hadn't come in on the last coal barge.

Sid had told her the whole story, and Dora had been as moved as the rest of them. When Lily added her speculation about why Les had been the one to do the dumping, Dora nodded.

'Let's hope once he comes clean – they both do – they can start again,' she said.

Lily hoped so too. Fingers, toes – they were all crossed.

'But it's all worked out for the best, if you ask me,' her mother went on, reluctantly rejecting one length of wool as too short to bother with. 'Tonight, I mean. Beryl was out like a light the minute she lay down, and I didn't fancy waking her up to talk to him. One thing's for sure, everything always looks better in the morning.'

Another thing was for sure. In an uncertain world, one thing that never changed was Dora's reliance on her favourite sayings.

Chapter 20

Beryl certainly looked better: when she came downstairs next day, she seemed much more like herself. Dora had ironed her dress and found its belt in Beryl's bag, so she was back to her normal nipped-in shape. She must have had her make-up in her bag, too, because she'd put on a bit of powder and rouge and combed her hair. It wasn't the usual slavish Veronica Lake look, but it was a serious improvement on the day before. The most encouraging thing for Lily was that Beryl hadn't done it for Les, because she didn't yet know he'd agreed to come round. She'd done it for herself.

Lily lit the flame under the kettle. She hadn't slept very well, worried about disturbing her mum, so she'd lain on the edge of the bed all night. She'd dropped in and out of sleep with such a jolt that a couple of times she'd thought she'd fallen out of bed entirely and had expected to find herself on the floorboards. She had a crick in her neck and her eyes felt as if they'd been rolled in sand. But she wasn't the one who mattered.

'How are you feeling?' she asked.

'A whole lot better than I did,' admitted Beryl. 'Your mum's quite a character, isn't she? I see where you get it from now.'

'Thanks!'

'No, it's a compliment,' said Beryl. 'But go on, tell me. I suppose Les said no. Can't say I'm surprised. I did tell you.'

'What? No—'

'Well, he didn't rush round last night, did he? You were supposed to wake me up—'

'Oh, Beryl! I'm sorry – no, you don't understand. No, he didn't come last night, because he couldn't. But he's coming this morning.'

'Never!'

'He is.'

'No! What did you say to him?'

'We told him you weren't well, like we'd agreed, and he didn't ask anything else. Just said he'd come.'

'I don't believe it,' said Beryl. 'He never did! Why's he changed his tune?'

'You'll have to ask him yourself, won't you?' said Lily, trying to look as innocent as she could.

But she was more and more convinced that she and Jim were right. When his dad went back to sea, Les had had to go back on Susan duty in the evenings while his mum went out to her cleaning jobs, and he hadn't dared tell Beryl the truth: the heartbreak and the hardship his family went through every day because of his sister, and would do as long as she lived. He must have been frightened that Beryl, who seemed to care so much about how things looked, would be one of those who was hard on people like Susan. Still, that was for him to explain. Funny, thought Lily, that Beryl believed she was the one with the big secret when Les had one of his own.

As the front room was the only place for Les and Beryl to talk in private, Jim unpinned the blackout for the first time in nearly two years, and Dora sent Lily outside to beat the rag rug and shake the cushions. Lily noted with amusement that Beryl didn't take any part in the preparations: she was too busy washing her hair, incredulous that Lily used soap and not proper shampoo.

'No wonder you have such trouble!' she'd exclaimed. 'I'll get you a bottle of Amami. Then you'll see a difference!'

Lily was more anxious for her mum to get her hands on Beryl's ration book than she was for a bottle of shampoo. Beryl's appetite had returned – she was obviously making up for the day before. She'd had two fat pieces of toast for breakfast but half an hour later said she was starving again and could really fancy a slice and some condensed milk, if Dora happened to have any?

Lily watched enviously as Dora cut another thick piece of bread and opened the tin, but her mum told her not to worry. Assuming Les came good, Beryl would soon be married and off their hands. Lily laughed to herself. And Jim had ticked her off for running ahead! Assuming Les came good? Her mum would make sure of it. It wouldn't be Beryl's dad with a shotgun making him do the decent thing, it'd be Dora with her rolling pin.

Not suspecting what Fate had in store for him, let alone the formidable Dora, Les arrived promptly at ten o'clock. He looked more like his usual self too: a smart jacket, a clean shirt and the glossy slicked-back hair. Touchingly, though, he was clutching a bulging paper bag. He'd bought Beryl a present.

'One guess,' said Lily, closing the front door behind him. Beryl was waiting in the front room. 'Chocolate caramels!'

'Not likely!' said Les. 'That's no good if she's feeling off!'

He untwisted the top of the bag. Lily saw some soda mints, a bottle of J. Collis Brown's Compound and some Beecham's pills.

'Goodness, Les! You've got a whole medicine cabinet there!'

Les delved in his pockets. From one, he produced

some cough sweets and a bottle of aspirin. From the other, a bottle of glycerine and thymol and a pot of Zam-Buk. He was obviously taking no chances.

'Medicine's one thing we know about in our house, with Susan like she is,' he said. 'I was that thrown to see you two last night, and with Susan and everything, I didn't even ask what was up with Beryl, so I brought the lot.' He looked anxious. 'How bad is she? She's not still laid up?'

'No, no,' said Lily. 'She's in the front room. Feeling a lot better. And she'll feel better still once she's seen you. I hope,' she added quickly.

Suddenly remembering that Beryl must be listening, waiting to deliver her news, and that she was holding things up, Lily indicated the door.

'Go on in,' she said. And, disappearing down the hall, left him to it.

'Turning up like a quack with a pocketful of potions!' she told Jim, who was polishing his shoes in the yard. 'What's Beryl going to make of that?'

But Dora, picking more beans – they really had done very well – approved.

'If she's got any sense, she'll be grateful. This Les is going up and up in my estimation. Let's hope he stays there.'

With Beryl and Les closeted in the front room, Lily didn't know what to do with herself. What she really wanted was to position herself outside the door with her ear to the crack, but to stop herself from doing that, she had to keep busy. She spent half an hour stringing and slicing beans for Dora to salt and then, at a loose end, was forced to watch Jim caulking the nooks and crannies of the henhouse – to prevent red mite, he said. Sid was outside too, on the old canvas stool. First he polished his belt buckle, then his belt, then his shoes, and then his belt buckle again. He said it was second nature now – he'd got used to daily kit inspections – but Lily knew he was as nervous as the rest of them, and simply trying to keep himself occupied.

Dora had just brought them out a glass of left-over lemonade and was wondering out loud when or if they'd ever hear church bells on a Sunday again, when there was a stagey cough from the kitchen doorway. Like a weathervane in a strong gust, everyone swivelled round at once. Beryl and Les stood there, gazing at each other like the hero and heroine at the end of a soppy film. Les managed to look both sheepish and proud, and Beryl . . . Beryl met Lily's eyes and simply mouthed, 'Thank you.'

'I'm going to be a dad!' Les cried. 'And you all knew! You might have told me last night!'

'Hardly our place, was it?' grinned Jim. 'But – well, congratulations! Both of you!'

Lily ran across and hugged Beryl, Dora following. It was going to be all right! The relief was over-whelming. Sid shook Les by the hand.

'Excellent timing,' he said. 'The announcement, I mean. Because for once we happen to have some beer in the house!'

'What, no champagne?' asked Beryl, looking at Sid doe-like from under her eyelashes.

Thank goodness, thought Lily, Beryl was back on form. Shameless flirtation – with Lily's own brother, and with the father of her child standing next to her! But she was delighted. Seeing Beryl so suppressed had been very unsettling.

'Don't worry, love,' said Les. 'We'll manage something better for the wedding!'

Lily smiled at her mum. No rolling pin needed. Les had come good!

Sid disappeared inside to fetch the beer anyway and Dora followed him to cut a few sandwiches. Beryl had to keep her strength up, she said – not to mention the very idea of the lads drinking on empty stomachs.

Beryl and Les, enthroned on the kitchen chairs Jim had brought out, held hands and held forth.

It was much as Lily had suspected, but in a way, even more touching. Les, he admitted bashfully, had held a torch for Beryl since he'd first seen her across the staff canteen – well, you could hardly miss her, as he remarked, while Beryl patted her hair and tried and failed to look demure. But he hadn't thought he had a hope – someone like her, and someone like him?

'Look,' he went on, but keeping his voice low, 'You both know about the delivery thing, so I don't mind telling you, when Robert Marlow come up to me after Christmas and offered me a way of making a bit extra, I jumped at it. By the time Dad came home on leave, I'd got a tidy bit put by and, well . . .'

'He asked me out, didn't you? Back row of the Roxy, don't think I don't remember!'

'Yeah, we had some good times, didn't we?' said Les fondly, and a bit more sloppy gazing and grinning went on.

Any more of this soppy smiling and they'd get lockjaw, thought Lily. Was this what a proposal did to you? Jim must have felt just as uncomfortable with all the mush, because he cleared his throat.

'And then the racket came to a stop and it all came crashing down.'

Les dragged his attention away from his beloved and back to the Collinses' backyard.

'One fell swoop. The little extra had dried up, my dad went back to his ship, I was back with Susan in the evenings. I didn't have much choice. I had to break it off.'

'Dope!' said Beryl affectionately. 'Should have told me straight, shouldn't you?'

'Yeah, I should,' agreed Les.

'But then I should have told you about my dad, what a so-and-so he is. And how he treated my mum. Fell against the table all those times! Yeah, right.

What's worse, in the end, a sister who's not quite all there, or a mum who's not there at all, dead 'cos of the way her husband knocked her about?'

If working at Marlow's had been a revelation to Lily in one way, what went on behind the closed doors and curtains of streets not that different from her own was turning out to be another.

'You've both had a lot on your plates,' she said. 'More than I could ever have imagined, and I'm sorry for that. But what now? There's even more, with the baby to think about.'

'Agreed,' said Jim. 'If you're tied to the house, Les, to help your mum . . .'

'We've talked about that,' said Les. 'It's not perfect, but we can live at my place. Susan sleeps in with Mum half the time anyway, so I've got the big attic room. We thought . . .' At his 'we', Beryl snuggled closer. 'We thought we could make it into a bedsitting room – a sort of flatlet.'

'A place of my own,' breathed Beryl. 'Away from my dad at last.'

So it wasn't all mush, and for Beryl the baby wasn't a tie but an escape – an escape of sorts, at least. Except . . .

'It's not quite your own, though, is it?' Lily pointed out. Someone had to say it. 'I mean, how are your mum and dad going to take all this, Les?'

'I dunno till I tell them. With dad, it'll have to be a letter. But to be honest, I think my mum'll love it.'

He paused. 'We don't know how long we've got our Susan for. Anything could carry her off. So for Mum to have a new life in the house, well, it'll be a help, I think.'

Everyone was quiet at that. Beryl squeezed Les's hand. Lily looked away, at the brilliant red flowers on the wigwam of beans, at a butterfly which was sunning itself on the roof of the henhouse. Even the woodlouse making its wobbly way across the yard bricks by her feet seemed a miracle to be grateful for. She swallowed hard. Her throat hurt with trying not to cry.

Jim was the first to speak.

'I'm sure that's true,' he said quietly. 'And I don't want to keep dragging things back to practicalities. But you'll have to leave work, won't you, Beryl? So what about . . .'

'Money? Yeah, we've talked about that too,' replied Beryl. 'Well, this war's done me a favour for once. They can't go chucking me out just 'cos I've got married, can they? Can't get the staff as it is. I mean, why else would they take her on?'

She jerked her head towards Lily.

'Thanks!'

Before, it would have been a comment that stung, and it would have been meant that way. Now Lily knew it had been meant as a joke.

'But they can't do without you now, can they?' Beryl went on. 'Mr Marlow's right-hand woman! Going to be running the place before long!'

'That's right,' said Les, grinning. 'I'll be coming to you begging for overtime! Or I'll get another job on top of Marlow's, part-time, anything, I don't care. All I want is to look after them – Beryl and the baby.'

Beryl beamed.

'He's a good 'un, isn't he? Course, I'll have to leave once I start to show.'

'I've told her she's got to see a doctor, pronto,' Les chipped in. 'Check everything's all right. And work out a date for when it's due.'

He lifted Beryl's hand and kissed it.

'Around Easter time, I reckon,' said Beryl, 'If I've done my sums right. 'A spring baby . . .'

'And a wedding as soon as, I presume!'

Dora had arrived with a plate of sandwiches. Sid followed with the beer, glasses and more lemonade – he must have nipped out to the pub on the corner.

'Now, look here, Jim,' Dora began as he passed the sandwiches around. 'You'd better get a shake on, finish that henhouse and get us these hens. Because I'll be needing plenty of eggs for the cake!'

Lily had to laugh. Never mind military manoeuvres, her mum was planning her biggest campaign yet, catering for a wedding.

And loving every minute.

Chapter 21

It was Dora who best summed up that Sunday, of course.

'Folks in and out all day!' she declared. 'Like cuckoos from clocks!'

The first of the 'cuckoos' were the lovebirds – Les and Beryl. They departed to collect Beryl's things at about half past two, but not before they'd eaten their share of the rolled shoulder of pork for which Dora had pooled the family's coupons for Sunday dinner.

'Don't fret, love,' Dora had reassured her daughter as they peeled extra potatoes to eke things out. 'She'll get more coupons now she's expecting. We won't be subbing her out of ours for ever.'

Lily hoped not. Eating for two? Beryl was scarcely

pregnant, but she seemed to be eating for twenty-two, and Les the same, and he wasn't pregnant at all! Still, at least, Lily consoled herself, they now knew, or at least hoped, that Beryl wouldn't be with them for long. Les, in an impressive show of manliness, had taken charge.

The plan was to fetch Beryl's things in the middle of the day while her dad was still at the pub, or, if at home, sleeping off its effects in his chair. Then they were coming back to drop Beryl's stuff at Lily's before heading off again to introduce Beryl to her prospective mother-in-law – and vice versa. Lily privately thought it was a lot to expect Mrs Bulpitt to take in. To learn all at once and out of a clear blue sky that her son had not only a girlfriend but a fiancée, who by the way he was intending to marry in pretty short order, because she was having a baby.

But Jim, whose thoughts so often mirrored Lily's, ventured further and – wisely – had voiced them as they sat round the table.

'Erm . . . so . . . sorry, Les, but how exactly are you going to break it to your mother? It's quite a lot to drop on her in one go, isn't it?'

Well done, Jim.

Les, to give him credit, had thought of that too.

'No, you're right,' he said, through a gulp of tea. 'I reckon the girlfriend – fiancée – wedding bit'll be plenty to start with.'

Tell his mum the good news, in other words.

'We'll only tell her about the baby,' chipped in Beryl, 'when we're back from honeymoon. Then when the little angel arrives . . .'

Angel? The same little angel she'd been trying to get rid of yesterday with gin and hot baths?

'. . . We'll let her think, like everyone else, it's a honeymoon baby that couldn't wait any longer!'

Lily could see from the look on her mother's face that she didn't think anyone would be fooled for a minute, but Lily nodded along, as did Sid and Dora, and even Jim. Beryl meanwhile was looking adoringly at Les. The transformation was extraordinary, as if her brain had been sucked out of her head and been replaced by – what, wondered Lily. Candyfloss? Jelly? Her womb? Still, it was Les and Beryl's affair. They'd made their bed, and . . . ah yes, sleeping arrangements until the wedding. What was the plan there? Was there one? But that was another matter the future bridegroom had grasped.

'We can't have Beryl living off you,' he declared. 'If you could put her up for a couple more nights, Mrs Collins, I'll make things good at our house.'

Lily was shocked. Glad as she'd be to have her room back, Mrs Bulpitt would have to be a pretty remarkable woman if she agreed to Les and Beryl cosying up together in their 'flatlet' before they were married. Dora wouldn't have entertained the idea for a second if Sid or Reg had proposed moving a 'fiancée' in. But Les, who was turning out to be a strategist on a par with the most experienced Army general – or at least Ordinary Seaman Collins – had a different scenario in mind.

'Susan often sleeps in our mum's bed anyway,' he explained. 'but I'll get her a bed of her own, make her a proper cosy corner in there with a few of her things. Then Beryl can have Susan's room till we're married, and in the meantime, we can make the attic into—'

'Our little love nest,' cooed the bride-to-be.

Lily couldn't believe it. Less than twenty-four hours ago Beryl hadn't had a good word to say for Les, convinced he'd abandoned her and trying to get rid of his baby. It was a good job sugar was rationed. With this much sickly-sweetness swilling around, everyone's teeth would be dropping out anyway!

She sneaked a look at Jim. He was looking down at the floor but she could detect a wry smile. He'd have something to say about it later! But then again . . . at least Les was turning out to have 'a lot of common' as her mum would have put it, meaning 'sense'. His plans certainly sounded practical and – oh, good luck to them, thought Lily. They'd need it – both of them!

Finally, off they trotted to Beryl's, the happy pair, heads together, hands entwined. Two proper lovebirds, thought Lily, remembering what Beryl had once cattily called her and Gladys . . . Gladys! She was due in an hour's time for tea. Time for that cuckoo clock to strike again . . . and for Sid to knock on the head this fledgling idea that Gladys could somehow be his sweetheart.

Once again, Gladys had put a lot of effort into her outfit. Lily thought it suited her much better than what she'd been wearing the day before, because at least Gladys wasn't trying to look like someone she was not. She'd gone back to her usual faded summer dress, as well-worn as Lily's, but from somewhere – her gran again? – she'd acquired a cardigan, which though a rather strange shade of mustard, at least brightened things up. The white shoes, carefully re-Blanco'ed, were getting another outing, at the expense of Gladys's toes, and she also sported a mother-of-pearl brooch – definitely her gran's. Still, the effect was a lot more suitable than the pink creation, and Lily complimented her.

'Thanks,' said Gladys. 'I mean, who knows when we'll see Sid again?'

Never, was Lily's ungracious hope, if he didn't sort this out!

Obviously, though, nothing could be said until the Great Cake Cutting had taken place, and as they all tucked in, the discussion naturally moved to Dora's anxiety about what sort of cake she could possibly produce for Les and Beryl's nuptials.

Flour wasn't a problem, and the one good thing about the need for speed was that dried fruit wasn't yet on ration. Icing sugar was a different matter. Getting hold of some was going to take all Dora's ingenuity, and they all knew it.

'And there's the little bride and groom figurines for the top . . .' Dora mused. 'I'm trying to think who's got married round here that I can borrow from.'

'Never mind the cake,' said Lily. 'What about the dress? That'll be all Beryl's interested in, how she looks.'

'Where are they getting married?' asked Gladys, who'd had a quick run-down on the morning's momentous events from Lily but was still trying to catch up.

'The Town Hall, I presume,' supplied Jim. 'I mean, surely even Beryl hasn't got the front to get married in church?'

'Wherever it is she'll expect a car to get her there in style,' said Sid, mopping up cake crumbs with a wetted finger. 'And back.'

'A car? What about petrol?' Lily challenged him.

'Ah, wedding cars don't count,' replied Sid. 'But they can't go far – it's all got to be done and dusted inside two hours.'

How did he know these things? Lily wondered how close he'd got to talking wedding plans with some of his girlfriends, before smartly extricating himself.

'And what about the reception, Mum?' she asked. 'There won't be that many of us. Have it here, perhaps?'

'Now you're asking!' Dora began counting on her fingers. 'Les and Beryl, his mum, his sister, Lily, me, Jim, Gladys . . .' She smiled at Gladys, who beamed. 'How many's that? I've lost count. It's no good, I'll have to make a list.'

As Dora got up to fetch pencil and paper, an emboldened Gladys put the only question that really mattered – to her.

'What about you, Sid? Do you think you'll be able to come?'

'Wedding of the Year? Wouldn't miss it for anything! On the other hand – I can't see my CO being too happy. It's not like she's a relative or anything, is it?'

Gladys somehow managed to mask her disappointment and bucked up when Sid spoke again.

'Right, Mum, we'll leave you to your list. The cake was out of this world. But . . .' He began to stack the plates. 'Back to reality. How about giving me a hand with the washing up, eh, Glad?'

It was a good thing Sid was carrying the tray, because, as Lily and Jim watched – Dora was absorbed in her list – Gladys was walking on air. Jim raised his eyebrows.

'The moment of truth?' he mouthed.

Lily held up her crossed fingers.

'Hope so,' she mouthed back. Then, louder, 'Fancy a walk?'

Yesterday she'd had to take her mind off what

might be going on in the front room: today it was the scullery.

'You're right, you know, Lily.' Her mother's voice cut into her thoughts. 'It's the dress that's going to be the biggest problem.' She put down her pencil. 'If I'm not careful, my foot's not going to be off that treadle!'

'Where to?' asked Jim.

They'd used the front door so as not to disturb the conclave in the scullery, then doubled back down the entry to the cinder path that ran between the backs of Lily's row of houses and those in the next street.

'Anywhere but the park,' replied Lily.

She'd had too many conversations in the park lately – good and bad.

'That only leaves the canal,' said Jim. 'Come on.'

Lily hugged her cardigan round her. The sun was getting lower and the evenings chillier. Soon they'd be going through another winter – please God not as harsh as that first, freezing winter of the war, nor as wearing as the last one, with the constant broken nights from the bombing, although, thankfully, in Hinton the actual damage hadn't come to much.

She had Gladys to thank for the cardigan. Not the cardi itself – that was another cast-off from Renee, and not a very exciting one, Lily had thought at first, being plain beige, though it did have a pretty little

293

scalloped collar and cuffs. But Gladys had given her the idea. Lily had suddenly realised that if she put it over her dress and buttoned it, she could leave her dress buttons undone – so much comfier! Now her only problem was keeping up with Jim's loping stride.

'What do you think's going to happen?' she asked, trotting along beside him.

'With Sid and Gladys?'

Jim stood back to let her go first down the steps to the towpath. Ahead of them a shire horse, released from his barge-pulling duties, was enthusiastically cropping what grass he could find.

'There is no Sid and Gladys! At least there'd better not be – he's promised me he'll let her down gently!' countered Lily. 'I meant Les and Beryl.'

'Well, it's a rum do, isn't it?' said Jim. 'Hello there, old boy!'

He stopped to pat the horse, which raised its head minutely in acknowledgcment. The bridle jangled.

Lily looked at him sidelong. He was so . . . how could she put it? . . . so comfortable around the animal. He must really miss the countryside.

But he'd set off again and Lily scuttled to catch him up.

'I mean,' she persisted, 'Beryl seems like a changed person, but how long's that going to last?'

'I know,' agreed Jim. 'She's so bound up in the romance of it all, isn't she, and the speed . . . We'll see what she's like when she's seen the set-up at Les's.

And it all depends how his mum takes the whole thing.'

'True,' nodded Lily. 'But, well, Beryl's got to get on with it, hasn't she? She's lucky Les has come good.'

'He's certainly saying and doing all the right things. Let's hope the good-news-first idea works, and his mum lets Beryl move in.'

'The sooner the better!' Lily burst out. 'She could give that horse a run for its money!'

'I had noticed,' grinned Jim. 'And I thought eating you out of house and home was my job!'

Lily smiled back. They always seemed to be thinking the same – especially about food. And as if to prove it . . .

'Let's walk along to the cut,' Jim suggested. He groped in his pocket and produced a string bag. 'Then up to Cavendish Road? See if any windfalls from the big houses have fallen our side of the fence!'

By the time they got back, the string bag pleasingly heavy, Dora's cuckoos had been on overtime.

Les and Beryl had had to make several trips, she reported, first with Beryl's things in various bags and a bulging case; then Les had gone back for an armchair earmarked for their attic flat but presently residing in the Collinses' front room, then once more for a trunk, no less. Finally, they'd headed off to Les's as planned, by which time Sid and Gladys had long since emerged from the scullery, with Sid announcing he'd be walking Gladys home. He had not yet returned.

What did that mean, Lily wondered in some panic. But as her mother and Jim gloated over the apples, with Jim planning a blackberrying expedition along the railway embankment in due course – dicey with the barbed wire and the stern notices, but worth the risk, he thought – she concluded she'd have to be patient a while longer.

To be fair, Sid wasn't too long. Lily had hardly finished wrapping the apples in scraps of salvaged paper when she heard the latch on the back gate click. Jim was reading in his room and Dora had gone over the street. She'd had an inspiration. Rather than her having to make a wedding dress – and out of Lord only knew what – Renee's mum might know someone who could lend one. Lily privately thought that Beryl would be having none of it. She'd want new, and Lily knew exactly which one – slipper satin overlaid with Nottingham lace, three-quarter sleeves and a deep V-neck, like the one currently on display in Marlow's bridal room, with a long veil secured by a sparkling tiara. Knowing Beryl, she'd somehow get her way.

Sid came in whistling a merry tune, and seeing the apples, brightened up even further.

'Apple pie!' he exclaimed. 'Next time I'm home, I hope that's on the old me-n-u.'

Lily had every sympathy with Sid's focus on his stomach – half the time, it was all anyone thought about – but really! He didn't just take the biscuit, he took the whole tin.

'Sid! For goodness' sake!' she began. 'Gladys? What did you say? Have you sorted it?'

'Bless her.' Sid sat down at the table. 'She's such a nice girl.'

What? Don't say he'd caved in and agreed to be her boyfriend after all!

'She's going to do it,' he grinned. 'Write to Cobby.'

'What . . . ? Who's . . . Cobby . . . ? What have you done?' cried Lily. 'Oh, start at the beginning, for heaven's sake!'

'All right,' agreed Sid. 'Sit down, Lil, 'cos it's a good 'un.'

Lily did as she was told and Sid started on his tale.

'Like I say, she's such a sweetheart. I did have one nervous moment, 'cos I could tell the way she was looking at me all goo-goo-eyed when we got out the back that she thought it was going to be one of those "Alone at Last" situations, like in the films.'

Lily knew only too well. Gladys had breathily recounted enough of them from her picture-going.

'So . . . ?'

'So I cut her off at the pass. Said that much as I was grateful for her writing to me, I felt bad about it.'

'Because she was wasting her time?'

'I didn't put it like that – what do you take me for?' Sid looked indignant. 'No, I told her about Cobby, and asked if she'd write to him instead.'

'How can she write to someone called Cobby?'

'Well, that's not his real name,' Sid explained patiently. 'His real name's Bill. But with a surname like Webb, what else am I going to call him?'

Of course. Obvious – if you were Sid.

'So you've, what, fobbed her off on this . . . Bill?' said Lily. 'What's he going to make of it?'

'I'm doing them both a favour, Sis!' Sid sat forward. 'He's a great bloke, Bill, but he's got no one. He's never known his dad, and his mum gave him up, or had to give him up, when he was born. He was brought up in a children's home. So, like I said to Glad, here am I getting all these letters and what-have-you from home. Mum, you, even Reg drops me a line when he can be bothered. And then Gladys as well . . . but when the post's given out, never a thing for poor old Cobby.'

'That's so sad!'

'Yeah, and that's exactly how Gladys looked when I told her. Except more so. A tear in her eye.'

'She's very soft-hearted.'

'I know. Anyway, she said like a shot she'd be happy to write to him. And I said he'd be happy I'd found him a penfriend – with the emphasis on friend, so she didn't start getting the wrong idea about him and all.' He grinned. 'But who knows . . . could be

298

the start of something beautiful. A double wedding, if they get a move on!'

So that was Gladys sorted, thought Lily with relief, and she had to hand it to Sid, very neatly, and in a way which might actually make two people very happy.

Now there was just the other happy couple to think about. Lily didn't doubt Beryl would have a lot to say when she got back from the Bulpitts'. It was going to be some time yet before this extraordinary twenty-four hours could be put to bed.

Chapter 22

But there was no sign of Beryl, even after they'd put up the blackout. After the eventful weekend, they were all exhausted. Sid would be setting off early the next morning; Jim and Lily had work to get up for, and Dora announced they should all go to bed. Luckily, she'd seen this coming, and had told Beryl about the back-door key they kept behind the loose brick in the privy.

'I hope she's not too late. She's got work tomorrow as well,' fretted Lily. 'So's Les.'

'That's their lookout. He'll take care of her, one way or another, I'm sure,' said Dora and, after they'd drunk their cocoa, she swept them all upstairs.

In her mum's room, Lily lay sleepily watching her

mother brush her hair. While she and Sid had inherited their father's mop – strong and wavy – Reg and Dora shared the same fine, straight hair. Lily was tired out but, soothed by the rhythm of the hairbrush, she had to admit she was happy. Things had all worked out.

Dora put down the brush, hung up her dressing gown on the back of the door, and got into bed.

'Light out?' she said. Lily nodded. It was all she could do to make that much effort as she snuggled down.

'Night, Mum,' she said. 'And thanks for everything. Beryl, I mean.'

'I don't know.' Dora put out the bedside light and eased herself down on her side of the bed. 'Never a dull moment with you, is there?'

Lily smiled into the dark. It was a good job her mum didn't know quite how many not-so-dull moments she'd been spared since Lily had started at Marlow's.

To give Beryl her due, she couldn't have made a sound when she came in; or maybe Lily had been in too deep a sleep to hear the creaky stair and the wonky floorboards on the landing. But next morning when Dora shook her awake, Beryl, her mum advised, was already downstairs.

'Don't tell me,' grumbled Lily. 'Starting on her third round of toast!'

When Lily got down, sure enough, Beryl and Jim were at the table. Sid had already gone, leaving Lily a mock-invitation in fancy copperplate writing to the wedding of Miss Gladys Huskins to Mr William ('Cobby') Webb, followed by a string of exclamation marks. Shaking her head – he really was the limit – Lily stuffed it in the pocket of her skirt.

She'd managed to tell Jim about Sid's elegant fobbing-off of Gladys as they'd put up the blackout the previous evening, but she knew she'd have to hear all about it all over again – and not in those terms – once she got to the shop and Gladys had her in her sights.

First, though, she wanted to hear how Beryl, crunching toast plastered with yesterday's dripping, had got on with Mrs Bulpitt. But Beryl was holding forth about her dad: she'd left him a note which in pretty bald terms told him that as he obviously didn't want her there, that was fine by her – and he needn't bother trying to find her, either. Dora pursed her lips. She hated to hear of family fallings-out, but Mr Salter did sound a brute who didn't deserve much better.

Jim diplomatically excused himself from the walk to work. He sensed, he said, that Lily and Beryl might have 'womanly' things to discuss. Lily certainly hoped not – she knew far too much already about Les and Beryl's love life, though she supposed that wouldn't necessarily stop simply because they were already having a baby. She felt a bit funny when she thought

about Les bringing Beryl home and kissing her goodnight – probably more – on their front step, or in
the starlit yard, so she made sure to steer her on to
other things straight away.

'Well?' she asked as they emerged from the entry
into the street. 'Go on then. Les's mum. How was
it?'

'Les played a blinder,' said Beryl, tucking Lily's
arm close against her side: Lily had obviously been
promoted straight from Arch Enemy to Best Friend.
'He left me in the caff at the end of the road so he
could break it to his mum by himself. So by the time
he came and got me, she'd had a bit of time to take
it in.'

'That was clever,' said Lily.

'Yeah, I'm seeing a side to him I never knew,' said
Beryl wonderingly.

They were all seeing a side to Les they hadn't
known, not just his love for his sister, but other
touching revelations. Determined to save every penny
towards the wedding and the baby, he'd confessed
he'd only taken up smoking and bought his flashier
clothes to impress Beryl and hated the feel of
Brylcreem on his hair. Savings, he grinned, he could
make straight away!

'He really wants to take care of me, Lily, and . . .
well, after my dad, it makes a change, I can tell you.'

Lily pressed Beryl's arm wth her own.

'Good. But his mum . . . ?'

'She was lovely. Basically said she hoped we'd be very happy. And she's fine with Les's idea about the attic. We'll have to share the kitchen, but I mean, I'm not going to get in her way there. I'm no great cook, me!'

Lily could imagine. No problem with eating the results, though!

'And what about his sister?' she asked.

'Susan . . . oh dear.' Beryl shook her head. 'There's a thing, eh? I mean, you see ones like her about, don't you? But I'd never really had anything to do with them.'

Lily nodded.

'Me neither.'

'But,' Beryl went on, 'Les introduced me, told her we were going to get married, wouldn't that be nice. Well, I dunno if it meant anything to her or not, 'cos she kept on looking at me like I was some . . . some Jerry paratrooper dropped through the roof or something. And then Les said I should sit down and have a chat with her. Well, that's all very fine, but it was a bit one-sided, if you know what I mean.'

Lily refrained from pointing out that that was usually the case with Beryl, who, true to form, carried on.

'But she was like, fascinated by my hair, and she kept trying to touch it. Her mum told her not to, but I didn't mind, so I got my comb out of my bag, and we combed her hair, and then mine, and then she sort of kept winding my hair round her finger and laughing. Kept her happy for ages! She's a bit like a baby herself, isn't she?'

'Yes, I'm afraid so,' said Lily.

She had to admit she was relieved – and impressed. One of her fears had been that Beryl might be – well, almost repelled by Susan. But then she'd been thinking of the old Beryl – the tough, flippant exterior that wasn't really Beryl at all.

'I only hope my baby's OK, after all the nonsense I tried.' The new Beryl sounded truly anxious and Lily squeezed her arm again.

'I'm sure it will be.'

'Yeah. So, anyway . . . one thing at a time, like Les says.'

Lily could see 'Les says' was going to be a recurring motif in the coming weeks.

'I'm going straight to see Miss Garner, tell her I'm getting married,' Beryl continued. 'And Les'll tell his boss. We'll square it to have our dinner hour together, get passes out, go up the Town Hall, and see how soon they can fit us in.'

'You're not hanging about!'

'If we want people to believe this honeymoon baby stuff, we can't, can we?' Beryl reasoned. 'And I've got some good news for you.'

'Oh yes?'

'Mrs Bulpitt – she says I'm to call her Ivy – she knows where she can borrow a camp bed, so Susan can sleep in with her from tonight. I can move my stuff round there this evening and you can have your room back.'

'Oh, that's marvellous!' Lily couldn't help herself.

Beryl had the grace to smile.

'I don't want to take advantage, Lily. I can never thank you or your mum enough for what you've done for me this past weekend.'

'Oh, Beryl. Honestly. What else was I going to do?' said Lily.

'I tell you what you can do. You can be my bridesmaid. You will be, won't you? Please?'

Lily was glad she had some news of her own because, if Lily was Beryl's New Best Friend, Gladys was full of her changed status too – Official Penfriend to Sid's pal Bill. Thank goodness, she obviously had no intention of calling him Cobby.

'Did Sid tell you about him?' Gladys asked.

She and Lily had been sent to the stockroom: the winter stock had begun to arrive. Never mind toys, even children's clothes were starting to look war-like, Lily thought, as she unpacked little leatherette helmets for boys, too much like flying helmets for her taste.

'He did,' she replied. But if she'd hoped this would cut Gladys off at the pass, as Sid had done, she was disappointed.

'I bet he didn't show you a photograph!'

'No, he didn't,' said Lily, surprised. 'Why, have you got one?'

'Only this. Sid said I could keep it. It's a bit blurry, but . . .' From her pocket, Gladys reverently produced a creased snap of a bunch of lads grinning inanely and raising their glasses round a pub table. Lily peered at it. A bit blurry! You could say that again – perhaps the photographer had had one too many.

'I can recognise Sid . . .' she said doubtfully.

'And can you see his twin? That's Bill!'

Lily peered again. At the other end of the group from Sid there was, if she looked very hard, someone who also had fair, crinkly hair.

'Is that him, on the end?'

'Yes, the spitting image of Sid, don't you think?'

Lily had to hand it to Sid. That was a doubly clever move.

'He's quite like him, I suppose.'

Gladys took the photo back and studied it, smiling soppily.

'I've already written, posted it this morning,' she confided. 'I wonder how soon he'll write back?'

Crikey. Lily hoped Sid hadn't been held up on the way back to base. Otherwise 'Cobby' would be getting a letter from his pen pal before he even knew of her existence.

'Well, I think it's lovely of you to take him on as a favour to Sid,' she said tactfully. 'But don't you want to hear my news? You'll never guess what

Beryl's asked me! She only wants me to be her brides-maid!'

But – danger alert! Sure enough, Gladys's thoughts soon moved from delight for Lily ('So she should! It's no more than you deserve! Oh, but what will you wear?') to thanking her stars for the pink crepe dress and wondering if not only Sid, but Bill, would be able to get leave on the day, if Beryl didn't mind inviting him . . .

After another hour of Gladys's ceaseless chirping, however, Lily was ready for a break. Thankfully Miss Temple arrived to check that they'd put everything away on the correct shelves and had saved every scrap of wrapping. After a thorough inspection, she declared herself satisfied, and sent Lily off for dinner. Gladys was left to sweep the floor.

As Lily now knew, Monday was rissole day. 'Grissoles', Jim called them, but still made remarkably short work of his plateful: by great good fortune, her dinner hour had coincided with his. He'd had to go down to Despatch a couple of times during the morning, so had seen Les.

'Hmm,' he said, when Lily had recounted Beryl's reported reception from her mother-in-law-to-be. 'I sensed a bit of reserve about how Mrs B. took it, actually. I mean, Beryl's turned down the volume a bit since she found out she was pregnant, but she might not be quite the blushing bride Mrs B. had in mind for her son.'

'What choice has she got, though?' reasoned Lily. 'Anyway, the main thing is that Beryl will be out of our hair by tonight. And I'm sorry, that's all I care about.'

'Well, enjoy the peace while you can,' replied Jim, adding innocently, 'I hear you're going to be bridesmaid. What are you going to wear?'

Fair question. And one which had already started to exercise Lily.

Staff shopping was only allowed, strictly speaking, before ten thirty in the morning, but in the circumstances, Lily thought it was worth asking Miss Frobisher another favour. She wanted to use her afternoon break to go down and look at the paper patterns on Haberdashery. She was pretty soon going to have to ask for a day off for the wedding, after all, and if Miss Frobisher knew she was going to be a bridesmaid, she might be more inclined to look kindly on that, especially as Gladys would be asking for the same day as well.

But news travelled fast in Marlow's and when she got back from her dinner, releasing Gladys for hers, Miss Frobisher was the one who informed Lily that Beryl Salter was getting married – and soon. She'd heard it from Mr Bunting.

'She won't be leaving on her marriage,' Miss Frobisher said. 'She's never going to be Employee of the Month, that one, but the store can't afford to lose anyone, the way things are.'

Little did the buyers know that Beryl would be leaving soon enough for another reason – but that news was for another time, thought Lily.

'I did know, actually, Miss Frobisher,' she replied. 'And once they've sorted a date, I'll need to put in a leave request to go to the wedding. If I may.'

'Really?' Lily had the satisfaction of seeing the unrufflable Miss Frobisher look truly ruffled. 'I'm . . . well, I had the impression you and Beryl didn't exactly hit it off.'

She didn't miss a thing, did she?

'We've had our ups and downs,' said Lily tactfully. 'But, um, we've got more friendly lately. In fact, she's asked me to be her bridesmaid.'

'I see!' Lily had to hand it to Miss Frobisher. She recovered herself pretty quickly. 'Well, that's exciting. What are you going to wear?'

Chapter 23

Miss Frobisher really was a good sort. When four o'clock came she caught Lily's eye and gave a tiny nod, the sign that Lily could go. Afternoon break was only ten minutes and as running, or even speedy walking, was strictly forbidden in front of customers, Lily would have to put the dash in Haberdashery once she got off the sales floor. She took the back stairs three at a time and arrived panting on the ground floor, composing herself before pushing through on to the sales area.

Haberdashery, like every department, was putting its best face forward. Although some of the basics like elastic and pins had vanished – as had many of the more luxurious fabrics – the buyers had been

inventive in filling the gaps. So had some canny manufacturers. Lily didn't have time to linger over the
pin-on flowers and buttons which glowed in the dark
('Be Seen in the Blackout!') or the ribbon remnants
where she'd had such rich pickings. She headed
straight for the pattern books. There were plenty of
those – one way to get round clothes rationing was
to re-fashion what you had, even if you didn't have
the skill to make from new.

Lily knew there'd be no chance of her getting her
bridesmaid's dress made with new material – or made
at all. It would most likely be something borrowed
which didn't fit, but which couldn't be altered because
it had to go back, or something her mum was allowed
to alter, but only because it was on its last legs and
its final outing. All she hoped for from this expedition
was to get some ideas. If she was allowed to express
an opinion, she might at least be able to indicate
what she didn't want. The trussed-up-chicken look,
for a start, was one she was keen to avoid.

Rapidly flicking through, the ideas came thick and
fast. Sweetheart neckline . . . pretty; round neck, cap
sleeves . . . not bad; oh, no, goodness, no! Not the
Bo-Peep look, puffed sleeves and spotted net up to
the neck with a frill and a mimsy bow. She wasn't
having that!

'Hello? It is you, isn't it?' The voice came from
behind her.

Lily jumped and turned round. Violet!

'Miss Tunnicliffe!'

'It's Lily, isn't it? Lily Collins, that's your name? Oh, I'm so glad I've seen you! I've been wanting to thank you ever since . . . well, you know. The raid.'

'Thank me?' Lily was stunned. 'Oh, but that was ages ago . . . and there's no need!' Then, feeling she'd been ungracious, she added, 'I mean . . . I hope you're feeling a bit better about things these days.'

Violet smiled. She was very pretty when she wasn't screaming.

'Now things have quietened down, I am, thanks. A lot better. This is the first time I've been back to Marlow's, though. It's a sort of test.'

'Well, that's very brave of you,' said Lily. 'Have you come on your own?'

'Not quite. Mummy's having her hair done. I'm meeting her for tea upstairs.' Violet glanced at the pattern books. 'Are you having a new dress?'

Bless her, she didn't have a clue, did she, thought Lily.

'No, I was only looking for ideas,' she explained. 'Out of interest. I'm going to be a bridesmaid. But I expect I'll end up in something borrowed.'

'Well, you must borrow mine!'

'What?'

'I was a bridesmaid the summer before the war. It was a lovely day. Lovely dress, too.' Violet stood back and considered. 'Yes . . . I'm sure it would fit you!'

Lily gulped.

'Look – Miss Tunnicliffe – it's very kind of you, but I couldn't possibly accept. In fact, if you don't mind, I'm not supposed to talk to customers like this.' She looked around nervously. 'If anyone sees us, I'll be for it. And I'm afraid my break time's up. I've got to get back.'

'Of course. Silly of me. I don't want to get you into trouble.'

'No, well, thank you. And for the offer. It was lovely meeting you again.'

She made to go, but Violet touched her arm.

'Lily, wait. I'm serious about the dress. Truly I am. I'd . . . I'd like to do something for you. To say thank you. When's your . . . do you get a day off in the week?'

'Not really,' said Lily awkwardly. 'Only Wednesday. Half-day closing.'

'Perfect! Mummy's got a WVS meeting in town on Wednesday. Meet me at Lyons' after you close. I'll bring the dress.'

'But—'

'One o'clock, Lily! Or just after! See you then!'

Lily wasn't to know, but hers wasn't the only unexpected encounter that afternoon. At about the same time as she was being accosted by Violet, her mother was pouring tea and offering a plate of biscuits to her own surprise visitor – Ivy Bulpitt.

'So what do you make of it?' asked Dora as they settled themselves at the table. Good job she'd put a clean cloth on it after the ravages of the weekend – and done a bit of baking that morning. Yesterday's cake had, of course, all gone.

Ivy helped herself to a biscuit and dunked it in her tea. You could see from the shape of her that she was someone who liked her food. Dora liked hers too, but she was still as thin as a lath.

'Well, seeing as she's expecting . . .' Ivy, obviously practised, retrieved her biscuit just before it collapsed and poured it into her mouth. 'There's nothing else for it, is there?'

'Oh, so Les told you,' said Dora, surprised.

She knew he and Beryl hadn't planned to. He must have waited till he and his mum were on their own, or Ivy had got it out of him.

'No!' said Ivy scornfully. 'He didn't have to! It's as plain as the nose on your face! What's the big hurry for otherwise?'

Dora smiled to herself. It could have been her talking. She could tell she and Ivy were going to get on.

'I haven't said a word to them, of course – it'll all come out in the fullness of time,' Ivy went on. 'I daresay they'll try and kid everyone it's a honeymoon baby – as if anyone's going to fall for that!'

Exactly what Dora had thought.

'I have to hand it to them, they're making the best

of it, and I'm proud of my Les for the way he's worked things out. Mind you, he had to grow up fast when our Susan was born,' reflected Ivy. 'And he's had to be the man of the house since Eddie went to sea.'

'Yes, I gather he's had to take on a lot of responsibility.' Dora sipped her tea. 'And now some more. But he's a very nice young man. A credit to you.'

Ivy's pudgy cheeks pouched some more as she glowed, and her little button eyes almost disappeared. Is there a mother anywhere who doesn't cherish a compliment about her children?

'Well, thank you,' she said. 'He hasn't had it easy. But which of us has, eh? You're on your own with your three, Les tells me, and Beryl with no mum all these years. Her dad's a right so-and-so, I hear. She doesn't want him near the wedding!'

'No,' agreed Dora. 'So what do you make of her?'

'Well . . .' Ivy was looking hopefully at the biscuits. Dora pushed the plate towards her. She'd had to use mashed potato as well as flour, and treacle instead of sugar, which made them taste sort of burnt, and chewy, but Ivy seemed to be enjoying them regardless.

'You can see she's a bit of a madam,' she was saying as she munched. 'Just the sort our Les would fall for. But the babby'll soon bring her down to earth. And if it doesn't, I will!'

Dora's mouth twitched. She had no doubt Ivy would keep her word.

'We'll finish this pot, and then I'll show you my list,' she said. 'For the wedding. We can divvy up who's doing what. And once that's out of the way, and they've officially told you their news, we can sort out what's needed for the baby.'

'I've kept a few things of Susan's,' confessed Ivy. 'Little things I couldn't bear to part with. Thank goodness I did, now.'

'I've started sorting my wool,' offered Dora. 'And my Cousin Ida's a great knitter. Baby things'll make a nice change from balaclavas.'

'Well, it's very good of you to get involved,' said Ivy, picking crumbs off her bosom and popping them in her mouth. 'I mean, Beryl's nothing to you, is she?'

'We've all got to pull together, haven't we? Especially these days.'

'That's what they say, but it's not everyone who'd put themselves out. Kids, eh? Who'd have 'em?'

'I wouldn't be without mine,' said Dora determinedly.

'Me neither, even with our Susan like she is, but honestly . . .' Ivy shifted in her chair and, entirely oblivious, adjusted her corset. 'They wear you thin!'

Not much evidence of that!

'Les and Beryl don't know what they're letting themselves in for,' Ivy sighed. 'I'll tell you one thing, Dora, and it isn't two. I'm glad I'm grey already. I'd only be greyer!'

Dora smiled and stood up.

'I'll freshen the pot, shall I? Then we'll start on this list.'

Lily got back to the department, but only at the expense of a serious stitch in her side. She'd had to take the stairs four at a time on the return trip, and she was still a minute late. The unforgiving wall clock told her so, but thankfully Miss Frobisher was absorbed in measuring Mrs MacRorie's eldest for his new school uniform and didn't seem to notice. It didn't mean she hadn't, since she had eyes in the back of her chignon, but Lily was safe for now. Beryl, however, had spotted her return and beckoned her over. Lily shook her head, mouthing 'Daren't.'

As resourceful as ever, though, Beryl approached Mr Bunting and said a few words. He inclined his head and the next thing was, Beryl had sidled over and dragged Lily behind a tower of model-making kits.

'We've done it!' she whispered. 'A week this Wednesday, eleven o'clock at the Town Hall! Half-day closing, so you'll only need a half-day off – Gladys and Jim the same!'

Lily tried to look pleased for Beryl, and she was – but what was it about Wednesdays all of a sudden? Not that she'd decided if she was actually going to meet Violet this coming Wednesday.

That is, she'd have to go along out of politeness, if only to say that she couldn't stay, let alone borrow the dress. The very idea was incredible, impossible. How could she? How would she explain how she'd come by it to her mum, who didn't even know Violet Tunnicliffe existed? She couldn't lie about it to Jim, Gladys and Beryl – Jim and Gladys wouldn't be a problem, but to expect Beryl to keep it from Dora? Some hope! Quite apart from which, the kind of wedding at which Violet Tunnicliffe might have been a bridesmaid was bound to have been a very swanky affair, with dresses to match. Lily had little or no experience of weddings, but she knew one thing: it was very bad form to outshine the bride.

The bride . . . who was rabbiting happily on beside her.

'Mind you, me and Les'll take the rest of the week off – well, we've got to have a honeymoon, haven't we?'

'A honeymoon?' squeaked Lily. 'How are you going to afford that?'

'Didn't you read the staff manual? Not like you, Goody-Two-Shoes!' teased Beryl. 'You get a marriage grant from Marlow's. And since it's the last spare cash we're going to have, we've decided to spend it.'

This didn't sound like one of those 'Les says' moments.

'We have? Or you have?' demanded Lily.

Well, what was the point of being someone's Best Friend if you couldn't speak your mind?

'Oh, all right, clever clogs. It was my idea. But we'll

only go away for the one night. The other days we'll be settling in at his place, getting things straight. And the rest of the Marlow's money'll be going straight into War Savings for the baby, don't you worry.'

So far, so sensible. And Lily didn't believe it for a moment. Her brief foray into the wedding pattern books downstairs had made her realise, from the sketches, all the other paraphernalia that Beryl would want – shoes, gloves, flowers . . . they'd all have to be paid for somehow. Still, she consoled herself, her mum was masterminding proceedings. She'd rein in Beryl's wilder excesses, she was sure.

If she'd known that at that moment Dora Collins and Ivy Bulpitt had their heads bent over Dora's list, and were already doing a rough costing, she'd have been very reassured.

Chapter 24

Monday evening was almost as much of a flurry as Sunday had been, what with Beryl and Les coming and going all night and, with Jim's help, carting Beryl's mountain of stuff round to Alma Terrace.

But before that began, Dora sat them all down and explained her visit from Ivy and how the two of them proposed dealing with the catering. Les had already confirmed that the landlord of his local, The Grapes, had said that as the wedding was midweek, they could have their reception in the Tap Room for free. If the chap was counting on selling a lot of alcohol, he might be disappointed, thought Lily, unless by a miracle Sid managed to get a twenty-four-hour pass, not to mention Bill. Gladys was certainly counting on them both being there, and Beryl had given weight to the argument.

'Who's going to give me away otherwise?' she asked when Les had departed with the first load, and the rest of them were eating tea. 'Give me his address, I'll write to the top brass if I have to!'

'What's wrong with Jim?' enquired Lily, but Jim shook his head.

'No can do,' he said. 'Les has asked me to be his best man and I can't be in two places at once. And trust me, you don't want to hear me make two speeches.'

'And you're already official photographer, aren't you?' said Beryl.

'If I can a get a film. But I'm working on it with the chap on Photographic.'

There were times when working at Marlow's really did help. Film was expensive now supplies were short, but it wasn't going to cost any more at Marlow's than anywhere else – and Jim would get a staff discount. And thinking of Marlow's, and the Bridal Room . . .

'Your dress, Beryl,' Lily ventured. 'Any thoughts?'

With the issue of her own dress looming and the danger of the understudy outshining the star, she had to ask.

In reply, Beryl stood up and went to the trunk which had been standing in the corner since the day before, too big to stay in the hall.

'I was going to wait till we'd finished tea,' she said. 'But here we go . . .'

Kneeling down, she undid the clasps. Jim leaned out of his seat; Dora and Lily got up from the table. As Beryl lifted the lid, the trunk seemed to explode in a froth of tissue paper and net. She lifted out a long veil edged with lace and attached to a cap-like headdress with more net, bunched like wings, on either side. From the style, Dora realised straight away what it must be.

'This is years old!' she exclaimed. 'Was it . . . your mum's?'

Beryl nodded. Laying the veil to one side, she unfolded more tissue paper and stood up, holding up a dress in a style which Lily had only seen in old photographs – a boat-necked, straight up-and-down satin bodice with elbow-length sleeves, with a drop waist and a lace overlay falling in points to an ankle-length hem.

'I found the trunk after she died, right in the corner of the attic under a load of other stuff,' Beryl explained. 'My dad got rid of all her other things, but he never knew this was up there.'

Dora was examining the fabric.

'But Beryl, this is beautiful!' she exclaimed. 'Beautiful! The work in this . . . !'

'My mum was a tailoress,' said Beryl. 'She never had the chance to pass on any of how it's done to me, bless her, but she always was beautifully turned out, even though my dad kept her short. And she made me the most beautiful things. I can see them now . . . a little velvet party dress I had . . .'

She tailed off and Lily looked at her mum, more grateful than ever that she had her.

'That's why I wanted to work at Marlow's,' Beryl went on. 'To be around lovely things again. I was hoping for Fashions – even Childrenswear would have been something. But the vacancy was on Toys, and that's where I've stuck. With dolls' clothes!' She stroked the fabric of the dress. 'There's no chance of a move now – or of me having much nice stuff myself for the foreseeable. Still,' she brightened. 'If the baby's a little girl, I can enjoy dressing her up, can't I?'

Tears were tickling the back of Lily's throat. Poor Beryl. More dreams dashed.

'So. Do you think you could make something of it, Mrs Collins?' asked Beryl.

'What? Me? You honestly want me to cut this up?' Dora sounded disbelieving. 'I'm no professional, you know. I'd be terrified to touch it!'

'You'll be brilliant,' said Beryl. 'I can tell you exactly what I want!'

It wasn't tears tickling Lily's throat now, it was laughter. Not so much as a thank you – she blithely assumed Dora would take on the responsibility and do all the work!

'I saw a picture in a magazine . . . it's in my bag. Wait till you see it! Dreamy, it is! I'll get it!'

She rushed off upstairs, humming 'Blue Moon', and leaving the rest of them staring at each other.

'Classic Beryl,' said Jim. 'I don't want to impose, but I'm going to, anyway!'

'I know. Will you be all right with it, Mum, seriously?' asked Lily.

'Well!' Even Dora didn't have a saying that could sum this situation up. 'I don't know. All I was expecting was to have to alter something, take it in, let it out, let it down . . .'

'You'll be lucky!' joked Jim. 'This is Beryl we're talking about! I've been waiting for her to tell me to get out there by night, intercept an enemy agent and bring back his parachute for the silk!'

'I'll do my best,' shrugged Dora. 'Looks like I'll have to. But I don't know what we'll do about you, Lily, now. I was going to try and cobble you something together, but I've only got a week and a bit! There'll be no time for that!'

'Don't worry about me, Mum,' Lily reassured her. 'You concentrate on Beryl.'

'Are you sure, love?'

'Absolutely,' Lily replied.

'We'll have to hope you can borrow something that fits,' fretted Dora. 'I'll ask around, but I don't know anyone round here that's got a bridesmaidy sort of thing your size.'

'I'll sort myself out,' said Lily quickly. 'You've got more than enough to do.'

She had her answer for Violet, and she had her answer for her mum. She could tell her quite truthfully that she'd managed to borrow a dress from someone she knew through Marlow's. Well, it was sort of true. Roll on Wednesday.

Chapter 25

'Lily! Over here!'

It was ten past one and Lily had had to run to get there at all. It had been agony, waiting on the department till every coloured light on the panel below the wall clock had been illuminated, signalling that the last customer had left the store and that clearing up and covering up could begin. Finally, it was green for 'go'.

'I'm sorry I'm late,' she panted, sliding into the seat opposite Violet, who was calmly pouring her a glass of water as if she lunched like this often. Maybe she did, and they knew her in here. Somehow she'd managed to bag a coveted table by the big plate-glass window of the upstairs café.

'Don't worry, I knew you wouldn't be here dead on one,' she smiled. 'Now, I hope you don't mind, but they get so busy I thought I'd get our order in. The set lunch. Soup and fish – they say it's cod but it's more likely to be coley!'

This was all very chummy. And was going to be expensive: Lily had hoped she might get away with a cup of tea and bread-and-butter. But Violet, a much more confident Violet these days, Lily was beginning to realise, seemed to be in charge and she'd have to go along with it. After all, the cost of a lunch wasn't that much if you set it against the cost of a dress.

Violet was waving to the waitress to show her they were ready for their food.

'But before it comes,' she said. 'Here it is!'

From under the table, she produced a small, grey-checked suitcase.

'Have a peep!'

Lily stood up again and placed the case on her chair. Both nervous and excited, she lifted the lid. Neatly packed inside was the dress. Lily couldn't believe it – it was a miracle! She couldn't fully take it out here, in the middle of the restaurant, but she could see enough to know. It was moiré taffeta, cool and slippery to the touch, with a simple sweetheart neckline and dear little cap sleeves. If she'd had all the time in the world, and all the money in the world, and all the dresses in the world to choose from, it was precisely what she would have picked. No fuss, no flimsy fabrics, most importantly, no frills. Best of all, it was her favourite periwinkle blue.

'Oh, Violet!' she gasped, then hesitated. 'May I call you Violet?'

'Of course! I hope we're beyond all that Miss Tunnicliffe business!'

Lily could see the waitress approaching with their soup. She swiftly closed the lid of the case, tucked it under the table and sat down again. She waited till the woman had lifted the lids on their little soup pots and taken them away before she began.

'It's absolutely beautiful,' she said.

'It's not bad, is it?' smiled Violet. 'I liked wearing it, anyway. It's full length, by the way – no restrictions on material then!'

'It's beautiful,' Lily repeated. 'Are you serious, though, about me borrowing it?'

'Not this again!' Violet lifted her spoon.

'No, really,' Lily insisted. 'It's too kind . . . I mean, I hardly know you!'

'Oh, don't be silly. What's that got to do with anything?'

'Everything!'

Violet smiled again.

'Nonsense! I've always wanted to do something for you after what you did for me that day. So embarrassing . . . in public like that.' She shook her head as if to shake away the memory. 'But I've had some . . . some treatment since then and . . .

well, it's helped. I think. Anyway. Do start! It'll get
cold!'

Lily obeyed. The soup was more of a broth, but
it was hot – and very tasty.

'Well, if you're absolutely sure, thank you, again,
from the bottom of my heart,' she said. 'I never
expected anything – certainly nothing like this. And
the fact is . . . well, I don't know what I'd do otherwise. My mum's got her work cut out making the
dress for the bride.'

'There you are then. And I know it'll suit you –
and fit you to a T!'

Now she'd seen the dress, Lily could see the truth
of it.

'It's not just that,' she said. 'I mean, you're right,
but – you couldn't have known, but it's my favourite
colour!'

'Even better!' cried Violet. 'It was meant to be.
Now, if that's settled, tell me all about yourself – and
this wedding.'

As their soup bowls were cleared away and the
fish arrived, Lily told her – about her family, her
friends, life at the store, and, of course, all about the
wedding – when it was happening, who was getting
married, who'd be there. She edited out a few details,
naturally, but managed to give a fairly full – if some-
what sanitised – version of events. She felt she was
doing all the talking, but she didn't like to ask too
much about Violet, though she learnt that she'd been

destined for some kind of course – cookery or floristry were mentioned – but that had been scuppered by the war. There was no question of her doing any kind of serious war work, or joining the Forces, even when she was of age, so she was helping her mother with her WVS work and Red Cross activities.

The waitress had long been eyeing their table – there was a queue of people waiting to be seated – but Violet ignored her till she pointedly asked if they wanted the bill. Lily found she didn't want to go – for the past hour, she realised, she'd actually felt quite grown-up, someone almost important, who could sit about in cafés and afford a half-decent meal. Oh well, back to reality – half the bill. She reached for her gas-mask case and her purse.

'What are you doing?' Violet had brought out a tan suede handbag and took from it a matching purse. 'This was my invitation, so my treat!'

'Violet. When you've . . . After all you've done . . . I can't let you! It's too much!'

'Too bad! It's done!' Violet laid some coins on the little dish and snapped her purse back into her bag.

She wasn't having any argument, and when they parted in the street, Lily clutching the suitcase, Violet pulling on her gloves, she went to shake Lily by the hand, then thought better of it, and gave her a swift kiss on the check.

'All the best, Lily,' she said. 'And have a wonderful wedding.'

'Thank you, Violet. Thank you. Oh, but – how am I going to get the dress back to you?'

'Oh, don't worry about that for now,' smiled Violet. 'We'll sort something out. Just enjoy your day.'

'Thank you.'

Lily was so moved she could hardly get the words out. As she walked home, the case bumping against her leg, she couldn't believe her good fortune. Such kindness from a virtual stranger. Such a lucky chance to have bumped into Violet again. And such a good thing she'd gone to work at Marlow's in the first place. None of this would have happened otherwise – none of it.

As with everything since Beryl had arrived unannounced on their doorstep, the next week passed in a whirl. Hunched over her trusty Singer, Dora was a blur of pins and fabric, and before their eyes a new and modish dress started to emerge. Beryl had, as Lily had suspected, requested a fitted bodice, V-neck, and the straightish skirt puffed out into something fuller by turning the net from the veil into a petticoat. Beryl's veil would be shoulder-length.

'And covered buttons down the front, I ask you!' Dora was heard to mutter when Beryl had left after the first fitting. 'She can whistle for those!'

'It shows what confidence she has in you, Mrs C,' put in Jim, turning on the wireless for the news.

'Confidence my eye! Who's she think I am? Madame Vionnet?'

Dora turned back to her stitching. She had to make the most use of the available light – mending or darning were one thing, but it was hopeless trying to sew anything delicate once the blackout went up.

Meanwhile Lily kept her dress a secret. She'd managed to smuggle the case into the house without anyone seeing and for a few days she kept it hidden while she got her story word-perfect and tried to anticipate any questions her mum might ask. Then, cunningly choosing a moment when her mother was engaged on a particularly tricky bit of hand-sewing, Lily gave her the 'someone through work' story and held her breath, waiting for the interrogation. But with her catering concerns pressing on her mind, and her foot welded to the sewing machine's treadle, Dora was much too preoccupied to question her further. She did stop momentarily to thank their lucky stars, and comment on the weight of the material, and the pretty colour being Lily's favourite, but that was all. She'd got away with it! All the same, Lily knew she'd have to tell Beryl – and Jim and Gladys – where the dress had really come from. There was no one she knew who actually worked at Marlow's that she could have borrowed from, certainly not a dress of this quality – and they'd be the first to realise it.

So, swearing them to secrecy, Lily gathered the three of them in her room one evening and told them

the full story of Mrs Tunnicliffe's unexpected gratitude after the incident in the shelter. She'd kept quiet
all this time to protect Violet, not wanting to paint
her as a hopeless neurotic, but having seen her again,
and especially after their lunch, she felt Violet was
much more robust these days. She could only conclude
that whatever treatment Violet had had, combined
with the timely tailing-off of the worst of the bomb-
ings, had made all the difference. So now she was
able to present the Marlow's episode as a one-off and
say that Violet had panicked simply because she'd
been trapped in an unfamiliar place with no idea of
when or if she'd get out.

Gladys just gasped, but Jim nodded.

'I always thought there must be more to it than
you'd let on. Poor girl. Horrible for her. In public
like that.'

'I know,' agreed Lily. 'I've felt like screaming myself
sometimes, stuck in the Anderson with Mrs Crosbie
and Trevor. Enough to give anyone the heebie-jeebies.'

'Well!' Beryl was open-mouthed. 'So that's how
you didn't get the sack. I always wondered. But
honestly, Lily . . .' She touched the material. 'You're
a guy one, you are. This dress . . . it's . . . well . . .'

'Beautiful,' breathed Gladys.

It was. After Gladys had gone home and Jim had
gone off downstairs, Lily tried it on again in front
of Beryl. It fitted like a glove.

'It's gorgeous, Lily,' said Beryl. 'Oh, we're going

to look a right couple of swells! And do you know what, it's given me an idea. Your mum hasn't started on the bodice yet. Forget the V-neck, I'm going to go for a sweetheart neckline myself!'

Lily smiled weakly. Oh well. She'd make it up to her mum somehow.

Chapter 26

It was a perfect September day. It would have been a perfect September day even without a wedding to look forward to – veiled, milky sunshine, with leaves shimmying down on the lightest whisper of a breeze. It had all been worth it – all the fuss and flurry, the occasional frustration and the fit of desperation when Dora had heard about the sweetheart neckline – all worth it.

Beryl had spent the night before the wedding back at Lily's. Jim gave up his bed this time and nobly slept on the front room sofa as everyone agreed that Lily, with her bridesmaid duties, deserved a good night's rest, as did Dora after her forced labour on the sewing machine. Sid wasn't there, thankfully, to take up bed space, though thankful hadn't been the word when there'd been concern (for the Collins and Bulpitt households) and terror (for Gladys) that he might not make it at all. He'd already had some leave after his extended sick leave, after all, but, as usual, Sid's charm – or cheek – had somehow wangled it. The day before, he'd managed to get a message to them, the message they'd all been praying for. He'd done it! He'd wrestled a twelve-hour pass – 6 a.m. to 6 p.m. – out of his superiors, and he wouldn't be coming alone. He'd be bringing Cobby – or rather, Bill – with him. Sid promised that come hell or high water, or even both, they'd be there in good time – 'reporting for duty'!

To give her credit, on the wedding morning, Beryl was the epitome of the blushing bride – so nervous that she refused breakfast, her hand trembling as she did her hair. She was shaking when she stepped into the dress; when Lily and Dora placed the veil, held in place with a (borrowed) diamanté comb, on her head; when she pulled on her (borrowed) net gloves; when she slipped into the (borrowed) satin sandals. But with every addition she was more and more transformed until finally Lily and Dora were able to stand back and take it in.

'You look stunning,' said Lily.

'Do you think so?'

But Lily knew Beryl. Now she was fully dressed she wasn't shaking any more, and she wasn't really asking. She knew she did.

Dora went off to get ready and now all that was left was for Lily to get into her ensemble. The heavy material felt strange but luxurious against her skin as Beryl did up the buttons at the back and tied and re-tied the bow to her satisfaction. Then she swivelled Lily round and only then allowed her to look in the mirror. Lily didn't know what to think. She'd never worn anything like it before. She didn't look like herself, and she didn't feel like herself, and she said so.

'You know why, don't you?' said Beryl. 'You're really pretty, Lily, but you don't make the most of yourself – and the dress is only half the story!'

All this time, Lily had longed to tame her hair, to have better clothes, to look older, but she suddenly felt defensive.

'I like myself as I am, thanks!'

'I don't mean you have to start wearing a load of slap. I can see that's not your style. But – gild the Lily a bit, if you like. Like this.'

Carefully, after draping a towel across her front, Beryl applied a dab of rouge to Lily's cheeks, powdered her nose, and offered her pot of Vaseline so Lily could gloss her lips. Then with brush and comb and what she called 'setting lotion' she smoothed and tweaked Lily's hair into more manageable curls. It was only quick reflexes on Lily's part and her insistence on wearing her own periwinkle-blue ribbon that saved her from being asphyxiated in a cloud of hairspray.

Beryl gave in but took Lily by the shoulders and stood her in front of the mirror again to show off the effect she'd achieved.

'See?'

Someone Lily barely recognised looked back.

At that moment there was a shout from downstairs.

'Hello? Anyone home?'

Sid! He'd made it!

Lily flew down, leaving Beryl to admire her own reflection again. That should keep her busy for a while.

'Who the heck . . . ? It is you, Lil?' exclaimed Sid as she arrived. 'Blimey, Sis, what a bobby-dazzler! I wouldn't have known you!'

'I don't know myself,' said Lily. 'Don't worry, I'm going to wash most of it off!'

'Well, before you do, say hello to Bill.'

'Sorry!'

Lily spun round and took in the young man, also in sailor's uniform, who'd been hanging shyly back. So this was 'Cobby'. Now they were face to face, she had to admit he did look a bit like Sid – a more gingery Sid admittedly, with the pale freckled skin that went with it, and a much shorter Sid, but then Gladys wasn't as tall as Lily. But like Sid he had a cheeky smile which dimpled his cheeks.

'Pleased to meet you,' she said, holding out her hand. He shook it.

'Same. And very pleased to be here. Thanks for inviting me!'

He sounded like a Londoner – or from somewhere down South, anyhow. But there was no time to ask exactly where he came from or find out any more about him because Dora, in her best dress and hat, scurried in, hugging Sid and shaking Bill by the hand, asking about their journey (hellish) before scooping Bill up and hurrying him out of the door. Les had managed to get a wedding car through one of the other drivers at work, but it was only for Beryl, Sid and Lily – Bill and Dora would have to walk and needed to get going. Jim had already left to collect Les and take him for a swift half before shepherding him to the Town Hall, where he'd deposit him safely inside and await the bride's arrival, camera at the ready.

'Well, that's a first,' said Sid, sprawling in a chair. 'A visitor in the house and Mum didn't manage to force-feed him a sandwich and a cup of tea!'

'Don't worry, he can make up for it later,' said Lily, thinking of the feast to be laid out in The Grapes. 'We all will. Mum and Ivy – Mrs Bulpitt – have done wonders with the food, Sid, you won't believe it – there's ham and sausage rolls and—'

She managed to stop herself before she mentioned the trifle – Sid's favourite, and made with possibly the last tin of peaches and cans of cream they'd see in a twelvemonth, as Dora had noted. No one liked to ask quite how Ivy Bulpitt had got hold of them, so no one did. She'd even got glacé cherries for the decoration.

'And the cake? Iced? Ribbons? Bluebirds and turtle doves? Bride and groom in a little arbour on the top?'

'The lot.'

'No!'

'Wait and see!'

'Wait and see what? Are you expecting someone?'

Beryl was standing in the doorway, her satin bodice shimmering and her lacy skirt sighing to a halt around her. Sid leapt to his feet.

'Blimey, Beryl, I'm speechless,' he said, going over and kissing her. 'You are the most beautiful bride – quite took my breath away. Lord knows what you'll do to Les.'

Beryl glowed.

'I don't want to let him down,' she said.

'You couldn't,' said Lily, meaning it.

Beryl smiled and came into the room. She wouldn't sit down for fear of creasing her skirt, but crossed to the window and looked out at the backyard, at the henhouse, completed now and waiting for its occupants, at the vegetable bed where Jim had turned over the soil ready to plant spring cabbage, at the patched roofs of the houses the other side of the alley.

'This wasn't quite how I planned it, you know, my wedding,' she said softly. 'I always imagined I'd have a bigger do – church, vicar, choir, bells, lots of guests, slap-up meal . . . It never occurred to me I'd be expecting, either!' She shook her head. 'All a dream, really . . . I don't know how I ever thought it was ever going to be like that anyway.' She turned back to them and smiled. 'But now it's here, truly, I wouldn't have it any different.'

'Really?'

Maybe Beryl hadn't just been admiring her reflection up there, thought Lily. Maybe there'd been a different sort of reflecting going on.

'Honestly. Everyone who matters to me'll be there. My real friends. More than friends – you feel like family.'

'Oh blimey!' cried Sid. 'Let's not get all sentimental, please. You must be desperate, Beryl, if you want to be part of our family! Talk about the Crazy Gang!'

'Sid!' Lily reproached him.

But Beryl was smiling and didn't seem to mind.

'Flowers, please, Lily,' she said, perfectly calm now. 'The car'll be here in a minute.'

It was only afterwards that Lily realised it might have been an idea if she'd asked what was expected of her as bridesmaid, or if they'd had some kind – any kind – of rehearsal. But in the end, what did it matter if she'd been a bit slow on the uptake when Beryl had turned to hand over her bouquet – the bouquet they'd cobbled together out of what Dora could cadge off a friend of Cousin Ida's who still had a bit of a flower garden. Lily had also had no idea, really, what to do when Les and Beryl, now man and wife, had kissed and they'd all clapped, and the register had been signed and the happy couple had triumphantly led the way out. Jim, however, seemed to know and, as best man, offered her his arm. Mesmerised, Lily took it, dimly aware that behind them, Sid had given his arm to his mum, Ivy was shepherding out a bemused but beaming Susan, and Bill, rising to the occasion, was squiring a beet-root but also beaming Gladys.

Everyone but Jim had already been inside when Lily had arrived with the bride, so she'd missed the moment when her friend, in the pink crepe again, had first clapped eyes on her sailor suitor. Oh well. She'd be hearing all about it, she was sure . . . for days to come.

But this was Les and Beryl's day – and they looked the image of happiness as they stood on the Town Hall steps in a hail of rice – no confetti, of course. Les, like Sid, declared himself 'bowled over' by his beautiful bride. He looked pretty natty himself, in a pinstriped suit with a snowy hanky billowing from his top pocket. And, as promised, he was laying off the Brylcreem these days. Mrs Bulpitt, who'd spent the entire service adjusting her corset, was poured into a most ill-advised and extraordinary costume of broad horizontal stripes in—

'What colours are those?' Lily whispered to Jim

as he assembled them for the group photograph, a tricky shot as there weren't quite enough of them to blot out the sandbags heaped up against the doors.

'Can't really tell, can you?' he whispered back. 'Plum pudding and brandy sauce? Cocoa and Horlicks?' There was something about Mrs Bulpitt that made you reach for food as a comparison, and Lily giggled. Even the hat perched on top of her frizzy grey hair had a little stalk like a mushroom.

'I love her,' she said. 'She doesn't care, does she?'

'No,' grinned Jim. 'Anyone else her size'd look like a cooper's barrel in that get-up, but somehow she gets away with it.' He looked down to fiddle with his camera. 'I only get one chance at this, so I've got to get the exposure right . . .' Then he added casually, still looking down, 'You look very nice, Lily, by the way. Very nice.'

Lily was glad she'd scrubbed the rouge off. Her cheeks were suddenly on fire.

When Jim had finally got his photograph, after much cajoling of Susan, who'd gone shy, they all stood about chatting and watching Sid and Bill acting the fool, throwing sticks into a horse chestnut to bring down the spiny conker cases. Suddenly Gladys pulled at Lily's arm.

'Lily! Have you seen . . . Isn't that . . . ?'

Lily looked across and there, on the pavement, giving her a little wave, was Violet.

'Oh, what?' she gasped, horrified. 'Keep Mum occupied,' she hissed. 'I'll have to talk to her.'

* * *

'I told you, didn't I?' smiled Violet as she approached. 'I said it would fit and I knew it would suit you.'

For all the awkwardness of the situation, Lily smiled back. She knew it was true.

'It's gorgeous, Violet,' she said sincerely. 'I've had so many compliments. I don't think I could have had more if I was the bride!'

'Well, you deserve them. Though she looks wonderful too, of course. And your mother made the dress? What a genius.'

'Well . . . it had its moments,' said Lily diplomatically. She paused. 'I wasn't expecting to see you here.'

'You don't mind, do you?'

'Mind? Of course not. I'm honoured!'

'Oh, don't be silly!' exclaimed Violet. 'I had to come. I wanted to see you anyway, but as well as that, I wanted to explain because . . . well, I'm going away for a bit. To stay with my aunt. She's getting on, and she's on her own, so she needs the company.'

'Oh! I see. Does she live far?'

'Bath.'

'Violet, how lovely!' Lily clasped her hands. 'Jane

Austen! Maybe you'll have some romantic adventures like one of her heroines!'

Violet laughed.

'Well, that would be fun. Though . . .' she smiled mischievously. 'I think you'll be married before me, Lily, the way that photographer boy was looking at you.'

Lily felt her cheeks flare again.

'Jim? Nonsense! He's just a friend!'

'Yes, of course he is. That's what they all say,' said Violet knowingly. 'Anyway, you'd better get back to them. I mustn't keep you.'

'Well, no, but – hang on, what are we going to do about . . . You'll need the dress back before you leave.'

'No, I won't,' replied Violet. 'I'm not going to be wearing it in Bath, am I? I don't think they have balls at the Pump Room any more.'

'Maybe not, but . . .'

'Anyway,' she went on. 'I'm not going to wear it again, am I? You keep it.'

'What? Don't be . . . I couldn't possibly!' exclaimed Lily. 'It's far too . . . when am I going to wear it again?'

'Who knows?' Violet gave her a mischievous smile. 'Maybe your friend'll marry one of those handsome sailors and need a bridesmaid!'

'Gladys . . . ? I'm not sure about that! But look, Violet, really. You can't! You can't give it to me!'

But Violet was walking away.

'Sorry, I just have!' she called back over her

shoulder. 'I'm leaving tomorrow, and you're far too busy today for us to stand here arguing. In fact, I think the bride needs you.'

Lily swung round. Beryl was standing by the car, with Les ineffectually trying to help her pick up her skirts so she could get in without getting them grubby. Lily turned this way and that, wanting to run after Violet, needing to go and help Beryl . . . and all the time conscious that her mum was watching from her vantage point on the steps. Dora had seen everything. Now there'd be some explaining to do.

Chapter 27

'Well, Mrs Collins? How do you think it's going?'

'Never mind that!' Dora turned to Jim, who'd materialised at her side. 'Who's that girl Lily was talking to?'

Lily had made her choice. Beryl had been shoehorned into the car and it had borne her and Les away to the reception with Lily and everyone else waving after it.

There was nothing for it.

'She's the person who lent her the dress,' Jim answered truthfully.

Dora's eyebrows shot up.

'Never!' They both looked after Violet. She'd reached the corner now; Dora watched her disappear before turning back to Jim and fixing him with one of her looks. 'Well, don't try and tell me she works at Marlow's! I could see from here that suit she had on was tailor-made!'

As usual, Dora had taken it all in at a glance.

'I don't think Lily actually said she worked at Marlow's, did she?' Jim pointed out. 'She's someone Lily met through Marlow's.'

'Met . . . ? Wait a moment . . . She's not – she's not a customer, is she?' asked Dora, scandalised. 'Don't tell me Lily's been pushing herself forward! That girl of mine! I read the staff manual as well, you know. "Cultivating any kind of special relationship with a customer is strictly forbidden!"'

Jim briefly thought of the 'special relationship' that Sir Douglas and his circle had enjoyed.

'Look, Mrs Collins,' he said. 'I'll be straight with you. Yes, the girl's a customer, but if she's taken a bit of a shine to Lily, it was that way round. Lily asked for nothing and she's done nothing wrong. The offer of the dress was quite spontaneous.'

'Well!' Dora folded her arms. 'That's your story and I'm stuck with it, am I? I'll get it out of Lily, you see if I don't! Little minx!'

'There's no more to get,' said Jim simply. 'I promise you. Lily tried to refuse, but it was no good. The girl wanted to do it. She was happy to help.' He paused. 'You may not have noticed it, Mrs Collins – maybe you're too close – but there's something special about your daughter. People like her. She can't help it and they can't help themselves.'

Dora swallowed hard. Sometimes, thinking about her children, about how proud she was of them, about how well they'd turned out despite the difficult times since their father's death, made her want to weep. Jim could see it and gave her time to recover herself.

'The world's not a very nice place at the moment,' he said gently. 'So why not just be grateful for a simple act of kindness, and not question it too much?'

'Mum . . . ?'

It was Lily, come to face the music, or so she assumed. But her mother merely gave a little tut and, reaching in her bag, brought out her comb. She applied it vigorously to Lily's hair, which had had enough of behaving, and was trying valiantly to escape its ribbon.

'This hair of yours!' she said. 'It'll be the death of me. All the setting lotion in the world can't do better than I can with a comb and bit of spit.' Finally satisfied as Lily writhed under her attention, she tucked the comb away, adding, 'Nice of your friend to come and see you, wasn't it?' And then, as Lily gaped, 'Well, let's get going, or Les and Beryl will think we've deserted them. I don't suppose Susan's the fastest walker.'

She moved off towards the rest of the wedding party. Sid and Bill had split open the conkers. Far from collecting them – the starch in them went to make cordite, incredibly – they were juggling with them, to Susan's ecstatic delight, while Gladys and Ivy looked on. Lily stared after her mother's narrow back, then looked at Jim.

'Did you . . . ? What did you . . . ? Violet . . . ?'

'No names, no pack drill. Forget it. It's sorted,' he said.

'How? What did you say?'

'Never you mind,' said Jim, and rather smugly, she thought. Oh, he could be so annoying! But if he'd saved her from an interrogation . . .

He gave her that crooked grin of his that crinkled up his eyes.

'You heard your mum – let's go. Last one to The Grapes is a cissy. Oh dear, I was forgetting – pity you've got that long skirt to hold you back, isn't it!'

It was a very jolly afternoon – the best Lily could remember since the start of the war. After the food – no, the feast – had been marvelled at and enjoyed, and everyone had gone back for more – and then more again – the famous cake was finally produced, carried in proudly by the mothers between them. Ivy had managed to get enough icing sugar to cover the top, but the sides were cleverly masked with cardboard and ribbon and from somewhere she'd borrowed a little plaster bride and groom, who were in the dove-bedecked arbour which Sid had specified.

351

After Les and Beryl had cut the first slice, and it was being put on plates, Les chinked the cake knife on his glass.

He knew what was expected of him . . . they all did.

'My wife and I . . .' – cue catcalls from Sid and Bill – 'my wife and I want to thank you all for being here on our special day. I've got to thank the mums for such a fantastic effort with the food' – cue 'hear hear from everyone – 'and the flowers and everything – and especially to Mrs Collins for helping make Beryl the most beautiful bride in the world. Not that she needs any help in that department!' – cue much simpering and blushing and 'Oh, Les!' from Beryl, and nudges from Sid to Lily – and not just about the bride and groom.

Gladys was gazing across at Bill, who was gazing at the trifle bowl and plainly longing to run his finger round the rim where a few traces of cream remained. Gladys's longing was also plain, but of a transparently different kind – leaping ahead to the moment in the future when Bill would be standing up and saying the same thing about her. Lily marvelled at her friend. Bill had written back one brief letter in reply to Gladys, which hadn't said much beyond that he'd be glad to have her write to him, and she'd only met him for the first time a couple of hours ago! But as Sid had predicted, in Gladys's head she was already well on the way to being Mrs William Webb. Still, at least Bill was a real-life boy, not some unattainable film star, or, worse, Lily's own perfectly-friendly-but-that's-as-far-as-it-goes brother. And Bill seemed a thoroughly nice boy at that. But Les had resumed his speech.

'Talking of departments . . . we only met, me and Beryl – and Jim and Lily and Gladys – through working at Marlow's. I think it's fair to say' – he glanced at Jim and grinned – 'we didn't all hit it off straight away.' Beryl glanced at Lily and grimaced. 'But I think I can say now we're all mates, and me and Beryl are very grateful for that, especially to Lily and her mum for giving Beryl a roof over her head when she needed it. So it might seem funny to be grateful to a shop, but without it, we wouldn't be here today. Marlow's has been very generous, too, with a marriage grant to each of us. And that's not all – they've sent along a little surprise.' He nodded to the landlord, who whipped his filthy tea towel off his shoulder and from under the bar produced a rattling tray of saucer-shaped glasses.

'Champagne?' Sid rubbed his hands. 'That'll get the party started!'

The landlord had disappeared, and came back with not one, but two foil-crowned bottles, which he proceeded to open with surprising skill, given that he must be more used to pulling halves of mild.

Susan nearly jumped in the air when the corks

353

popped, but Jim, to whom she'd attached herself like a limpet mine, calmed her down by saying it was just very fizzy pop and nothing to worry about. When everyone had a glass, Jim managed to prise Susan off his arm and transfer her to her mum. He then chinked for silence himself.

'I don't know what order these speeches are meant to happen in, and Sid might fight me for the honour, but as best man' – cue 'That's what you think!' from Sid and 'Yeah, who says?' from Bill, who was really loosening up now – 'As best man,' Jim continued, undeterred, 'it's my duty to thank the bridesmaids – in this case, bridesmaid – and pay them some lavish compliments. Well, I'm not a very complimenting sort of chap, but you'd have to be a mole in a blindfold not to see that Lily looks lovely today, and I know she's been a great source of support to Beryl.' Cue 'Hear, hear!' from Beryl and mortified blushing from Lily. Jim, in fact, was looking a bit pink himself – and no one had had so much as a sip of champagne yet, which Sid wasn't slow to point out.

'Blimey, get on with it!' he cried. 'Me and Bill have got to be on a train soon, so let's get some of this posh stuff down us! Ladies and gentlemen, without further ado, I give you . . . the bride and groom!'

'The bride and groom!'

At last they took their first sip. Lily felt the bubbles tickle her nose; Gladys coughed and spluttered and was banged on the back by a grinning Bill. Their second physical contact of the day – she'd be reliving that tonight! Ivy had downed her glass almost in one and was holding it out for a refill.

'Come on!' She jabbed a finger at the landlord. 'And don't be so shy with it this time. That last drop hardly touched the sides! Anyone'd think it was rationed!'

Too soon – much too soon for Gladys, certainly – Sid and Bill said they'd have to be making tracks. They had to allow for cancelled trains and delays, or as Bill put it, they'd be painting coal white for the next three weeks. The wedding party gathered on the pavement to wave them off, Beryl kissing them both, thanking them for coming, and admonishing them for breaching etiquette by being the first to go. From the pub doorway, Lily noticed Gladys looking on enviously. Lily ached for her. She knew Gladys would never dare be that forward with Bill, much as she might want to be. As Sid emerged from Beryl's enveloping cloud of satin and Soir de Paris, Lily shot him a look and cocked her head minutely in Gladys's direction.

'Gladys!' he exclaimed, cottoning on at once. 'What are you hanging back there for, eh? Come and give a couple of brave sailor-boys the send-off they deserve!'

He pulled her forwards, giving her a peck on the cheek. Clever Sid. By making it about the two of them, he'd given Gladys the perfect excuse for doing the same to Bill.

'Bye, Gladys,' Bill said now, taking her by the hands. 'Keep those letters coming, won't you? And on my next leave . . .' His next leave! Oh, heart be still! 'We'll go for a drink, shall we? I can't promise it'll be champagne though!'

Lily felt a ton of tension drop from her shoulders. Bill had gone further than she'd ever dared hope. She knew that Gladys would have happily drunk dishwater to go and sit in a pub with a boy, but Bill had effectively asked her out – her first date! Thank goodness for Bill, thank goodness for Sid, thank goodness for Les and Beryl – and the baby, or none of this would have happened. And – Lily looked over at Jim – as Les had said, thank goodness for Marlow's.

They tried to resume proceedings, but the party lost a bit of its fizz after Sid and Bill had gone. Lily braced herself for a torrent of over-excited babble from Gladys, but it seemed Bill had achieved the impossible – he'd actually silenced her. She was simply too stunned by the day's developments to recount them yet, and took herself off to a corner to relive them frame by frame. Lily concentrated on relieving Mrs Bulpitt, who'd got a bad case of hiccups, by taking Susan off her hands and improvising a game of Snap with an assortment of the pub's beermats. But before long, she had to hand her over to Jim. Les and Beryl also had a train to catch and she was on bridesmaid duty again.

'He won't tell me where we're going,' said Beryl, as Lily helped her out of her dress and into her going-away outfit in the pub's box room. 'Mind you don't traipse that dress on this filthy floor!'

Lily hung the dress on the back of the door.

'Hasn't he given you any clues?'

'Well, he said I didn't need a passport, that's all I could get out of him!'

Lily knew, because Les had told her – they were going to Stratford-upon-Avon for the night. He didn't think there was much point in going to the seaside: apart from the fact that the journey would take up most of the available time, where was the fun in staring out to sea over a beach bristling with barbed wire and probably mined? Stratford had escaped the Blitz, people said, because Hitler admired Shakespeare, so, according to Les, it was the safest place in the country for his wife and unborn child. Lily thought it was a shame Shakespeare hadn't come from Coventry, which was only down the road, after all, and hoped Beryl wouldn't be disappointed. She couldn't see her finding much to enjoy in the home of the national bard unless the shopping was good. But maybe on honeymoon you never left your room. That was the impression the cheap novels Beryl devoured gave you anyway – she'd left loads of them lying around at Lily's. Lily looked away, feeling hot again, as Beryl fastened her suspenders and wriggled into a dress of self-striped jade green.

'That's new, Beryl. Where did you get it?'

'Good, isn't it?' said Beryl, doing up the buttons. 'It's my old bedroom curtains! Well, my dad won't be needing them and there's a perfectly good pair at Les's already. I had someone make it – I didn't think it was fair to ask your mum. And look – button-through, and I've had big darts put in, see, so it can grow with me for the baby!'

They said having a baby changed you. It seemed to have changed Beryl for the better already, and Lily hugged her.

'I'm so happy it's worked out for you, Beryl,' she said. 'I couldn't be happier.'

'Nor me,' said Beryl. 'And it's all thanks to you, Lily.' But before they could get too sentimental, she added briskly, 'Now, my wedding dress. You're in charge. Cover it up with that old sheet, and get it back to your place, OK? I've kept it clean this far, and I don't want a mark on it, or you're for the high jump.'

As Lily had noted before, the old Beryl was still there, still bossing everyone she could – except for Les, to whom she seemed in thrall. Lily didn't think Ivy would stand for it for one moment, but it had occurred to her that there might be one advantage for Ivy in taking Beryl in. It might be a help with Susan. Babies were a lot of work, or so everyone kept saying, and while Susan couldn't be left in charge, she could surely fetch nappy pins and be trusted to rock the pram. Having something to do might actually be good for her.

But that was all to come. For now, it was enough to know the day had passed off without a hitch. Susan had behaved, Sid had behaved, Gladys had a boyfriend, or as good as, Lily had a beautiful new dress and Jim had somehow pacified her mum on the subject . . . She sighed with satisfaction. It had been a wonderful wedding. Life was going to seem very dull now.

'Wasn't it a lovely day?' she sighed to Jim as they made a pot of tea when they got in. 'I can't wait to see the photographs.'

Jim lit the gas under the kettle.

'I could have done with a wide-angle lens for Ivy, but . . .'

'Don't be rotten!' laughed Lily. 'She's a dear.'

'I know. Beryl's struck lucky with her as well as Les.'

'It's going to be strange now it's all over.' Lily arranged the cups on a tray. 'Nothing to look forward to.'

'Oh, I don't know,' said Jim. He was spooning tea. One spoon for each of them – no 'one for the pot' these days. 'There's always Sunday.'

'What's happening on Sunday?'

'Didn't I say?' Jim had his most innocent face on, so Lily was instantly suspicious. 'It's all arranged. We're going to the country. To get the chickens. Well, don't look like that! They're hens, not homing pigeons!'

Chapter 28

Time was a funny thing, thought Lily. The ten days between Beryl's arrival on their doorstep as a fallen woman and her emergence on to the Town Hall steps as a respectable married lady had passed in a flash, punctuated only by Dora's desperate cries of 'I'll never get it all done!' and sporadic appearances from Ivy to announce more black-market booty. There were only three days between the wedding and the proposed trip to the country, but by contrast, time seemed to be standing still.

The shop was quiet; that didn't help. The Sale was long over; the children were back at school, their uniforms and sports kit bought; Christmas was still ages away. All there was to do was dust the fitments, tidy the rails and parcel up the odd purchase. Even Miss Thomas and Miss Temple had time on their hands. They'd quizzed Lily and Gladys relentlessly about the wedding – what everyone wore, what they ate, who'd said what to whom, but at least they were a new audience for Gladys's breathy account of her new beau.

Lily was keen to find out more about Bill, but Gladys hadn't got much to tell her that she didn't already know. To be fair, Bill had only spent a few hours in Hinton and a lot of that had been taken up with the wedding itself, but the main trouble was that Gladys had been too overcome to ask him anything. All she was able to tell Lily was that Bill had, as Sid had said, been raised in a children's home, but, as soon as he could, had run away to sea, or as good as. He'd found casual work, first on the canals, then on river tugs, and then, more enjoyably and less strenuously, on pleasure boats. With all that experience, the Navy was the obvious fit for him. He'd signed up as soon as he could and eventually found himself in the same base and billet as Sid, and promptly re-christened 'Cobby'.

Lily could have predicted what came next, because she'd seen and heard Gladys do it with Sid. Sure enough, Bill's final destination, in Gladys's mind, was Commander William Webb, RN. Gladys didn't actually say that when he collected his medals and commendations from the Palace, she'd be by his side, but Lily could supply that bit for herself.

But she was happy beyond belief for her friend. Bill must have liked Gladys too, because he was really delivering the goods now, or rather the postman was. By Saturday she'd had not just a postcard but an actual letter saying what a good time he'd had, and that he'd let her know as soon as he could get leave. Gladys had never known such bliss.

When more winter stock arrived, the juniors and the salesgirls practically fought each other for the privilege of having something to do, but there was soon disappointment. Neither the quality nor the quantity met Miss Temple and Miss Thomas's exacting standards.

'I know, I know,' lamented Miss Frobisher. 'But if you'd seen what I had to choose from . . . All the mills and factories have gone over to making uniforms or Army blankets. Trust me, I did what I could.'

The salesladies clucked and said they were sure she had, but shook their heads all the same when Miss Frobisher had gone.

Jim's department was facing the same problem and had been for some time. Pretty much the only furniture available was second-hand, acquired from people who'd fallen on hard times selling off their stuff to make ends meet. And if you were after anything metal like a coal scuttle or a companion set, well, good luck to you!

'Come back when the war's over, I almost told one woman today,' Jim said as he and Lily walked home after work on Saturday evening. 'If it goes on much longer, Marlow's is going to have to change its slogan. Not "Only the best" but "The best we could do".'

But Lily was hardly listening. In twelve hours they'd be setting off for the country – three trains, then a bus if they were lucky – if not, trying to hitch a lift – and then a bit of a walk, as his parents' cottage was well out of the village, Jim had explained apologetically.

Lily didn't know what he had to be sorry about: it all sounded wonderful. She was already imagining a half-timbered cottage with roof-thatch like eyebrows over lead-paned windows and a wonky brick path to the door, which had roses round it, of course, and birds trilling away in a bowed apple tree. She had the setting, no problem; it was the people in it she found harder to imagine. She was dying to ask Jim more about his parents, or to ask to see a photograph, but from the way she'd had to drag his reluctant confession about his home life and background out of him, she somehow guessed he didn't find it easy to talk about, and she didn't want to pry. And what was the point of seeing a photograph this late in the day? She'd be meeting his mum and dad soon enough anyway.

* * *

Jim pushed open the warped wooden gate and stood back.

'After you,'

'No, you first.'

'Go on, Lily—' He broke off and looked at her with his head on one side. 'Hang on, you're not nervous, are you?'

'No! Of course not!'

But was she? If a fluttering heart and a slight sick feeling meant she was nervous, then Lily supposed she must be. All the way in the train – or rather, trains – being delayed, being shunted about, waiting on misty early morning platforms, she'd felt nothing but excitement and anticipation, but now they were actually here, actually standing at the foot of the – she'd been right about that, anyway – the wonky brick path . . . What would Jim's parents be like? Suddenly, even more than her first days at Marlow's, it was important, vitally important, that she made a good impression.

But as they dithered, the front door opened.

'At last! I thought you were never going to get here!'

It was Jim's mother, wiping her hands on her apron and coming down the path.

'Oh, Jim! Jim!'

Jim smiled and went to hug her, but she took him by the wrists and looked at him critically. 'You've lost weight!'

'Mother!' Jim reproached her. 'How can you say that? And in front of Lily! Her mum does nothing but feed me up!'

Mrs Goodridge swiftly backtracked.

'I didn't mean . . . no offence, I'm sure!'

She turned to Lily with a quick smile.

'So you're the Lily I've heard so much about.'

Had she? It was news to Lily. What on earth had Jim said?

'Pleased to meet you,' she said, holding out her hand. She could hardly counter that she'd heard lots about her, because she hadn't.

'Come on inside, the pair of you,' urged Mrs Goodridge, turning back to Jim. 'Your father's not so good – it's these damp mornings. He's by the fire.'

Lily followed mother and son up the path, listening as Jim commented on the garden, not quite the cottage garden of hollyhocks and roses she'd imagined, but mostly dug up for veg just like Lily's own backyard. The cottage itself, though, was as she'd pictured it: whitewashed, long and low, though again not quite as picture-perfect as the one she'd conjured up. She couldn't help noticing that the thatch was bald in places, the window frames sagging, and the wonky path very wonky and slippery with moss. Yet Jim's dad was supposed to be an odd-job man . . . Lily supposed it was, to quote her mum, the old story of the cobbler's children going ill-shod. After he'd done the paying jobs, Jim's dad had no energy left for the upkeep of his own home.

Inside, the cottage was in better order, if rather dark, and so low-beamed that Jim had to stoop, but there was a warm fire in the grate with a collie dog, its tongue lolling comically, stretched out beside it. Jim's dad put aside his *Farmer's Weekly* – he obviously still took an interest in all things agricultural – and struggled up to greet her.

'Oh, please don't get up!' Lily urged, but he was already on his feet, as tall as Jim, and as thin – though you could tell he'd once been a much broader man, and his skin hung loosely on his bones. He had a terrible pallor, too, almost grey, but his eyes, like Jim's, were deep-set and sincere and he managed a firm handshake.

'Welcome,' he said warmly. 'Any friend of Jim's . . .'

Lily beamed. He had a rough, country voice, rounded at the edges, though there was a rasp in it which was obviously unhealthy. Jim settled him back down in his chair. His mother, cursing the trains and the remoteness of where they lived, and fretting about the dinner being spoilt, disappeared towards the kitchen, refusing all offers of help.

'I can't sit around and be waited on!' protested Lily.

'You stay where you are!' she said firmly and disappeared.

That put me in my place, she thought, but Jim

said he knew his mum, it was no use trying to argue with her. He pulled round a little chintz-covered chair for Lily and a cane-seated one for himself and, as Jim's dad asked all about Hinton, and Marlow's, and Lily's family, and she answered, Jim chipping in, she started to relax.

Over dinner, on the other hand, she was the quieter one, taking it all in. She let them talk amongst themselves about people she didn't know and things she didn't understand – sugar beet and seedbeds and milk yields and something called 'tilth'. Achieving a fine one was very important to farmers after ploughing, apparently. Jim seemed to understand all about it, and Lily thought again how much he knew, how modest he was about it, and how little she knew about him, really. His dad had to have long periods where he did nothing but hold a handkerchief to his mouth, cough, and struggle for breath, and he didn't eat much, Lily noticed. She, on the other hand, was quite happy to concentrate on her plate – juicy chicken, roast potatoes, parsnips, carrots, cabbage, stuffing . . . no wonder Mrs Goodridge thought they were starving Jim in Hinton!

After a sizeable plum crumble – to Lily's astonishment she learnt that Jim's mum made her own butter in a churn – Lily, as a guest, was again barred from the kitchen. Instead, Mrs Goodridge carried Jim, comically signalling 'Help!', off to assist with the washing up. Obviously gathering all his strength, his dad offered to walk Lily round the garden and after she'd helped him into his coat, cap, gloves and two mufflers, out they went, the old collie dog trailing at their heels.

With Mr Goodridge supporting himself on a stick, they made slow progress, but it helped Lily to begin to grasp just how differently the war was felt in the country, with nature's larder outside the door. She marvelled at the size of the cabbages, and Jim's dad explained that it was down to the Vale of Evesham's good loamy soil. It certainly did look darker and richer than the dry, stony seedbed in Lily's backyard. When it came to the outhouse, it was the same story. Dora did her best with the little that was available, but with all autumn's abundance, Jim's mum had started to put by row after row of apples and endless bottled fruit and chutneys. There were two fat rabbits hanging by their hind legs, and what Mr Goodridge informed her was a brace of partridge – and there'd be pigeons and pheasants to come, he said, some for free, shot by farmers or knocked down on the roads. Hens skittered away under the apple trees at their approach, which reminded Lily about Jim's henhouse. As she praised his efforts, his dad nodded approval of the protective caulking, and warned Lily of the importance of checking the netting every day as hens were great escapers – 'and not a brain between them'.

In a while, Jim came out to join them. Lily looked

at him with new eyes. It was true that like he'd said, his family, for all his distant Marlow connections, obviously weren't any better off than hers. Their cottage was homely rather than grand, the chairs creaky and the knives and forks at dinnertime as bent and tarnished as the ones they used at home. But despite that, for Jim to have exchanged all this bounty, all this clean fresh air, all the golden-greenery-brownery of the trees and fields beyond the hedge and the purplish blush of the distant Malvern hills – for Hinton? How could he stand it? Didn't he long to go back?

She had no chance to ask him, because his mum came out too and chivvied them inside, fearful of his dad's chest. She could see now that his mother was a worrier, poor thing. Her worry reflex had been triggered, presumably, by her husband's war experience, his ongoing poor health and the insecurity that brought, and it had never quite reset. Lily could appreciate fully now what Jim had hinted at when he'd told her about the begging letter she'd written to Cedric Marlow. He was to have been their hope and their salvation. How frustrated she must be that her appeal had wrenched Jim away, when the plan had been to educate him for a country life, a farming life, like the one his father could no longer sustain. That would have kept him close and given her an interest – and Jim's company – in what, despite the plentiful food and beautiful views, Lily could see now was basically a hard life. His mum was stuck in the middle of nowhere, caring for an invalid and running the house, while also doing the man's work about the place: lugging chicken feed, tending the veg and collecting firewood. Jim was the future, her only future, and he had gone. While of course Mrs Goodridge wouldn't have wanted Jim to be unhappy, ever, maybe part of her had secretly hoped he'd hate Marlow's and come home.

They settled Jim's father back in his chair and he fell straight asleep – the exertions of the day had obviously worn him out. The three of them were now standing in the small scullery and Jim was in discussion with his mum about how much they could carry back with them. Obviously disappointed that he'd said they had to go already, she was trying to press on him some cream, butter, jars of jam, even one of the rabbits. Jim was pointing out that much as they'd like to, they couldn't carry it all. The whole point of the day was to collect the chickens, and they still had them, and a bag of meal, to get from a nearby farm.

With her new appreciation of what things must be like for Jim's mother, Lily noticed her lips reduce to a thin line at Jim's polite but emphatic refusals. She'd perhaps been quite pretty once, but worry had grooved deep lines in her face and she looked much older than she must have been. Her hands looked red and sore, too; Lily had seen the dolly tub and mangle in the outhouse on her tour and Jim's dad had explained, quietly, that his wife had to take in washing 'because I'm such an apology for a man these days'. Lily had tried to reassure him that she was sure he could never be that, but he'd smiled sadly and said, 'It's not the life Alice expected, I'm afraid.'

All in all, it hadn't been the day Lily had expected, either, and there was much for her to digest on the journey home, not that there was much chance. Trying to keep hold of the chickens wriggling and squawking in two separate sacks, a further weighty sack of grain, and a canvas bag stuffed with the provisions Jim's mum had insisted on, plus their gas masks, made anything like staying upright on the lurching trains impossible. With their writhing and bulky burdens, they were hardly the most popular people to share a compartment with, and by the time they boarded their final train to Hinton, Jim thought it best they didn't bother trying to get a seat, but stood in the corridor. It turned out that wouldn't be easy either, as the previous two trains had been cancelled, so Lily spent the journey with her face pressed into the rough tunic and smelly armpit of a soldier who was clearly the worse for drink.

After that, the air on the platform when they finally reached Hinton, for all the smuts and smoke, felt almost as sweet as the air in the Vale of Evesham, and Lily took deep breaths while Jim retied the string on the neck of one of the chicken sacks.

'Can you manage this one?' he asked her. 'The lively one? I'll take the other, the sack of grain, and this blessed mobile canteen Mum gave us.'

'Of course!' said Lily, though she felt as if she was still travelling – her legs were wobbly from so much standing and the 'clackety-clack' of the train was still reverberating throughout her body. It was after dark and they'd have to walk home, which would take ages in the blackout, but at least it would clear her head. 'It was very kind of your mum, Jim. She meant well.' Maybe now was finally the time to broach it. 'I suppose she feels it's all she can do for you now you live away. See you don't starve!'

'You noticed it, then?' Jim distributed his load over his shoulders and in the crook of his arm and set off, Lily following. 'I thought you would. Yes, I'm the apple of her eye.'

'I could tell.'

'Quite a responsibility. She's never really forgiven me for leaving, I don't think,' he went on sadly as they reached the street. 'She's a disappointed woman, my mum. Nothing in her life has worked out as she thought. Everything she touches turns to dust – like writing to Uncle Cedric. That's how she sees it, anyway.'

'Oh, Jim. I'm sorry. But it must be hard for her, with your dad.'

'Of course. And I feel a heel about it. It's hard physical work caring for him, as well as the worry that he won't make it through another winter, and the worry about paying the doctor to make sure he does. I've been sending them what I can to help.'

Lily hadn't known that, but it made sense, now she thought about it.

'I'm afraid she had a bit of a go at me in the kitchen,' Jim went on.

'Oh, yes?'

For the first time, Lily was grateful for the blackout. She knew how hard Jim found it to talk about personal stuff, but the visit home seemed to have opened up something in him. There was no doubt, though, that if she was about to hear what she was dreading, it would be easier if she had to concentrate on where she was putting her feet than having to look him in the eye. Something in Lily told her not to say any more, but wait for him to continue.

'The irony is that she only wrote to Uncle Cedric because she didn't want me starting at the bottom, in manual farm labouring. Well, take Broad Oak Farm, the place we were talking about at dinner.'

It was the place where getting the 'fine tilth' had been a problem.

'Ted Povey, the farmer there – two sons – both insisted on going off to fight when they needn't have. One was killed at Dunkirk, the other was captured, and died in a PoW camp somewhere. Ted's daughter has had to leave school to help in the dairy, and he's got a Land Girl working the land. It's like a slap in the face for my mother. With farmers so desperate for labour these days, if I'd started on the bottom rung back then, I could be farm foreman there by now.'

And up the road from her, thought Lily. She thought it because she wasn't sure she'd be able to get any words out, and when she did, she gripped the neck of the sack very tight, fearful she might drop it.

'Are you . . . ? Did she ask you . . . Are you tempted to go back?'

'No! Not at all!'

In her relief, Lily almost did drop the sack. She lunged for it and clutched it to her, forgetting that hens had beaks and claws – and used them.

'Ow!'

'Are you all right?'

'Fine,' she lied, hoping the tearing claws hadn't ripped through into her jacket, which her mum had lent her for the day, on pain of 'keeping it nice'. She shifted the sack back into a tight grip in her hand. 'Sorry. You were saying . . .'

Jim sighed.

'I had to tell her it's too late. I'm getting on at Marlow's now, had my promotion, and do you know what, I actually like it there. Farming's all very fine, it's a great life when it's all going well and the sun shines. And I know it's a vital job in the war, vital. But I'm past all that now. I'll always love the countryside, and miss it, and I'll send her money, happily, every penny I can. I feel bad about her, of course I do, but I can't live my life for my mother, Lily. I've got my own path to walk.'

Lily bit her lip, hard. She couldn't speak for relief.

They were passing through the centre of the town now, past the Town Hall where only a few days ago they'd seen Les and Beryl married. A crowd was spilling out on to the pavement. Posters announced that the local MP had been speaking about 'The Progress of the War'.

Jim went first, trying to push a way through the throng, but a young couple, arm-in-arm and deep in discussion, weren't looking where they were going. They barged into Jim, Lily shunting into his back.

'I'm so sorry!' the young woman cried, and scolded, 'Robert!'

Lily peered through the gloom. Robert Marlow! He was peering at them, too.

'Jim! It is you, isn't it?'

'Evening,' said Jim.

Ouch – this could be awkward.

'Do you two know each other?' asked the young woman. 'Well, go on then, Robert, introduce us!'

Robert cleared his throat.

'Evelyn, this is Jim Goodridge. And his friend is Lily. Lily Collins. They're, er, colleagues, well, ex-colleagues, now I've left, from the store.'

So Jim was a colleague, was he, not a cousin –

Robert was still trying to deny the connection, thought Lily indignantly.

'Oh, how nice! Evelyn Brimble.'

Evelyn held out her hand. Jim shook it, but Lily was paralysed. Brimble was hardly a common name. She could only be Sir Douglas's daughter! Could it be . . . no, impossible. Too fantastic . . . but then . . . Was this the answer to what had been puzzling her and Jim? Robert had cooked up the delivery scheme in some attempt to get close to her? They certainly seemed like a couple now.

Luckily Jim had more presence of mind.

'You're been at the talk, I take it,' he said. 'What had he got to say?'

Evelyn rolled her eyes.

'Don't ask me. We had to put in an appearance for my father's sake. I'm sure I should have been, but I'm afraid I wasn't listening very closely.'

Robert looked at her indulgently.

'Politics not your thing, is it, darling?'

Evelyn shuddered.

'Not at all. And I'll be honest, far from discussing world events just now, we were debating where to go for a late supper!'

Lily couldn't think of a thing to say, but nothing was needed, since the hen she was carrying filled the gap with another anguished squawk. Evelyn nearly jumped in the air and clutched Robert's arm.

'My God! What's that?'

'A hen,' said Lily, as if it were the most normal thing in the world. 'Jim's made us a henhouse. We're going to have our own eggs.'

Evelyn let go of Robert's arm and let out a peal of laughter.

'Aren't you brilliant! Exactly what the Government's always telling us to do! Why haven't you got me some hens, Robert?'

Robert looked indulgently on her again as Lily tried to picture Evelyn with her golden curls and dainty hands mucking out dirty straw.

'Evelyn! You wouldn't last five minutes!'

'You're probably right,' Evelyn admitted. 'Anyway, we mustn't hold these good people up. The hens need to . . . what's it called . . . roost?'

'Very good,' said Jim, smiling. 'Well, if you change your mind, let me know. I can get hold of some nice laying birds for you.'

Evelyn laughed her tinkly laugh again and they all wished each other goodbye.

The crowd had dispersed while they'd been talking and the street was deserted again. In the inky sky a few stars and a tentative new moon were the only illumination. Lily and Jim stood and looked at each other wonderingly.

Lily was the first to speak.

'Are you thinking the same as me?' she asked.

But she knew he would be.

'Oh, yes,' he smiled. 'I'm sure I am.'

'It was all about her,' said Lily. 'All of it. That's why Robert came up with the delivery scheme. To get a foot in the door at the Brimbles'.'

'It has to be,' agreed Jim.

'After all that.' Lily was half-amazed, half-admiring. 'It was over a girl!'

'Oh, well.' Jim looked down at his shoes. He scuffed one about on the pavement. 'It has been known, you know. It wouldn't be the first time a chap's made a bit of a fool of himself, or done something that seems a bit crazy, all to impress a girl.'

The hen Lily was carrying let out another squawk.

Suddenly it dawned on her. Did he mean . . . he didn't, did he? He couldn't. He couldn't mean . . . something like building a henhouse?

Les and Beryl, Robert and Evelyn, Gladys and Bill (hopefully) . . . but Lily and Jim? Really? Really? Her heart gave a thumping jump in her chest and she felt warm and shivery all at the same time. Thank goodness it was as dark as it was.

'Jim . . . ?' she began, but she knew that would be it. He wouldn't say any more, and to be honest, she wasn't sure she wanted him to. It might feel right for everyone else, but right now Lily wasn't quite sure she was ready to be half of a pair. She was happy just being herself – as long as she knew Jim would be there.

'Come on,' he said. 'We've had a long day. Let's get ourselves home.'

Author's Note

The woes of retailers in general, and larger stores in particular, seem to be constantly in the news, but not so long ago every city and reasonably-sized town had its own independent department store. Many have disappeared, but some still thrive – Walker and Ling of Weston-super-Mare, Brays of Malvern, Jarrolds of Norwich.

In Wolverhampton, the place to shop was Beatties which, like Marlow's, had started out as a small family drapery business. Over the years, it expanded into a twelve-strong store group across the Midlands before being swallowed up by House of Fraser. Shoppers in Wolverhampton, though, identified so much with the store that, after protests, the Beatties name was retained on the facade. When House of Fraser collapsed in 2018, another vigorous local campaign helped the store win a reprieve from closure.

After the initial House of Fraser takeover, Beatties gave their archive to Wolverhampton City Council, which a few years ago mounted an exhibition. I'd grown up with my mum's excited cry of 'Beatties' sale!' ringing in my ears, so, out of curiosity, and with no thought at the time of writing a novel – any novel – I went along.

The exhibition was in one small room, but I was there for hours, revelling in the detail of advertisements from the 1900s, sales bills from the 1940s and press cuttings from the 1950s. And when I did sit down to write a novel, that exhibition, mixed with childhood memories of shopping in similar stores and Saturday jobs serving in them, meant that the story of Lily Collins and Marlow's, but during wartime, was the one that I found myself wanting to tell. I really hope you've enjoyed reading it.

Now read on . . .

If you enjoyed

A Store at War

read on for the first chapter
of the next book in the series,

Secrets in Store . . .

Chapter 1

'Reg! It's Reg! He's here!'

Lily couldn't help herself. She'd been stationed at the window for the past two hours, as tense as a lookout in a South Coast pillbox. Now she tore to the back door the second she saw the latch on the back gate start to quiver. The hinge didn't even have time to squeak.

'Mum! Jim!' she hollered excitedly over her shoulder. 'He's home!'

Then she was flying out over the yard bricks, her feet skidding on the frosty surface. A few days ago, the whole country had been blanketed in snow, nearly five inches in their Midland town of Hinton, which had cast feverish doubt on Reg being able to get home at all. The snow had shrunk back now, leaving a scummy tidemark on the fringes of the yard, though it was still cold enough to make her eyes sting.

But Reg was here, finally, and guaranteed a warm welcome. His forty-eight-hour leave was in place of the family celebration they'd hoped to have at Christmas – insofar as anyone was celebrating Christmas in this third (the third, already!) winter of the war. If anyone had thought in 1939 that they'd still be fighting . . . Still, at least up till now it hadn't been as cold as that dreadful first winter, or as nail-shredding as the second, at the height of the Blitz.

'Lil! For goodness' sake, get back inside! You've only got your slippers on!'

The first words from her brother, and he was telling her off! No change there, and Lily had to smile. But she wasn't surprised: Reg, bless him, was the oldest in the family, and had always been the sensible one, the responsible one – he'd had to be, after their father had died.

Her other brother, Sid, would just have clocked the slippers' red pompoms, called her Frou-Frou or Fifi – he was always messing about with names – and made some crack about her pinching them off a French sailor. The fact that the British Navy, in which Sid was serving, issued its men with a plain flat-topped cap was a matter of some grievance with him, even though Lily was sure he'd have felt a right cissy in a hat with a pompom on it.

But Sid was away down south at HMS *Northney* on Hayling Island, and much as they'd tried, he and Reg hadn't been able to coordinate their leave to get home together. When she gave in to despair, which wasn't often, Dora, Lily's mum, sometimes wondered out loud when or if she'd ever have her three children under the same roof again. But it was no more than everyone else had to put up with, and as Dora was more likely to be heard to say in one of the many maxims she could produce to suit any occasion: 'What can't be cured must be endured.'

'Come on inside, then!' Lily hung on Reg's arm. 'We'll get the kettle on.'

'I wouldn't say no.' Poor Reg looked chilled through. His train must have been delayed – they mostly were, these days, if not actually cancelled – and he'd probably had to hang about on a freezing platform. 'Where's Mum?'

'She's upstairs, trying to keep herself busy and not watch the clock—'

'No, I'm not. I'm here.'

And there was Dora Collins, expectant in the scullery doorway. She was in her best dress in honour of the homecoming, with a Jacqmar scarf at the neck, no less, her Christmas present from Lily. Ever since she'd started at Marlow's, the town's smartest department store – or so it liked to claim – Lily had promised herself that as soon as she could afford it, she'd buy her mum something nice. And when Marlow's had given every junior a small bonus 'in gratitude for your hard work throughout the year in these difficult times', it had been earmarked straight away.

Lily had only joined the store the previous June. She hadn't been expecting anything extra in her pay packet, so the few extra shillings had been a very welcome surprise. But Marlow's was like that. It prided itself on looking after its employees, even though profits must be well down – for the simple reason that as the war ground on there was less and less to sell. Still, the buyers, like Miss Frobisher, Lily's boss on Childrenswear, did the best they could and the shop's reputation meant that if anything did become available, from tea trays to tobacco, children's coats to combinations, Marlow's was one of the first places a supplier would contact.

Reg crossed the yard. Sid, again, would have wrapped his mum in a hug, regardless of the rough, chilly wool of his tunic, but Reg, like Dora herself, was more reserved. He even looked like her, with soft brown hair, though his was now cropped short. Sid and Lily, on the other hand, had inherited their father's curly mop. Reg pecked his mum on the cheek before she stood back to let him in.

'Come in, love, out of the cold,' she urged. 'And let's have a good look at you.'

Only that telltale 'love' told Lily, and Reg himself, how much their mum had missed him and how very pleased she really was that he was home.

* * *

In the scullery, Jim was lifting the kettle from the gas
and wetting the tea: he was going to make someone
a wonderful wife someday, Sid always joked. Jim
wasn't a member of the family, but as their lodger,
he was starting to feel like one. He was another
employee at Marlow's, seventeen and already Second
Sales on Furniture. The arrangement suited them all.
Widowed when Lily was still a baby, Dora had learned
to be tough and independent. But with both her sons
away, she felt happier and safer with a man about
the house – and Jim wasn't only useful for the odd
pot of tea. There was no doubt that the two raised
beds in the yard were going to be a lot more produc-
tive this year under his watchful eye. Not only that,
he'd built them a henhouse. They now had fresh eggs
– gold dust, nectar and ambrosia all at once – and
useful as currency or for bartering as more and more
things went on the ration or disappeared altogether.

Jim held out his hand to Reg. They'd met once
before, in the autumn, when Reg had been passing
through on his way to yet another training camp.

'How's things?' Jim asked. 'Fair journey?'

'Oh, you know.'

It was yet another way in which Reg and Sid were
polar opposites. Where Reg was circumspect, Sid
would have treated them to a minute breakdown,
complete with music hall impressions of grumpy
guards and a star rating for the station tea bar.

'Well, the tea won't be long.'

Reg slung his haversack down on a chair.

'I've been saving some of my rations, Mum. And there's a bit of stuff from the NAAFI.'

He unbuckled the straps and took out a couple of lumpy parcels.

'Jam . . . chocolate . . . a bit of ham.'

Lily's mouth watered, but Dora wasn't letting Reg get away with that.

'Reg! You shouldn't have! No wonder you've lost weight!'

Weight loss was a crime on a par with sedition in Dora's eyes. Though the Army got first dibs when it came to rations, which was partly why ordinary households were having to cut back, she was naturally convinced that her boy wasn't being fed as well as she could have fed him if he'd been at home.

Reg gave one of his rare smiles.

'I haven't lost weight, Mum, far from it. I've toned up, put on muscle, that's all.'

Dora sniffed disbelievingly.

'Irish stew for dinner,' was all she said. 'I'd better have a look at it.'

She opened the door of the Belling and concentrated on extracting the promising-smelling stewpot while Lily and Jim discreetly stowed Reg's offerings in the pantry.

'Thank you,' Lily mouthed.

Reg grinned and gave her a thumbs-up.

Lily might not be as close to Reg as she was to

390

Sid, but jam, ham, chocolate or not, she realised just how pleased she was to see him too.

'All right, Mum, you win, hands down,' Reg conceded as he set aside his knife and fork. 'There might be plenty of it, Army food, but it's not a patch on your cooking.'

'Oh, get away with you! You'd eat horse manure if it was wrapped up in pretty paper!'

Lily bit back a smile. Their mum was no more capable of accepting a compliment than Lily had been of not shrieking her head off when she'd sensed Reg was at the gate.

'There's no more where that came from, you know!' Dora added, in case she hadn't dismissed the praise quite emphatically enough.

'I couldn't eat it!' Reg protested. 'I'm stuffed!'

Dora's eyebrows shot up.

'That's all they've taught you in the Army, is it, that sort of talk?'

Lily saw Jim and Reg exchange knowing, 'man of the world' looks.

'I should think that's the least of it, Mrs Collins.' Jim gave one of his wry, twisty smiles. 'Right, Reg?'

'You don't know the half of it! But don't worry, Mum, I won't be using any language while I'm home. Especially not now Lily's gone all posh on us, working at Marlow's. I didn't see you crook your little finger drinking your tea, though, Lil. Tut, tut!'

Lily flapped her hand at him and Reg ducked out of the way, laughing. He was relaxing now; they all were, with the warmth of some food inside them and the fire nicely banked up.

'So tell me, what's new at the swankiest store in town? What's the best-dressed baby wearing this winter, Lil? Had a run on cut-glass decanters for the folk with cut-glass accents, have you, Jim?'

This time Lily and Jim were the ones to exchange looks. So much had happened in Lily's first couple of months at Marlow's that the last few, apart from the flurry before Christmas and the January sales, had seemed quite tame in comparison.

She opened her mouth to reply but before she could begin, they heard the latch on the back gate click, followed by footsteps across the yard and then by someone opening the back door itself.

Lily's heart leapt. Surely not! It couldn't be, could it? Not Sid! Though it would be just like him to take them all by surprise. And who else could it be, turning up right in the middle of Sunday dinner?

'Only me!' trilled a voice approaching through the scullery.

Of course! Beryl! That's who.

Shy, tactful, reserved – not words you could ever use to describe Beryl. But what could she possibly want this time?